The Mumper

MARK BAXTER AND
PAOLO

PHOENIX

A PHOENIX PAPERBACK

First published in Great Britain in 2007
by Mono Media Books
This paperback edition published in 2011
by Phoenix,
an imprint of Orion Books Ltd,
Orion House, 5 Upper St Martin's Lane,
London WC2H 9EA

An Hachette UK company

1 3 5 7 9 10 8 6 4 2

A CIP catalogue record for this book
is available from the British Library.

ISBN 978-1-7802-2044-4

Typeset by Input Data Services Ltd, Bridgwater, Somerset

Printed in Great Britain by Clays Ltd, St Ives plc

The Orion Publishing Group's policy is to use papers that
are natural, renewable and recyclable products and
made from wood grown in sustainable forests. The logging
and manufacturing processes are expected to conform to
the environmental regulations of the country of origin.

www.orionbooks.co.uk

Acknowledgements

This book is dedicated to my mates. Lifelong mates, new mates, pub mates, football mates, work mates ...

It's for Gudge, Freddie, Dave, the O'sh, the Threadneedleman, Deano, Paul Hallam, Mr Miller, Mr Ezra, Alfie Davies, Oatsey Coleman, Colin Roy Churcher, Stan Vine, Nobby Palmer, Mickey Bale, Sagey, Mickey Demps, Jerry, Mad Dog, Johnny Mak, Johnny Fish, Bobby Cane, Bill Bateman, Teddy Herring, Jackie Mays, Eugene, Butch, Roscoe, Davie Watson, Woodyard, Charlie, Sailor Bill, Del, Ernie and Pop Stanhope. These people and others like them, shaped me, made me what I am, so you now know who to blame!

However, I will be eternally grateful for the education they provided.

It's also for the B. Man, the Saward Lad and Edwin Milner, all three of them trainee mumpers. They have put up with my dreams and schemes over the years, and have always supported me in them. A big nod to the Spurs man for the design work.

Many thanks also to BazDen and Olly. Thanks also to Vonnie, Nick, Lazza, Bugsy and Chuckle for their help with the glossary. It's for Scotch Iain, without whom a lot of what I have attempted wouldn't have worked. It's for all the wives, girlfriends and the saucepan lids of all above. It's for John Sullivan for all the joy his writing gave us. It's for my mum and dad, I truly stand on their shoulders today. Love to Glen and Tracey and Chloe and Tanya.

Finally Big Love to P. H. (ya mumper, ya) and to my wife Lou, the biggest love of all. Marvin and Tammi weren't lying when they said 'There Ain't Nothing Like The Real Thing'.

Mark Baxter,
South London, Spring 2007

I dedicate my work in this book to all the little mumpers who make my world a much better place, in particular, Antonio and Luigi (*uno e due*) Supino, Anaia, Sterling, and Asa Chandler, Clara and Niamh Taylor, Jo Jo and Grace Freeman, and Dylan.

Paolo Hewitt,
North London, Spring 2007

Both authors would also like to thank Clyde's family, Katie, Frankie and Pietro Clarke.

The Runners and Riders

For Gudge

John 'Gudger' Ginnaw died on 27 April 2011. Mark knew him all his life and considered him family. Gudger was Thimble's best mate, and they enjoyed many a song in many a pub together over the years. Both the authors sincerely hope they are enjoying a light ale or three in The Flying Dutchman in the sky.

I

The Flying Dutchman

Bagpipes ... bleeding bagpipes.

Every time I turn over in my bed or, God forbid, open my eyes, I can hear bleeding bagpipes.

Jesus Christ, am I suffering this morning. My brain is going like one of those heart monitors you see in the hospital dramas on the telly. Only mine seems to have all its wires crossed and crossed again. Suddenly, there's this one screeching long *bleeeeep* and just for a second everything flatlines ...

Thank fuck for that. It's only my alarm clock exploding into life. I force my eyes open once again and glance at the offending machine. It's now thirty minutes past ten on a cold September Sunday morning. I reach over and turn the bloody thing off. For a second there is silence, blissful, peaceful silence.

Then they come again ... bagpipes, bleeding bagpipes.

I lie there feeling terrible but there is nothing else for it, I have to get up, have to. I climb out of my bed and immediately feel like I've been run over by an articulated lorry. Which then reversed and rode over me again, just to make sure. I stagger across the landing of my parents' house to the khazi, which isn't easy when the floor is rolling up and down like waves in a choppy sea. I close the door softly behind me and look at myself in the bathroom mirror.

My face is the colour of chicken soup. I groan and look

down into the basin, trying to escape the man in the mirror, but that only makes things worse. The whole room feels like it is revolving around me. I have to go and sit on the bog for a minute to compose myself.

God, if someone shot me now they would be doing me a right favour . . . and I still have the sound of bagpipes ringing in my ears.

Through the wall, I can hear my old man coughing and shuffling around in his bedroom. I'm glad we have made an unspoken vow to avoid each other on mornings such as this. The last thing the pair of us need is to see someone looking as rough as we feel. I close my eyes and have enormous difficulty opening them again. Then I realise – I'm not sleepwalking, I'm sleep*sitting*.

My body is screaming for me to get back into bed, but I can't. I have an appointment at my pub of choice today, and I can't miss it. Within an hour and a half I will be in the company of three generations of men who mean the world to me, who educate me, make me laugh and keep me grounded.

Missing a date with them just isn't done. I have to get there and, by the look of things, the bloody bagpipes will have to come along as well. I step in the shower and let the comforting warm water try to heal me. I go back to my room, and even though the spinning has slowed down, I still feel dog-rough. And the reason for the hangover, I hear you ask? Simple. Please allow me to introduce the one and only Mr Gudger Ginnaw, a man I will be sipping the golden nectar with in about an hour's time. Gudge is a grafter who has worked in the Print for the past forty years, and despite reaching the respectable and pensionable age of sixty-five, he has shown absolutely no desire whatsoever to retire.

'Got a few years left on the clock yet, mate,' he tells

everyone when the subject is raised. I've known Gudge for ever.

He has a kind face, topped with blackish-grey hair that is always swept back, and he wears the thickest-lensed glasses I have ever seen. Sometimes when you look at him it actually looks like he has two jam jars perched on either side of his nose. He once stopped wearing the bins and began wearing contact lenses. He went down the pub with the contacts in but no one recognised him. So back came the glasses and people saying hello to him.

Yesterday, Gudge reached sixty-five. Cue massive celebrations. His friends and family all joined together to throw him a party at The Pembroke Club, which is just round the corner from East Street Market in Walworth, the birthplace of the one and only Charlie Chaplin. Top boy Michael Caine grew up not so far away. All roads lead to south London, as someone once said.

The Pembroke is nothing fancy but a nice little space all the same, all wood panelling and red fag-burnt carpet. In one corner, there's a stage on which sits an upright piano with nicotine-stained keys. Along the back wall there is a brightly lit bar.

The venue was chosen by Gudger's wife Doll, and we, his mates, helped organise the moriarty. It was important to us to give him a major blowout. The man is loved far and wide by all and sundry. From the start of the evening we had a variety of singers, piano players – even a local band – all entertaining the assembled in the hall. Round about ten o'clock we were waiting for the next act to start when suddenly a distinct buzzing sound could be heard that got louder and louder.

Now, Camberwell, my manor, is a cosmopolitan area, with a mixture of people from all four corners of the world.

Walking down my road, you'll hear all kinds of noises from roots reggae and ska to African beat and Celtic fiddles, all blaring out of shop doorways and flat windows. But in all my puff, I have never heard a sound like this one.

Around me people are smiling, but we are all thinking the same thing ... What the fuck is that? The noise gets louder and louder and louder until, amazingly, out of the back room of The Pembroke come fifty women, all dressed up in kilts, little black jackets and white socks, playing 'Scotland the Brave' on their bagpipes like there is no tomorrow.

Ladies and gentlemen, I give you ... The Dagenham Girl Pipers! But there's more.

At the head of this parade, with a kilt wrapped around his trousered legs, a little tam-o'-shanter on his head and carrying a massive silver-topped wooden staff, is the birthday boy himself, Gudger. He is actually leading the pipers around the pub. The crowd are in hysterics, laughing and joking as Gudger marches forward. Then it happens.

Gudge raises his big staff and then throws it into the air. Up and up it goes ...

Immediately, a cry goes up and people start diving for cover. They all know Gudger has remarkably poor eyesight and that there is no way in a million years he is ever gonna catch it. Gudger carefully watches the staff start to come down and then suddenly realises this fact himself. So he makes a run for it.

The staff hurtles down, landing on top of a table which six people are sitting around. Bottles of light ale and glasses throw themselves up in the air and cover their owners in liquid.

The staff bounces off the table and flies to a plug socket on the wall opposite. There is a crackle and spark, a tiny puff of grey smoke and immediately half the hall falls into darkness as the lights fuse. The people sat nearest the table are left covered in beer and bits of broken glass and all of us are now in the gloom as the Girl Pipers grind to a halt.

But you know what? No one moans, no one groans, because it's Gudger, and Gudger is loved by all. In fact, next thing you know, someone starts laughing and then another and then another until the whole place is laughing like there's no tomorrow, most of us doing so because we are extremely thankful not to have been in the immediate vicinity of the staff.

The Girl Pipers strike up again and Gudger comes over to retrieve the staff.

He says, 'Sorry 'bout that, boys,' and then he wheels around, places himself at the head of the pipers and leads them round the room as if nothing has happened.

The drinking starts up again and then my memory of the evening becomes distant, very distant.

Was I pissed at the end? Most certainly.

Was I an irresponsible man who should know better than to abuse himself like this?

Yes.

Am I now, having somehow got dressed and out of the house, standing outside my local, The Flying Dutchman, on a bright but cold September morning in 1985 with a hangover the size of London, waiting on Eric the landlord to open up and let me do it all over again?

Unfortunately ... Yes.

As I shiver against a wind blown in from the Arctic itself, I suddenly hear Sade's song 'Smooth Operator' cut across the icy morning air. I look up and note a car standing still by the traffic lights on Camberwell High Street, its window half rolled down, its driver nodding his head to the song's gentle samba beat. The lyrics float out of the car radio and go straight into my mind. It's the part that the Goddess sings ...

'No place for beginners or sensitive hearts, when sentiment is left to chance. No place to be ending, but somewhere to start.'

You know what? Those words are gonna sum this day up perfectly.

Now, I love this pub, The Flying Dutchman, but I have to say, it is no place for amateurs. It's a proper local with all kinds of characters up to all kinds of shenanigans. Unbelievable, some of the stuff that goes on in here, and one of the reasons that you get very few passers-by popping in. One look at the usual clientele is normally enough to make them seek refreshment elsewhere. That, and the state of the place.

Without wishing to cause Eric and the bar staff any offence whatsoever, it's fair to say that The Flying Dutchman has seen better times. It's what I would call an 'old school' pub, and it's been my family's local since the mid-fifties. I reckon it's been decorated twice since then.

The interior is basically made up of long fag-stained curtains that hide dirt-smeared windows. On the floor there's a sticky patchwork carpet held together by strips of black tape. There's tables and chairs that would probably disgrace a second-hand shop, and a bar so long that after a few sherbets it seems to stretch out into eternity. Behind the bar there is a sign that reads:

'No One Is Ugly After Ten O'clock.'

I always smile at that – usually round about ... ten o'clock.

I reckon every third light bulb is blown and the khazis are as cold as an outside bog in Siberia. People have been known to go into the gents as pissed as a pudding, and come out stone-cold sober. Still, after saying all that, I spend nearly every Sunday in here. It's my local, always has been, always will be, and that'll do for me.

As I wait for opening time I am joined by two other regulars, Sid and Davy. Davy is better known by all as Wavy Davy. I'll explain why later. Both have pale, sickly-looking faces. By that I mean their faces are much more pale and sickly than usual.

I nod to them. 'You all right, boys? Look like you're struggling a touch,' I say.

Davy lets out a small groan and Sid explains that the pair of them only left the pub at five that morning, having drunk their way to oblivion during another of the famous Dutchman lock-ins. Even if they hadn't told me that, I would have sussed it from the unleaded breath that is blowing from their mouths.

'I don't know why we didn't spend the night in the pub khazi, it would have saved us the bus fare back here this morning,' Sid moans.

You'd have frostbite by now if you had, I thought.

Finally, the outline of Eric can be seen through the front glass. There is that beautiful sound of a lock being cracked, and then the doors open.

'Lads,' Eric says in his usual style. Eric stands just under six foot, thin as a rake, with long black hair and a full black beard. He has what can only be described as a 'pub' face. That's a face that very rarely sees daylight, and which therefore develops a kind of grey pallor.

Nice fella, though, and a very adaptable player. I was once in a Dutchman lock-in and at four in the morning Eric ordered himself a Chinese takeaway. Now that's what I call a publican.

I bowl in, walk up to the bar and place my usual order of a vodka and diet, four bottles of warm light ale and two pint glasses to Brenda, the barmaid. Brenda's a big girl with a face that rarely cracks a smile, although she's pure gold once you get to know her. Mess with her at your peril, though. That woman can give you a verbal slaughtering so mean you'll do well to be out of hospital within a week.

The light ales, I should explain, are for Gudger and my old man. The pair of them always arrive just after I do. Always. In fact, if any of the others in my mob arrive before them I am pretty certain they would actually turn around and leave the boozer so as not to disturb the natural balance of things.

I walk over to our usual table in the corner and place the drinks down. I then take out a la-di-dah, dip one end in my drink, light the other and blow out a plume of grey-blueish smoke into the air. Then I and my hangover settle back and wait.

As usual, the pub fills up faster than a prisoner on the run. Within fifteen minutes I am surrounded by the faces I have known nearly all my life.

On my right the regular card school is already under way. The school consists of two Bills, a Frankie and a Charlie. The men are all in their fifties, are all taxi drivers and all have a few bob between them, that's for sure. They are all dressed in what I call 'taxi-driver chic', which translates as Gabicci sweaters and freshly pressed Farah strides.

Three-card brag is their game. They have a pint pot on the table holding the whip, and they never talk. They are all too busy being hypnotised by the cards they hold before their eyes. I nod to them but they don't see me through the hearts and the clubs, the spades and the diamonds.

To my left, the aforementioned Wavy Davy has already started swaying about on his stool, trying to find some gravity to cling on to. From a distance it looks like he's waving at you, hence the nickname.

Davy is as thin as a rasher of bacon and always dressed in jeans, a sweatshirt and market trainers. He is forever smoking a succession of prison-thin roll-ups and sits on the high stool by the bar, which has always struck me as reckless, seeing as he is the sort who just can't take his drink.

One pint of lager and within seconds he is wobbling all over the place. Everyone tries to keep an eye on him as he sways around on his stool because we all know that at some point in the day he will crash to the ground like the stock market on a bad day. Another regular face, Ronnie the Builder, now walks past me. He's on his way to the dartboard end of the pub.

'All right, son?' he says.

'Ronnie Boy,' I reply, acknowledging him. Ronnie is a mountain of a fella, got to be twenty-odd stone. The funniest thing is, he claims to be a vegetarian, so his massive bulk is not the result of endless fry-ups and kebabs. No, Ronnie simply loves a cream cake. He's got a ten-a-day habit. He's also the most un-builder-like builder I have ever met.

Normally they are all lairy, forever giving it the big 'un, trying to mug someone off. But things are different with Ronnie. He's got the character of an artist.

'Busy, mate?' I ask.

'Got a bit on, as it happens, but I'm struggling at the minute, son, really suffering, nothing's flowing at the moment, know what I mean? No inspiration at all. Really struggling ...' He shakes his head sadly. 'I painted this wall yesterday and the first coat went on lovely, I was really happy with the first coat. Loved the colour, and if I say so myself, my brushwork was first class, the paint went on a treat. But the second coat, nah, it just wasn't happening. Got halfway through and told the punter I couldn't finish it, told her sorry, like, she could have her money back but my nerve had gone . . . I think I've got builder's block, mate.'

With that, he strolls off, nodding his head sadly as I smile a sympathetic smile.

High up on the wall above the fruit machines the telly is on, the Ceefax pages gleefully reminding all the gamblers where their dough from the day before has gone.

I take a sip of my drink and all of a sudden Gudger is sitting beside me, landing in his usual seat like a homing pigeon.

'All right, boy?' he says and throws a tenner into the middle of the table. It joins the one that I had already put there to start the whip off. 'You look a bit under the weather, son. Good night last night, though, weren't it? Mind you, all I can hear right now are fucking bagpipes . . .'

I have to laugh. Here I am, dying from alcohol poisoning, and here he is, fresh as a daisy. He must have the constitution of Keith Richards.

'See those Lions lost again yesterday, polish, that mob, polish,' he continues.

I can't argue. Millwall are my team but they have been so pony lately I have actually stopped going to the games for the time being. I keep that fact to myself. If anyone knew, I'd be banned from the pub.

'Fucking hard work supporting that mob,' I tell Gudge, 'fucking hard work.'

'Ain't that the truth,' he replies gloomily.

I look up and break into a smile as I spot my old man walking over to us. As usual he is immaculately turned out. As am I. As is everyone else . . . well, apart from Wavy Davy. Round my way such things are important. It's the tradition.

You put on your best whistle and scrub up nicel,
Best and all that.

I got to say, though, that my old man always has the s.
on everyone in this particular race, and that's because he is
an extremely fussy fucker about his appearance. He will
spend hours getting ready to go out, making sure that you
never ever see him with a hair out of place, a crumple in his
clothes, or dirt on his shoes. Whatever the occasion, he will
always look immaculate.

'Allo, son … Gudger,' my old man says, sitting down.
'You alright, Pop?' I ask.

'Can't shake this bleeding cough off,' he replies.

'Sorry to hear that, Thimble. Getting old, my son,'
Gudger says.

'And I've got ten verses of "Scotland the Brave" going
around my nut,' the old man adds. 'Apart from that, I'm all
right.'

A smile breaks across Gudger's lips. 'Good night last
night, though, eh?'

'Blinding, Gudge, blinding,' my old man replies. 'Lovely
to see all those old faces. Wonder if they've got the electric
back on yet?'

Gudger calls my dad Thimble because if there is one
thing my old man adores, it is suits, especially handmade,
tailored ones.

'You were a bit quiet this morning, son,' my dad says,
looking in my direction.

I groan. 'I thought I was dying, Pop.'

'Blouse …' he says, smiling, 'not too clever myself, as it
happens …'

My old man draws some brown out of his pocket and
places a note in the whip. Then he starts to pour the light
ale into his pint glass before plunging his lips into the froth.

'Cheers, boys ... lovely drop that,' he says with a little sigh. 'Lovely.'

He is in his fifties now, works as a messenger for Barclays Bank but has also done some casual work on the Print in his time, thanks to Gudge, who got him in when my old man – as we all do at some point – hit some tough financial waters.

He puts his glass down and says through his foamy white moustache: 'What about those plums down the Den? What a poxy result that was, fucking Millwall, polish.'

My old man has been going to Millwall since the mid-fifties. Shortly after I was born, he passed his club on to me. I have never forgiven him. In fact, I asked him once why he had done that. After all, there are so many other clubs in London doing things Millwall don't do, like winning cups or league titles. How the fuck did I end up with this mob? We were in The Dutchman with Gudge when I put this question to him. My old man put down his glass and suddenly turned very serious.

'Son,' he said, 'you know the floodlights you can see from your bedroom window? Well, they belong to the club you will support all your life.'

Gudge took a sip of beer and said, 'Those Man United fans round here must have fucking good eyesight, then, eh?'

Gudge and the old man have been spars for centuries. In fact, I can't recall a time when Gudge was not in my life. You're probably trying to work out why the name Gudger, by now, ain't you? My advice? Don't bother. I asked him once where the name came from. This was his response:

'My old man was nicknamed Hudger McGudger the King of the Pharaohs, weren't he?' he casually replied. 'And it got passed on to me.' He then carried on drinking as if what he had just said was the most obvious thing in the world.

Hudger McGudger, King of the Pharoahs ... Well, that's cleared that up nicely, I thought to myself. One other thing Gudge is known for is his habit of wearing very dodgy shoes. You know the shoes the Africans go for, the grey snakeskin-style ones, with the little brass chain on them? Well, so does Gudge. He loves them.

'What's wrong with these, boy?' he'll shout if he catches you looking quizzically at them. ''andsome, them.'

I blame the glasses.

The supplier of these shoes is the next face in. His name is Fred Harris but he is known to one and all as Fred the Shoe. Fred is in his mid- to late-thirties and very dapper, the result of teenage years spent as an original Mod. Like my old man, Fred loves his schmutter, but above all Fred loves shoes. In fact, he loves them so much he owns a shoe shop, hence the nickname. I say shoe shop, but to be honest it is more like a social club, a place where all the old faces you are about to meet gather to chew the fat, take the piss, have a laugh, have a cuppa and maybe take home some quality shoes, made available to them at very reasonable prices. We all wear shoes from Fred's.

Very rude not to.

It being a Sunday, Fred sports a dark blue suit which looks like it came off the rack at Aquascutum. With it he wears a classic pair of burgundy beef-roll Bass Weejun loafers, a crisp white shirt and matching hanky in the breast pocket of his jacket to finish off the look nicely. Fred is no more than five foot five in his silk socks, but has kept himself fit and the weight off. His barnet is slowly leaving his head but as he always says, 'Grass never grows on a busy street!' He's married to Kay and they have a couple of teenage boys,

Mark and Sam. Fred's got a lovely easygoing nature, and is one hell of a piss-taker, a real funny fella.

Handshakes all round, and a kiss on Gudger's cheek from Fred. He plots up at our table and lobs his tenner entrance fee into the middle of it. Following close behind him is his best mate, Dave Norris. These two have been hanging out for ever, their collective memory stretching right back to war-torn London, you never had it so good, Christine Keeler in her chair, mohair suits, Georgie at The Flamingo, World Cup 1966, man on the moon, glam rock, three-day weeks, Ted Heath and Kevin Keegan.

'Hello, Dave,' my old man pipes up. 'Meant to say to you last night, mate, did ya see that Sinatra concert on the box in the week?'

'You'll have to speak up, Thimble,' Dave replies, 'I can't hear you over the fifty Dagenham Girl Pipers marching around in my swede . . .'

The whole table laughs at the same time.

'Yeah, I saw old blue-eyes, mate . . . 'andsome, weren't it, Thimble? Genius, the fella, absolute genius.'

Little Dave loves his music, in particular the old-style ballad singers of whom Francis Albert is the acknowledged guv'nor. Of course, there is also Tony Bennett and Nat King Cole to consider, but Francis Albert is his man. Such is his love for music, Dave will actually go miles out of his way to hear a good pub singer. Again, he is another sharp dresser whose Mod heritage is still in evidence. Today, he's wearing grey trousers with a crease you could slice bread on, a pastel yellow Lacoste polo and cardigan combination, tan tasselled suede loafers (courtesy of his close amico, Frederico of the Shoe) and a neat haircut. Dave lives with Sue and has done for years. Apparently he has never felt the need to get married.

When questioned as to his non-existent marital status, Dave reaches for the songbook dictionary in his mind and turns the page to the letter B. 'As Tony Bennett sings,' he states, '"*Out of the tree of life, I just picked me a plum*"', and that'll do me, boys,' is his take on the subject.

Dave is a black-cab driver, the only one I know in London known to go south if requested. Dave is also small (hence the nickname) in his mid- to late-thirties and has lived in Walworth all his life. I watch him go over to the bar to get the drinks in for Fred and him, which is when I spot the O'sh over by the fruit machine, O'sh being short for O'Shea, as in Mark O'Shea, another one of our table.

'Oi, O'sh,' I shout at him.

'Be with you in a minute,' he says without looking up, trying to make sense of all the flashing lights dancing in front of him. Bloody fruit machines.

In the old days, when I was a nipper, it was simple. They had a handle on the side. You pulled it. If you got three bells, three cherries, three apples, three whatevers, you won. These days there's so many lights and permutations going on, it's like overseeing the invasion of a foreign country by a nudged computer.

O'sh is the baby of our table, a year younger than me at twenty. Sensing that today the machine will be disobeying his commands, he gives it a slight kick, turns and ambles over to us.

'Here, Gudge, whose bleeding idea was it to get the bagpipes in last night, then?' the O'sh says as he plots up on one of the little stools by the table.

'Don't know, Goldfish,' Gudge replies, 'I s'pose it would have been old Dickie Springay. He books all the turns at The Pembroke. Why?' A little smile plays on Gudge's lips. 'Didn't you like 'em, then? I would have thought you would have bonded with your Celtic sisters and all that.'

'Slag off out of it, will ya,' the O'sh shoots back, obviously not impressed. 'What a racket, mate. Old Dickie needs looking at if he booked them.'

'Yeah, it was Dickie,' says Fred. 'I asked him afterwards. He told me he was going through his contacts book and under "D" he found "Doonican, Val". So he rung his agent.'

'Val Doonican! Fuck me,' splutters Dave.

'Straight up. He tried to book old Val, but turns out old Val and his rocking chair were already booked for a night down in Bournemouth, so he couldn't make it. So Dickie starts at the top of the page again and next thing you know comes across the Dagenham Girl Pipers, which is how we ended up with them.'

'I read somewhere,' Dave puts in, 'that the definition of a gentleman is someone who can play the bagpipes ... but chooses not to.'

'Could have done with that fella last night ...' says Fred.

'Top-flight contacts he's got, then, old Dickie,' laughs my old man.

'Could have been worse,' O'sh points out. 'We might have ended up with Diddy David Hamilton.'

O'sh is from Irish stock, got the ginger barnet to prove it. Today he is head to toe in a navy Fila tracksuit and his ever-present Nike blue-flash Glorias.

He's taken the same route as me to get to this table. As soon as he could, Tony, his old man, started taking him to the pub. Like his dad, O'sh is a big 'un, as can be seen from the prominent darby he takes everywhere with him.

'All that free school milk I had as a nipper, mate,' he says, justifying his stomach's ever-expanding nature, naturally failing to mention the copious amounts of lager he now consumes on a very regular basis. Fair to say the O'sh has

16

very much taken to pub culture. Slim Jim he ain't. Gudger calls him My Old Goldfish, on account of him having ginger hair and drinking like a fish. (Mind you, call him a ginger bastard, as we often do, and he will quickly shoot back, 'Oi, not so much of the ginger, mate. More like African Sunset, if it's all the same to you.')

O'sh is a fellow Millwall sufferer and my best mate, the great lummox.

Last but not but least to join us is Alfie Davies, or Alfie Hobnails as he's known to all.

He's in his seventies now but still as sharp as a knife and teak tough. He don't miss much, Alfie, believe me, and he is never seen without his flat cap on, never. Me and the O'sh reckon his missus Lil had it sewn on his head about forty years ago so that he wouldn't leave it somewhere. Under that very cap, he is rumoured to be as bald as a badger. He's got a right bugle on him, which every now and then he blows like a trumpet. How the hanky stays in his hand is a wonder of nature.

His face is very jowly and it wobbles like a ripe jelly when he laughs, which is quite often. Along with all the old blokes I know, he's got great big ears which I can never stop looking at, causing me to wonder if ears carry on growing for all of our lives or whether they actually stop at some point. Must ask the GP next time I go in for a check-up.

As for Alfie's clothes, it's fair to say he dresses more for comfort than speed nowadays. His wardrobe is all beige elastic-waisted trousers and jumpers with suede patches on the sleeves. Marks & Spencer is his outlet of choice.

One of the first things I noticed about him was that although you would often hear fellas of Alf's age telling their war stories, Alf never said anything on the subject. I found this strange. Most of the old 'uns have at least a story or two to tell about their war exploits, but Alf stayed shtum on the subject. After a while it got to me, and I asked him why.

He looked at me longer than usual. 'I wasn't allowed to serve in the army, was I? I was one of Moseley's Black Shirts. Fucking fought in the Cable Street riots of 1936, and all that,' he explained. Then he put down his pint and sighed wistfully. 'Young and silly I was, mate, got taken in by all that bollocks that was going around. Still going on today and I hope you never touch it, son. It's evil stuff. Anyway, because of that they wouldn't let me join up, so I was put into the Fire Service. As you can imagine, that wasn't a bundle of laughs, what with the Blitz and all that. The worst night was Saturday 10 May 1941. Fuck me, that was bad. Over a thousand people died that night, over eleven thousand houses destroyed. Couldn't cope, could we? How I came out of that alive I'll never know, son.'

Alfie picked up his pint and never said anything else on the subject ever again. It was only later on when talking to the others that I discovered he had single-handedly pulled a young mum and her daughter out of a burning building and won himself a bravery medal.

Alf might have had things in his past that would seem dubious to the likes of you and me, but I liked the man and I liked him because not only had he changed, but he told you how it was rather than how you or he wanted it to be.

'You're late, Alfie mate,' Gudger rhymes as Alfie shuffles into view.

'You're lucky I'm here at all, mate,' he replies. 'You nearly killed me with that fucking stick last night!'

'Was you under that, Alf?' says Fred, laughing.

'I was. What a soppy bleeder you are, Gudger. 'Bout time you started acting your age, and not your shoe size. Good gracious God, I thought I was a goner, mate.'

Alfie then smiles at Gudger and ruffles his head. Gudge smiles back. As I said earlier, no one gets the hump with Gudger for too long. He's one of those people who you forgive anything.

So there you have the people I drink with. A right mixed mob, three generations of local men, meeting up every Sunday lunchtime to create a tide of good feeling as we mercilessly extract the urine out of each other and drink the golden nectar. In fact, I would say that the art of piss-taking at this particular table has been taken to such a level, it should be taught in universities and schools. I kid you not. I can just see it in the student programme now.

The Art of Extracting the Urine 1900 to 1985. A two-year course.

I suppose after all this spiel, I had better introduce myself.

My name is Mark Baxter, known as Bax. Aged twenty-one, I'm six foot two, weighing in at around twelve and a half stone, and of a big build, just like the old man. My barnet is a sort of dirty-blond colour, cut into a number-three buzz cut by Alberto the Italian barber. Short and neat, just like the birds I like. I've got blue eyes, two of 'em, I'm pleased to say, and I've recently grown a little bit of fluff just under my bottom lip in homage to the jazz trumpeter Dizzy Gillespie, whose recordings with Charlie 'Bird' Parker back in the early fifties I am well fond of. Of course, the boys at the table didn't get the Dizzy reference at all. All I got was, 'Oi, Bax, you've missed a bit there, son.'

Plums ...

After leaving school as fast as I could, aged sixteen, I ducked and dived for a couple of years, earning a pound by whatever landed in my lap. Never did anything dodgy like selling the tackle, but you could say with some truth

19

that I have veered in and out of the straight and narrow. At the same time I had my name down to get into the Print. Gudge was my way in, but I had to bide my time. Everyone has to. You don't just walk into the Print. There are rules and regulations, traditions to follow. Whilst I waited I did all sorts, got my fingers into many pies, most of which, unfortunately, stayed cold. I mostly worked on stalls down at Camden Market, where I sold a bit of old bric-a-brac and quite a bit of quality second-hand clobber. I have also been known to do a spot of DJing, playing the old sixties favourites at various parties and a couple of local pubs, anything to make a pound, really. In 1982, aged eighteen, thanks to the man Gudge, I finally got the call to go into the Print, and I have been there these past three years. I love every minute of it.

I'm still living at home, and I am supposed to be saving for a deposit on a flat. Don't get me wrong, my P and M are the salt of the earth and I love them to bits, but even so I do feel the need to spread my wings. Only trouble is, I've got an addiction that needs feeding and it is a bad one. Nah, it's not the tackle I'm hooked on, it is something much worse: CLOTHES!

Always loved clothes, always. From my early days I've been a Mod. Got into it through Paul Weller and The Jam, really, back in 1979, 1980, and haven't looked back since. My pride and joy is the handmade whistle that I got a couple of years back from Georgie Dyer, the tailor all the south London Faces use. It's a thing of true beauty, made of brown mohair, three buttons on the jacket front, a centre vent at the back and trousers that show a bit of sock to match.

Sometimes I get it out of the wardrobe, hang it on the wall and sit and stare at it for hours. If I'm honest, I think I might be in love with my suit. You might see this as a replacement for the void caused by the lack of a woman in my life right now, and I would say you were talking absolute bollocks whilst agreeing with you wholeheartedly. Anyway, we're all rabbiting away at our table as usual when suddenly this skinny, round-shouldered fella nobody knows walks up to our table and says, 'Hello, chaps, ever thought about owning a racehorse?'

2

Oh for the Wings of a Dove

This fella who was stood before us must have been in his mid-fifties, and the first thing I noticed about him was his haircut. It was so bad, I reckon he had cut it himself with a broken bottle. He had a couple of front teeth missing, and that resulted in him having a bit of spittle around his mouth as he spoke. He reminded me of someone who might have been about in Dickens' time, carried a name like Henry Stump or something similar. He materialised at our table at precisely one-fifty p.m. and I know that because just as he stood in front of us, Gudge asked me the time. Before we go any further, I have to tell you that his question has now entered local folklore and is known by everyone in The Dutchman as The Silencer. That's because its effect was to silence every mouth sitting at that table. Never happened before. Never. Always someone in our mob talking, arguing, laughing, shouting and then this man comes along, asks one question and bang, next thing you know, not a sound to be heard. For the longest five seconds I have ever known, there was pure silence. It was Gudge who broke it in two.

'You what, mate?'

'You fellas ever thought of owning a racehorse?' he replied. 'You know, buying into one.'

'A fucking racehorse,' said Fred. 'You pulling my pisser, son?'

'No ... no I'm not,' the man coolly replied. 'Mind you, I had a feeling you'd say that. But I'm being straight up here. I know someone who has got this horse, and he reckons with a bit of tender loving care and plenty of dough, it will do well in the races.'

Everyone looked at each other and then started laughing at the fella, reckoning him to be either fucking mad, pissed, or on the gear, possibly a combination of all three. That's everyone except me, because I was too busy scanning the pub looking for the piss-takers who had put this geezer up to it. However, given the faces of the clientele who gather in my boozer, this was a pretty pointless exercise. Could have been any one of them.

'I've heard about you lot,' the fella continued. 'They call you the Jolly Boys, don't they? Come here every Sunday, always sit at this table, geezers who know a good thing if it came along, right?'

Actually, the geezer was a little bit off-beam as there was only one actual Jolly Boy at our table, and that was Gudger. The majority of the original Jolly Boys had either scarpered down to the south coast or taken the long road to Heaven.

That said, he had mentioned true local legends. The Jolly Boys started life around 1965 or '66 (no one is ever sure, as is the case with most local history), in The Globe public house in Darwin Street, SE17, not far from where we were now sitting. A group of fellas started to meet on a Sunday night at the pub, between the hours of seven and nine p.m. This group gradually grew to sixty in number, all fellas from the same side of the street in life. The venue changed from time to time but word of mouth ensured all knew where to land, come opening time. The origin of the name, The Jolly Boys, is lost in the mists of time, though Gudger remembers a family with the surname Jolly who were involved in the group. He thinks it was on account of them that the name was bestowed but you wouldn't want to put any money on it, if you know what I mean. Within this group, there were at least three quality piano players and a host of great singers. Whatever pub they were in, these artisans of the south would take turns to play and sing.

Soon, every decent pub in the area had a piano installed in one of the bars in case the Jolly Boys arrived. To this day there is still Jolly Boy activity, although not on the scale of yesteryear. Time has not been the gang's best friend. By 1985, a few of the old 'uns had retired to the sands and quieter times, and the rest of us had taken their place. We were friends and sons, Honorary Jolly Boys, if you like. The original survivors still meet up at various pubs and have golf weeks and even trips abroad, Lanzarote being a favourite destination. Some of them still wear their Jolly Boy ties. Gudge still owns a couple. One day, he took me aside and handed one to me.

Got to say it made me really proud to be considered a Jolly Boy. Until I saw the tie, and thought, I'll wear that ... when I'm indoors.

As I said, no one knew who this mush in front of us offering us a racehorse was. Which was kind of strange. In The Dutchman, you get used to certain faces offering all kinds of things, from snide Pierre Cardin shirts to packs of bacon, and we knew most, if not all, of the faces doing the selling. But a racehorse ... that was a new one on all of us. After we had stopped laughing at the fella, the man stood there, not wanting to move. That was when we realised he was serious and not taking the piss.

Glances were exchanged between us and voices discreetly lowered. 'Fucking junkie, ain't he?' O'sh muttered.

'Definitely on the tackle, got to be,' Dave said, taking a sip of beer.

'What the fucking hell are we gonna do with a racehorse, mate?' Little Dave asked.

'These slags will nick anything nowadays, won't they?' said Alfie.

'No,' said the salesman, 'no, it ain't nicked. Look, a mate of mine has got stables out in Newmarket. He's got a couple of horses he runs at flapping tracks, gambles them against the pikey's horses. Anyway, he's got this one horse he reckons could do well so he's looking for someone to invest in it, so he can run it legit. I'll be straight, this horse has come from a, excuse the pun chaps, an unstable background, so the normal owners won't touch it, so my mate has asked me to tout it around.'

We all looked at each other. All of us had heard a few tales in our time but this was off the plot. I've got to admit I was beginning to think I'd love to know how much the geezer was looking for for it, but that's me all over. Love a scam, get an idea in my head and I'm off. Even though the idea was ridiculous, I was still thinking, how much and could I get the price of a packet of fags out of it? But from the looks on the other faces, this was a non-starter, in more ways than one.

'I think we'll leave it, mate,' said Fred. 'Horses cost a bundle to stable, feed and all that. I looked into being in an owner syndicate before and it runs into the thousands. A couple of fellas I know once bunged a few bob into one, along with five hundred and ninety-eight other punters. I asked them once what they got back on their investment. A couple of bags of hot horse shit, they told me!'

'Fair enough,' said the seller fella, 'thought I'd give you a punt. Any point in leaving my name and number in case you change your mind, or might know someone?'

'Here y'are, mate,' I quickly said. 'Give it to me, I might know a couple of fellas.' Those around me sighed, all thinking the same thing: Baxter is off again, another fucking stupid idea, so please leave me out of it.

I wrote the fella's name and number down and stuck it in my back sky rocket. The horse seller, happy to have at least got a bit of interest, ambled off to the bar.

'Same again all round?' said Alfie, finishing off his bitter. 'Up you go Goldfish, save me legs.'

'What you saving them for, Alf?' O'sh replied. 'Fucking medical research?'

'Bollocks, you lump, get up there, you could do with the exercise. Look at the darby on you.'

'Funny thing is,' said my old man to no one in particular. 'I've always wanted to get into horse racing in some way or another. Out of my reach though, of course ...'

The old man then looked over at me, and straight away sussed what was running through my mind. Which, to be precise, was a racehorse.

'Look at that soppy prat,' he said, recognising the signs. 'He's only thinking of getting involved, ain'tcha, son? Tut bloody tut ...'

Despite his comment, I knew the old man well. If he had one weakness it was the gee-gees. He was a serious student of the sport of kings. I reckoned on it not taking much to get him involved.

'Well, what harm can it do?' I said. 'We could have a word with the trainer, see what he wants for it. If it's silly dough, we walk away, no harm done.'

'Fucking mad, you are, son. Always been the same, champagne tastes but only lemonade money in your pocket.

26

You're just like your grandad. He was the same. Head in the clouds, woke up in the dirt. How the fuck you gonna afford a gee-gee? On my life,' he said, shaking his nut and laughing.

'Ain't got a chance on my own, granted,' I said, feeling a slight shot of anger in my gut. 'But Fred's given me an idea. I mean, there is nothing to stop us forming a syndicate and lobbing out for it, is there?' I asked.

Everyone looked at me, uncertain as to whether I was being deadly serious or deadly stupid. Then Fred the Shoe piped up.

'I also said it costs thousands,' he explained. 'None of us has got that kind of spare dough, have we? Well, apart from Gudger, eh Gudge?'

Gudge just carried on drinking his light ale, not making eye contact. It had long been rumoured that Gudge had a few bob tucked away on account of his time on the Print. Made sense. The man had worked his ring off, doing all the hours he could get, never turning a shift down. When you had come from fuck all, like him and my old man, the easy money on offer at the *Telegraph*, the *Mail* or wherever, was too good to turn down. The blinding thing about Gudger was that he didn't keep all the gravy to himself.

Gudge came back at us. 'I ain't got cough all, boy. Done most of my spare dough betting on the bloody horses. I wish you joy with it, boy, but I ain't got nothing to give ya.'

'I'll tell ya what,' I piped up, 'I'll bell the fella and get a price and take it from there. Ain't gonna cost us a tanner to find out what he's after, is it?'

'Mate, you're a fucking nut-nut,' said the O'sh, 'a fucking great nut-nut.'

By this stage they were all laughing at me. I looked at them and just grinned, but I didn't reply. I think my best mate had a point because right then, just as he said it, I felt something inside me change, heard a voice whisper something along the lines of, *your life is about to do a three-point turn, son, better get yourself good and ready.* Unfortunately, I didn't clock the time for that particular occurrence. Glad I didn't, actually. You really would have thought I was a flash bastard then, wouldn't ya?

All of the following week, I was obsessing about that bloody horse. I'm murder, me; get an idea in my head and I have to follow it through. The more I thought about it, the more I wanted it to happen. The problem was, I now had to convince six other non-believers from my 'congregation'. Yet, despite their apparent lack of interest, I did get the vibe that a couple of them might be tempted to get involved. After all, my mob loved a bet and had a genuine interest in the sport. It just needed a couple to admit that to the others and we'd be on. Take my old man, for instance. At tea on the Monday night, he started making all the right noises, kept repeating he would love to get involved *if* he had the dough. That was when I decided to bell the fella at the stables and see what he wanted money-wise. If the price was reasonable, I would go on the offensive, try and talk the others round. I mean, if my old man had it in his mind, then who knows what the others were thinking?

The next day at work, I took the scrap of paper with the number written on it out of my pocket and rang.

'Hello, Dawson House Stables, Sefton speaking,' said the voice at the other end. (Sefton!? What sort of name is that?)

'Yes, hello ... er ... Sefton ... er ... mate,' I said, trying not to laugh, 'I've been given your number by a fella in a pub, reckons you've got a cheap horse for sale ... I might be interested.'

He paused.

'Well, I've got a couple of horses I'm looking for buyers for. You know anything about horses?' He sounded wary. His voice was what I would call proper Farmer Giles.

'Only losing money on them,' I replied, trying to lighten the moment. I didn't hear a chuckle come back down the line, so I cracked on with my story.

'Well, as I was saying, this fella in the pub, he reckoned you had a horse that might do okay, and you were looking for backers, so to speak.'

'That would have been my cousin Allan you met. Asked him if he knew anybody up in the smoke who would fancy owning one. That horse is a three-year-old jumper, big, headstrong bastard, but I've always thought he could do well, if he was looked after in the right way. Just a question of getting the money to do it, really.'

I have to say, what I had heard so far hadn't put me off.

'All right then, Sefton, well, as I say, I might be interested, wouldn't mind coming down for a butcher's ... a look at it in other words ... If the price is right, we could talk business, know what I mean?'

The voice at the other end sighed.

'Look, I'm a businessman, not a Punch and Judy show, and well, they ain't cheap to look after, y'know. You'll be looking at stabling it, me training the bloody thing, vet's fees and entry money to races ... (Come on, Sefton old son, spit it out, I'm thinking) ... I reckon, well ...' he sounded like he was puffing out his cheeks '... eight grand will do it ... how does that sound? What do you think?'

Eight grand! Eight large ones! I'll tell you what I think to that, Sefton my old son, I think, fuck me, that's a lot of dough. At least I knew the price now, and I figured with a bit of haggling I could get it down. The first lesson you learn on the stalls is that the first price mentioned is just the opening gambit. Just as in life, there is always room for manoeuvre. Take Sefton. He must be struggling for dough if he's got family going round dodgy pubs in south London trying to flog a horse.

He continued, 'You never know, you might even get some prize money, might get your dough back, if it wins, never know, but yeah, you're welcome to come and check the horse out.'

Sefton was sounding eager, keen to keep me on the phone. I'm thinking, I must be the first punter to call him about the horse, so he doesn't want to lose me at the first hurdle, all puns intended.

'Yeah, that sounds okay mate,' I said, lying and giving it the big 'un. 'Let me have your address and I'll shoot down at the weekend to see you and the horse.'

Already my mind was trying to figure out how I could sell the idea to the chaps. Sefton asked me my name, and then rattled off his address. It was a gaff called Ashley, up in Newmarket, just as we'd been told in the boozer. I put the phone down and looked up.

A couple of the lads from my office, Roy and Sagey, were looking at me in amazement. They had obviously overheard the conversation.

'Bax, did I hear that right, son, you're buying a horse?'

'You want to get some ointment for that nose of yours, son, don't ya?' I said. 'Listening to other people's phone calls. What you like?'

'Flaming hell, you are, ain't ya?' Roy said.

'Might be, son, might be.'

'Oi, hear that? This mumper is buying a horse,' Sagey

shouted to the assembled blokes dotted around the despatch room where I worked.

There followed a burst of loud laughter. No need to ask what Roy and the boys thought of the idea, then ...

'What you buying a horse for, son?' piped up Frank. 'You taking up hunting?'

'Tally-ho!' shouted a couple of the chaps. I just shook my head at them. Chuckle on brothers, I thought, chuckle on ... I'll show ya.

On the bus home from work, as I headed towards the deep south, I began trying to work out a speech to persuade the rest of the honorary Jolly Boys of the potential in buying this horse. Nothing came to mind. It was only when we went past Fred's shoe shop that I decided then and there to jump off and start my campaign. I wouldn't try and persuade the boys all at once, I would pick them off one by one, the theory being divide and conquer. If I approached six at once, I'd get slaughtered and verbally nailed to the floor. If I could talk Fred round, and then my old man, the idea might still have legs.

Fred's shop is located just before Camberwell Green and has been a shoe shop since the 1850s. I reckon some of the dust on the shelves is of that vintage as well. Inside there are mirrors, which were used in the booths so women could try on their shoes in privacy. Apparently, a hundred years ago, showing a bit of ankle constituted hardcore pornography.

Fred's always worked in the rag trade in some capacity or other, but he decided to go it on his own five years back. He's always got some cracking stock in. Being an old Mod, he knows his shoes, and being south London, he knows how to get them at cheap prices.

Today, his customers fall into two main camps. He still gets a lot of the 'Faces' going in there, people he has known socially from over the years. Like him, a lot of them grew up in the sixties, when being turned out well on a Friday or Saturday evening was the norm. Some, like Fred and Dave, have kept that tradition on; the others have let standards slip. I've often wondered how that happens. Women and children, I suppose.

People get married and the money that would once have gone on a new pair of shoes or a whistle, is needed elsewhere. I'd like to think that won't happen to me, and that I will find a way to buy quality togs for the rest of my days, whatever the circumstances. Fred's other main punters are the local Africans, many of whom love a bit of good British quality gear. He often says he wished he'd kept up the French lessons at school because half of them speak French as a first language.

'Make my life a lot easier, that would, if I knew what the fuck they were on about,' Fred says.

He also says that although they love his stock, they also love a bargain. Most of them have degrees in haggling. Mind you, with Fred's prices, even they are gonna struggle to knock him down. Don't stop 'em trying, though ...

Fred was on the phone when I walked into the shop. While I waited for him to finish, I looked along the shelves, which were lined with classics like Loakes, Grensons, Bass Weejuns and Alfred Sargents – real quality webs. There was also a selection of Gudger's favourites in every conceivable colour, snakeskin, moc croc with bits of suede, brass and silver stuck on them. Right bastards, them ...

Fred spotted me and waved in my direction as he hung up the phone. "Allo son, just finished work?'

"Allo, mate. Yeah, another day at the salt mines out of the way.'

'Good lad,' he says. 'Good lad.'

'Fred,' I said as nonchalantly as I could, 'I spoke to that fella with the gee-gee today, got a price.'

'Fuckin' 'ell, son, you don't piss about, do ya?' he said, chuckling. 'What's the fella want for it?'

Straight away I knew I was in. Fred had been thinking about the horse as much as I had. Didn't surprise me. He's a lot like me, Fred – if there's something of interest going on, he wants a slice.

'He wants eight large,' I told him.

'Eight, eh? Not giving it away, is he? What do we get for that, apart from a fucking great big horse?'

I explained that the dosh would take care of it for one year, and that included stabling, vet's fees, entry to races, as well as the training – the full bifta, in fact.

'I reckon if I get the others on board, then we can go in with an offer of six large, tell the geezer take it or leave it,' I stated. 'Listening to him today, he sounded keen to jog the horse on, and he must need the dough if he's got a fella going round boozers trying to sell it, eh?'

'Well,' Fred said, stroking his chin, 'been thinking about it a bit, as it happens; reckon I might be in, if the others go for it, of course.'

I knew it, I fucking knew it . . .

'Having a gamble runs in my family, don't it?' he explained. 'My old man loved a bet. He would bet on two raindrops falling down a pane of glass. Did I ever tell you the best betting story to do with him? When he was at home on leave, during the Second World War? Every night, he was down the Catford dog track, every night. Only there wasn't enough greyhounds around to make a race, maybe they had ended up on dinner plates, don't know, but anyway, he comes up with this plan. He gets six doves . . .'

'Six doves?' I said, in disbelief.

'Yeah, six white doves,' chuckled Fred. 'Him and his pal, Teddy Herring, talked the owners of the dog track into letting them have the main straight of the track netted off, all down the sides, and then over the top, like cricket nets, you know? Then they got the doves, gave them each a dollop of different colour paint, so as to distinguish between them, and invited the punters to have a gamble on them.'

'How the fuck did they get them to race in a straight line?' I said, and then automatically thought, hold up, he's pulling my pisser and I've fallen for it . . .

'You bastard,' I said. 'You're getting me at it, aren't ya?'

'Nah, mate, this is kosher,' said Fred, smiling, his voice going up a notch. 'The old man reckons what they did was this: they only raced female doves. You get someone to walk the length of the straight waving a male dove in the air, giving off . . . er . . . male dove smells. Female doves can't resist that smell, so when the male dove gets to the other end they release the female racing doves . . . They paid out on the colour that crossed the line first!'

'Bollocks! I ain't having it.'

'What d'ya mean, bollocks? It's all true,' he said laughing, his steely little eyes glinting.

'Fuck off,' I said. 'Fucking racing doves on a dog track . . .'

'On my mother's eyesight,' Fred said, and as soon as he said that I knew the story was true. Fred rarely used that expression and when he did it meant one thing – he was talking straight up.

'Right,' he said, 'the horse. I reckon we have a serious chat on Sunday with the others and decide if we're in or out for it, yeah?'

'Can't say fairer than that, mate,' I said. 'And if they don't go for it, I'll go halves on six doves with ya!'

We both laughed out loud again, happy with the thought we were on to a scheme, and who knew where that'd lead ya. Life had suddenly got interesting again.

'Ta-ta, son, I'll bell the others, make sure we get a full turnout at The Dutchy,' he said.

Just then, his shop phone started up again. I waved at him and turned to go out. That was when I heard him say, 'Hello, Jean,' and shout 'BAX! For you, mate. It's your mum.'

I came back and took the phone.

'Hello, Mark, it's me, Mum. Thank God I found ya, son, been ringing all over the place. Get here as soon as you can, eh?'

She sounded really upset.

'What's up, Mum?' I asked, worried.

'Just get round here, mate, eh?' she said quietly, and then the phone went dead. I put the receiver down, confusion and worry now surging unexpectedly and terribly through my stomach.

Fred knew something was wrong right away. 'What's up son?'

'Fuck knows, got to shoot lively though, mate, speak Sunday, yeah?' and I went.

I walked and ran as fast as I could towards home, running over the possibles of what could have happened. Had she been mugged or had a fall? I'd told her to keep her wits about her, especially this time of the day when all the freaks came out. Had one of the outlaws died? Was my brother Glen okay? Had something happened to him? All these thoughts and more were going round my nut as I went through the gate, and instead of pulling out my keys I rang the doorbell – quicker that way.

My old man opened up and let me in.

'Dad?'

He just shook his head. It was then that I saw he'd been crying for what looked like a day and a week, and it was then that I suddenly felt very empty.

3

The C Word

You don't expect to see your old man crying, do ya? I didn't, anyway. Dads don't cry, simple as that. Nor do they ever look as scared as mine did right now. I followed him into the kitchen. My mum was sitting there, wringing her hands, a look of such shock on her face that I felt my heart drop.

'Dad, what's going on, mate?' I said. There were a dozen thoughts going through my brain, but nothing prepared me for what he was about to say.

'Bad news, mate,' he said as he choked through the tears. 'I've just got back from the hospital, told me I got ... cancer, and it ain't looking too good, son.'

He struggled to say the word cancer, and I got as far as the word, then my brain shut down. Jesus ... My dad has got cancer. The one thing no one wants to hear, and my dad was saying it to me. His firstborn. I sat down at the table opposite my mum and looked past her shoulder into the distance, trying to get my head round it.

The old man had been ill for weeks. Months really, now I thought about it, but no one paid it too much fuss. At first, it was a touch of the flu, a cough that he couldn't seem to shake off. Then he had started taking some time off work, going to bed in the afternoons, saying he ached all over. Should have sussed then this was getting serious. My old man was a grafter. He didn't take time off work. His bastard work ethic saw to that. We knew he had problems with his prostate, like loads of fellas his age, but he was getting treatment and we just thought it was only a matter of time before he got back to normal. Now we knew different. Now we felt hopeless.

My mum looked at me, and a jolt went right through my body. They had been married since 1958, a lifetime, a fucking lifetime. All she had known was being married to my old man and bringing my brother and me up. Now we had grown and she had begun looking forward to a time when the old man no longer worked and there were days out to the country, trips to the park, green bowling lawns, lunch-time drinks, peace, quiet, sunshine. That simple dream, those simple demands, had just been brutally snatched from her. Now she was faced with the sheer horror of growing old alone, the only partner she had ever known gone for ever. At that moment I felt so sad for her.

'What they saying up the hospital?' I asked the old man, still dazed at the news.

'Bad, mate, bad. The problem is that the prostate trouble has developed into bladder cancer, and they've missed it. Haven't diagnosed it in time, and now I've got it bad. Spread real quick. They are going to start chemo rapid but they said … it might be too late. I might not have long …' He put his head in his hands and I saw his teardrops hit the lino on the kitchen floor.

'Fuck me,' I said, as a strange and awkward lump invaded the back of my throat. The old man was only fifty-three. He would have made plans to go on till at least his seventies. You do, don't ya? That's what you expect.

I know tomorrow is promised to no one, but you don't think you'll peg out at fifty-fucking-three.

The doorbell went.

I nearly jumped out of my skin. My brother Glen had arrived. He had rushed home from work, after getting the same call as I got from the old lady. As the old man told him the news, I went into the garden, sparked up a la-di-dah. After five minutes or so, my brother came out, tears rolling down his boat. The pair of us looked at each other, struggling to know what to say.

'Don't look too good, eh, bruv?' I finally said after thirty seconds, which seemed like thirty hours.

'Fucking nightmare, ain't it? That poxy doctor has got a lot to answer for, I know that much,' Glen said, anger hitting every one of his words.

The doctor he was on about was a specialist. He had been treating the old man's prostate for a few months now, and you would have thought he would have seen the problem coming. But the old man just kept coming home saying everything was sweet, it was all under control. Something had gone badly wrong here.

'Goes without saying, we'll have to keep an eye on the old lady,' I said.

''Course, whatever she needs, mate, I'll be there,' Glen said, a slight sob in his voice.

There's three years between Glen and me, but it might as well have been three hundred years sometimes. All our life we had been told we were like chalk and cheese in looks and temperament. I took after the old man, big build, pale skin, blondish hair, blue eyes. My old nan, Connie, used to tell me I would have been all right if the Germans had won the war, 'cos I looked just like one of those 'aliens' – she meant Aryans. Glen took after my mum's side of the family – dark, almost swarthy, with brown hair and brown eyes. My mum's side of the family somehow had a drop of French Canadian in it, which explained the dark features. Whatever it was, we didn't look like brothers. That wasn't the only difference. Glen had settled down early with his bird Tracey. They lived a quiet life at the end of the northern line in Morden.

Me, I liked a scheme and a scam. I still lived at home, and although I had had a couple of long-term-ish girlfriends, I hadn't met anyone I wanted to plot up with. Like I say, chalk and cheese, but whatever the differences between us over the years, now we closed ranks and became solid. The old girl called us in. She had made us both coffee.

'Your dad has to go and see another specialist on Thursday,' she said, her voice wavering badly.

'I'll go with him,' I said. 'I'll get time off work.'

My mum looked relieved. She was a worrier at the best of times, and knowing we would take care of stuff like that would ease her mind. We sat and drank our coffee in complete silence, the four of us occasionally looking at each other, but too stunned for words.

Suddenly, the old man got up. 'I'm going to see Gudge. Want to tell him what's occurring.'

A couple of seconds later, we heard the front door shut behind him.

'Gudge is going to be beside himself,' my old girl said to no one in particular.

How right she was. My old man and Gudge went back donkey's years. They were closer than close, their memories stretching right back. They had played in the same football teams, dated the same birds, drunk the same drinks in the same boozers, done the same jobs, pulled off the same capers, talked the same, sung together in pubs, gone on holiday together. They were mates, proper mates. I'll never forget the time the old man had money troubles and I came into the kitchen to hear Gudge tell him he could have all his savings. As I said, mates, proper mates.

Mum suddenly got this reflective look on her face. She started to speak, her voice nothing more than a faint whisper, sniffing and wiping teardrops away as she spoke.

'You know, your dad would never take me to his house when we was courting, he was too ashamed of the state of it. His dad was in the British Queen every Friday night, Saturday and Sunday as well, spending all his wages, treating everyone to a drink, but giving Connie nothing. He did nothing around the house, no painting or decorating, and it fell into rack and ruin. Your dad often told me Connie would stand in the kitchen cooking the family meals, with one hand on the frying pan and the other one holding up an umbrella to keep the rain off the grub as it came in through the holes in the ceiling. I don't know why I just thought of that,' she said wistfully.

Glen and I smiled but our mum did not clock us, just carried on quietly reminiscing, inhabiting a place we could never ever get to.

'He also told me they had no door on the toilet, did you know that? The room was so small, and with them all being so tall, when they sat down for a pony, they banged their knees on the door. Anyway, one night your grandad came home rolling drunk, went in there and then suddenly kicked the door off its hinges. Your dad and your uncle Len were too frightened of what he might do to them if they were to put it back up, so it stayed door-less. Your dad hated those days. That's why, when he started earning, he looked after Connie, gave her a few bob when he had the spare, especially after your grandad died of TB in 1959. I know you boys have laughed at your dad being so house-proud, but he couldn't believe he had this place, not when you think what he came from . . .'

She suddenly went very silent, put down her cup and

then literally fell off her chair, collapsed there and then in the kitchen. One minute she was sitting at the table talking to us, the next she was lying on the floor. Me and Glen didn't have a scooby what to do or what to say. Suddenly, I felt really young, really vulnerable. I didn't feel old enough to know what to do, and it frightened the fuck out of me. We picked her up from the floor and carried her to a chair.

We sat her down and started trying to calm her down, telling her not to worry, that everything would be all right. But it was hopeless. She sat there sobbing her heart out, asking again and again what was going to happen, how would she cope, crying out Oh my God, Oh my God, over and over again. We did our best to say the right things, how we would always be there for her, do whatever she wanted, get her whatever she wanted, but the one thing she wanted we couldn't give her, and it was 'cos of that I felt so fucking helpless and so fucking sad.

After a while she said she wanted to lie down, and she went to bed. Glen and me sat in silence. Words didn't form until my brother got up and said he was going to ring his missus, tell her the news. He broke down, a couple of times doing it. After he had put the phone down, he told me he had to get home. Sitting here was doing his nut in. We hugged each other, promised to bell each other and he was off. Suddenly, I was alone. I sat in the kitchen and it was as if I had been frozen in time. I felt numb. I felt nothing, I thought nothing. I just sat there and I waited. For what? I didn't know. The old man was gone for ages, but when he came back it was obvious he had been crying again.

He came in and asked where Mum was. 'In bed, mate,' I told him.

'I think I'll turn in as well,' he said. 'Better get some kip yourself, eh, son?'

After half an hour, I popped up to check on them both. Dad was asleep, but even in the darkness I could see the old girl was just laying there, staring at the ceiling. I closed the door softly. I went to my room, but I knew sleep would be impossible. It was still reasonably early, so I came downstairs and phoned Gudge. He answered after one ring.

'Hello,' he said quietly.

'Gudge, it's Markie, mate.'

'Oh, fucking hell, boy, what's going on, mate? I can't believe it. It's so fucking unfair, son. It's bollocks.' He sounded angry and confused.

'Gudge . . . what did he say to ya?' I asked.

'Oh, Christ . . . told me it was only a matter of months, boy. The hospital might be trying to make it seem longer, but nah, it's all over.'

Silence enveloped us both. I knew in my heart that was the truth all along. The old man knew, my mum knew and all we could do now was hope for a miracle.

I broke the silence the only way I knew how.

'See ya Sunday, Gudge, eh? Have a pint and a chat, mate, eh?' I was this close to sobbing, an inch away from breaking in two.

'Yeah, see ya Sunday, son,' Gudge said briskly, 'give your mum a kiss from me and Doll, eh?'

The phone receiver must have accidentally fallen from his hand because suddenly I heard a bang and then the sound of his crying. I stood there listening to this strange heaving sound, and as I did so the enormity of what was happening hit me even harder. It was the second time that day I had heard a grown man cry, and it seemed so wrong. It was such a strange noise . . . a noise you should never hear.

The phone went *click*. Doll, Gudge's wife, must have picked up the receiver and ended the call. I put it down and went back slowly to my bedroom. I undressed in the darkness, settled on my bed and waited for the longest night of my life to begin.

4

Chris de Burgh Was a Sex Pistol

For the next three nights, I just lay there thinking about what was going to happen. Nothing else for it; I had to face the unthinkable. My dad was dying, he wouldn't be around for much longer. That thought alone frightened the life out of me. After three nights and days of absolute torment, of not knowing what I was doing, where I was going, a strange thing happened. I woke with the overwhelming feeling that the only way forward was to get things done. Stop fucking talking about stuff and do it, mate! Do it for my father, honour him with achievements that he would salute me for from high above. I know that sounds contrived and over-dramatic, but we only go round once, as far as anyone can prove, anyway, so to crack on would appear to be the order of the day. Once I had come to this conclusion, I could clearly see the path I had to follow and it fired me up.

On the Thursday I went up to the hospital with the old man, and just from looking at the consultant's face when we walked in it was obvious it was all over. The dramatic changes were there for all to see. The old man was really struggling to breathe, and his face was pale and drawn. When he went into the changing room, the consultant asked me where my mum was. I told him she was ill, suffering terribly with her nerves, and that she couldn't face a visit to the hospital this morning. He looked down at his papers and told me they would be starting the chemotherapy as soon as possible but I should know the cancer had spread really quickly, you could see that by Dad's condition, and there was little they could do. Thanks, I thought to myself. I kind of knew that already, but I appreciated his honesty.

On the way out of the hospital, the old man stopped halfway down one of those horrible long, soulless corridors that only the NHS can provide and leant on a wall. Then he turned his face to it and thumped the wall with all the strength he had left.

'Jesus, it's all over, ain't it, son? All over ... finished. Promise me one thing, look after your mum. You hear me?'

How I didn't cry there and then is beyond me.

'Of course I will, Pop,' I sighed, 'you know that. Come on, let's get you to the taxi.'

We sat in silence in that black cab all the way home. Needless to say, the next Sunday the meet at The Dutchman was very subdued. He was missed. Although the old man had only told Gudge, the rest of the lads knew. Gudge had passed on the word. One by one, they offered words of regret and absolute sorrow.

'Gutted, mate,' Fred said, 'gutted.'

'Well, what can you do, mate,' I sighed, 'he's got it and it don't look good.'

'What a right bastard, tragic,' said Alf. 'I'm so sorry.'

I sat there accepting their kind and sorrowful thoughts, but in all honesty I wanted to be somewhere else. The Dutchman was no longer a haven of warmth and comfort, it was now an overpowering reminder of times past. It would never be the same again. It couldn't be. As we sat there with our pints of gloom in front of us, it was clear a big hole had opened up between us, and we all felt it keenly.

Frankie and Charlie from the card school ventured over

and offered their best. So did many others. The whole of Camberwell, it seemed, had heard the news.

'Once they get that chemo going, he might well be sorted,' O'sh said. I wanted to correct him there and then, tell him it wouldn't be sorted, that it was way too late, that the fucking medical profession had naused the whole thing up, messed up the diagnosis ... but what would be the point of that, eh? What would be the point?

They would know soon enough when the collection for Thimble Baxter came round. Anger suffused me, swept up me from toe to head, like poisonous mercury. I was angry at the doctors, angry at the disease, just fucking angry. I slammed my glass on the table. I had decided to say something that had been on my mind ever since the old man had told me what was really going on inside him.

'Chaps,' I said, making sure I got everyone's attention. 'This might seem like a strange time to bring it up,' I announced, 'but I want to crack on with this horse thing. Okay?'

My boys stared at me in disbelief. I knew what they were thinking – namely, that I was an insensitive bastard. I didn't care. I had to channel this overpowering urgency to get things done into something concrete. I had to get positive or die and be buried with the old man. It was one or the other, and buying and racing the horse seemed the ideal way to start. After all, the old man had begun to come round to the idea, and I reckon, given time, he would have gone for it.

'Look, you don't know this, but my old man was coming round to the idea, and—'

'I know he was,' Gudge said, interrupting. 'He told me he wanted to do it, for you.'

There was an awkward silence for a few seconds. Then the O'sh piped up.

47

'Look, a few of us have been struggling with the thought of getting involved, no point lying to ya, can't see what we will get out of it, mate. But Fred has told us what the fella is looking for money-wise, and, well, this has changed things, ain't it? Why don't we do it for your dad, do it for Thimble?'

I thought my heart was going to break in two.

'Tart,' I said, and the table laughed, breaking up the thick, gloomy atmosphere.

'I'm in,' said Alf. I smiled at him.

'Yeah, and me,' said Dave.

And one by one, they all agreed.

'Listen,' I said, 'I admire you all saying this, but only do it if you really believe in it.'

Gudger looked at me seriously. 'Son, we're all old enough to do what we want to do, right? Now then, we're buying the fucking horse. End of, all right?'

I felt my face go red, and I was suddenly thirteen all over again, the very age I was when I took my first drink in Gudge's company. Rule one, never question these boys.

'Right,' O'sh said, 'I'll get a van, and we'll bomb down there to have a look at the bloody thing. If it exists, we'll have it, right?'

'Jen,' I shouted towards the bar, 'same again, darling,' and then we raised what was left of our drinks on the table and clinked our glasses together.

We were now a syndicate.

Before the old man had his first chemo treatment, he had a bad night and started pissing blood. The local GP who came out to see him during the night decided he needed to be in hospital so they could keep an eye on him. An ambulance was called, and I went with him and my mum to Guy's Hospital. She was in bits. I wasn't far off.

The old man was checked into a general ward and given a dose of something to settle him down. My old girl stayed there, wouldn't leave him. I stayed for a while but then got a cab home. The ward was so depressing. Death was everywhere. Men lay there just waiting to pass away. The whole scene put my head in a spin. The next day I went to visit the old man again. To my joy, he actually looked quite well.

'It's all the bleeding morphine I've had, ain't it?' he explained. He nodded to the switch that he used to give himself a little boost and said, 'Good stuff, this. Eric should sell it down The Dutchy.'

I smiled at my dad, happy to see his humour was still intact. I told him we had formed the syndicate and that we were going down to the see the horse at the weekend, check it out.

'Blinding, son, blinding. I'm in with that, mate, you know that, don't ya?'

'Yeah Pop, 'course, mate,' I said as he smiled at me. It was good to see him so positive.

The doctors told my mum he would be in there for the next two weeks at least, that they would run some checks and then start the chemo. I had a feeling then that these were going to turn into long weeks.

To visit the horse, we had arranged to meet up the next Saturday, at eight in the morning, outside The Dutchman and then drive up to Newmarket.

O'sh was supplying the transport. I was first at the pub, the result of being awake from the crack of dawn, unable to sleep, with thoughts of the old man going round and round my swede. As I stood outside the pub, I noticed for the first time how it actually smelt, as if all the doors and walls had been painted with a beer-and-fag-ash emulsion. I breathed in the aroma deeply and have to say I found it hugely comforting. O'sh had managed to get a van from his yard at the Royal Mail, and he honked the horn loudly as he pulled up. I got in the front seat and we sat there waiting for the others.

O'sh asked how I was bearing up, and the look I gave him was enough for him to know pretty well how I was doing. We sat in silence until Alf ambled up.

'Here he is,' the O'sh said brightly. 'I see they found the wreck of the *Titanic* the other day. You were on that, weren't ya, Alf? I heard you were the ice-cube maker, only you got a bit carried away.'

I had to laugh.

'Cheeky pair of bleeders,' Alf said, smiling. One by one the others turned up. Gudge had a Tesco's plastic bag with him. His packed lunch, he said. This turned out to be a nutritious meal of twenty Bensons and a *Sporting Life*. Eric, the guv'nor of The Dutchy, had let us have two crates of Fosters at cost, so we were all set. Once we were all aboard, O'sh kicked the van into action and we bombed off. As we reached the Elephant and Castle, which is all of five minutes down the road, I heard the crack of a tin being opened. I turned and saw that Alf, Fred, Dave and Gudge already had a card game on the go.

'You cheating old spunker,' Gudge said to Fred as he scooped up the pot.

'Fuck off, it's you, you can't even see what cards you got through those fucking glasses you're wearing.'

Obviously the card game was going well. Suddenly another voice broke out from the back.

'O'sh, do us a favour, son, pull up, mate, I'm busting to have a slash.'

'Bleeding hell, Alfie, we're only at Tower Hill,' said Dave. 'Should have gone before we set off, mate.'

He sounded like a million mums on a million car journeys.

'You old mumper, can't you control your bladder? Where you gonna go for a piss round here?' Fred demanded.

'Listen, mate, when you get to my age you'll know all about bladder control. 'Til then keep it quiet, okay?'

'For Christ's sake, at this rate we won't get to Newmarket 'til Monday,' O'sh sighed.

Alf got his wish and was dropped off by Tower Hill tube station. He disappeared down into it.

After twenty minutes and plenty of, 'Where the fuck has he got to?' he popped up again and got back in the van. As he got in, Dave noticed Alf's shoes were squeaking.

'Those shoes are making a bit of racket there, Alfie?'

'Means you ain't paid for them, if they squeak,' said Gudge.

'What?' said O'sh.

'If your shoes squeak when you walk, it means you ain't paid for 'em,' Gudge repeated.

Dave looked at Fred. 'Got 'em off you, didn't he?'

Fred looked at the offending footwear. 'Yeah, at half price, that's why it's only the right one piping up.'

The whole van laughed, and it was good to hear such a lovely noise again.

O'sh pulled off, and soon we entered east London. 'Passports out, boys, all had your jabs?' Fred laughed.

'Shithole, ain't it?' muttered Gudger as he surveyed the streets in front of him. Personally I thought it looked a lot like where we had started from, but I couldn't say nish, as there has always been this south versus east rivalry. God knows when it started, but it usually comes to a head at

51

the Millwall–West Ham games, not a day for the faint-hearted.

'Where's all this rivalry come from, then?' I asked no one in particular.

'All that goes back to the old docks, mate,' Alf explained. 'Proper distrust among those from the south and those from the east.'

'You're old enough to know, son,' said Fred, winking at Dave.

'Alf probably started it all,' Dave said, and we all cracked a smile at that hit.

After the East End, and a bit of motorway, we came into greener pastures. Rich green countryside flashed past the window.

'Mint sauce! Mint sauce!' shouted the O'sh as we passed a group of sheep.

'Typical of you,' I said to my best spar, 'food is never far from your thoughts, is it, son?'

'Too right, Bax; in fact, got to say I'm starting to get a bit hungry here, boys,' O'sh announced.

No one took a blind bit of notice. They were too wrapped up in the card game.

'Look what that lump of wood has put down there,' exclaimed Fred.

The barb was aimed at Alf. 'How can you play that? You've got the brains of a rocking-horse, you have.'

The lager was beginning to kick in.

'I'll give you a lump of wood in a minute, you saucy bark,' Alf retorted.

'Alf!' said Fred.

'WHAT!' shouted Alf.

'Give us a kiss,' Fred said, and with that he jumped in beside me in the front.

'Had enough, Fred?' I asked.

'Not 'alf ... they're doing my swede in, son,' he said with a smile.

As ever, Fred was immaculately turned out. Black polo neck, grey worsted trousers, a Burberry mac and a pair of dark brown suede tasselled loafers on his feet. Funny, but I can actually remember meeting him and Dave for the very first time, and not because of what they said or did, but 'cos of what they were wearing. That day, Fred had on a double-breasted pinstripe whistle, white button-down shirt and black brogue lace-ups. Dave was in a pink shirt, grey crew neck, Prince of Wales strides and black loafers. As I was well into the Mod lifestyle, and had been for the past couple of years, these guys were fascinating to me. I would often ask them about The Scene Club, or a designer like John Stephens, and they would laugh and ask me how the fuck I knew about any of that. They thought it funny that someone of my age would be interested in things they had taken for granted over twenty years before.

As I now had his undivided attention, I took my chance to ask Fred something that had been bothering me recently.

'Fred,' I said, 'whenever I read anything about the sixties, it always makes out that it was an amazing time in this country's history, when class didn't matter and the young ruled the world and everyone was on the gear and the orgies. But surely if you were stuck in a tower block in Camberwell and working every day in a factory, it couldn't have been that much fun, or was it?'

'Ah,' said Fred dismissively. 'All that swinging sixties stuff was for the Chelsea lot down the King's Road, or the poncey pop stars. They had the money. I mean, if you had to get up for an early shift on the papers, you wouldn't be hanging out of a mini moke at five in the morning with a rainbow painted on your boat, would you? As for the whole sex game, round my way it was simple. If you got a bird up the stick you did the decent thing, you married her. If you ended up with a couple of kids in a council flat, you had to make adjustments.

'I love my clothes, still do, but with two kids, I had to make some serious choices.'

'Such as?'

'Got to buy grub? The scooter has to go, that kind of thing.'

On hearing this, Dave butted in from the back. 'It weren't all tough times though, mate, was it? Let's be honest. I used to love going to the clubs, buying the schmutter, going to see the groups and the singers, magic days. Best ever for me was Otis at The Ram Jam Club in Brixton. The fella was a genius ... and on top of all that, I always got my leg over down The Scene, they had mattresses on the floor in the corner, remember, Fred?'

'Too right, mate, too right ...' and a little smile lit up both their faces. 'Happy days, happy days ...' they both sang softly in unison.

I decide to leave them to their memories and noticed that, in spite of the stoppages, the O'sh had done well. The journey had taken about two and a half hours to the outskirts of Newmarket. All we had to do now was find the stables. I pulled out the directions Sefton had given me, and after a couple of wrong turns, we had found the lane that led up to the Dawson House stables. O'sh pulled the van over and the majority piled out and made straight to the nearest hedge, frantically pulling at their flies. The sight of everyone standing there exclaiming, 'Oooh, I need this, mate,' was the first sight leafy Newmarket got of The Jolly Boy syndicate of south London.

After watering the daisies, we all started walking up the muddy lane.

'Oh, look at my webs, mate, fucking ruined, ain't they?' Fred suddenly cried.

The brown suede tasselled loafers he was wearing weren't exactly suitable for the amount of mud and horse shit he was now wading through. We all fell about laughing. I've never seen anyone look so out of place.

'Don't you sell wellies in your shop, Fred?' Alf enquired cheekily.

'Funnily enough, not a lot of call for them on the estates of Peckham, you silly old duffer,' Fred replied.

Up ahead I could see a fella coming towards us, looking us up and down with a great deal of suspicion. I took a guess as to who it was.

'Hello, mate, you Sefton?' I shouted.

'That's right,' he said, 'and you are ...?'

'Mark Baxter, spoke to you on the telephone. We're the syndicate, looking to buy one of your horses.'

He looked relieved, if a little puzzled, by the motley mob standing in front of him. I introduced Sefton to the lads, and one by one they shook his hand.

'Right. Follow me, I'll show you the horse.' He obviously wasn't one to fanny about; it was straight down to business.

'You'd think he'd offer us a cup of tea and a bit of cake or something, eh?' Alf muttered as Sefton briskly marched off.

'Ain't too much to ask, is it?'

We followed the horse owner to a couple of big barns. In the yard, various youngsters were mucking out the stables and there were a couple of little Jack terriers dodging about, here and there. The sounds and smells of horses filled the air. As we walked past a barn, Gudge suddenly went arse over teacup, slipping on a combination of water, straw and horse muck. I think the Fosters he had drunk might also have had a part to play in his downfall.

'You want to watch that there, Gudge, you might slip over!' Dave helpfully pointed out, as the rest of us reached down to help him.

'Get up, you dozy plank. This ain't the time for a kip,' O'sh gently reminded him.

'Fucking kip! ... Gawd help us, I'm telling ya, you'll have more room in the van on the way back ... I'll be in the local hospital at this rate.'

I could tell Sefton was struggling a bit with all the verbals flying around him, so I apologised.

'Sorry, mate, they ain't used to all the fresh air. It's having a bad effect on them,' I explained.

'Um, right,' he said, not looking at all convinced that we were serious punters.

He walked us to a stable and told us to wait outside. He went inside and after a minute or two, he came out and there, right in front of us, being led on a long rein, was what we had come to see. The horse was a big 'un all right, black, with a smudge of white that ran all the way down its nose. Dave walked up to it and started patting it, calling it a good horse, and then he ran his hands down its front legs ...

'Yep,' he said confidently, before pausing, 'it's definitely a horse.'

'Fuck me, it's James Herriot!' Fred said. 'Nothing gets past you, son, does it? You should have been a vet, you. You're a natural ...'

'As I said on the telephone, he's a big 'un, sixteen hands, or thereabouts,' Sefton said, looking the horse over. 'Eight thousand pounds I'm looking for. That'll include a year's stabling, food, training and vet's fees. On top of that I'll also enter the horse in a couple of beginner's races.'

We all looked at each other, realising the time had come. I winked to the boys.

'Bit small, ain't he?' I said. 'I thought he'd be bigger.'

'Looks a little underweight to me,' Dave said.

'Careful, Dave, don't lean on him too much, he might fall over,' Fred said.

'Hang on, hang on … Look, boys, he's in good shape. I look after my horses well,' Sefton said.

'Sorry, mate. Listen, we ain't saying it's neglected, are we?' I said, looking at the chaps.

'Well, you did say he was a bit small,' said the O'sh, pulling my chain.

'I need you, don't I?' I said to him. 'No, what I meant was, I was expecting a bigger horse for the sort of wedge you are looking for.'

Sefton made a face which quite clearly said you obviously know fuck all about horses, a fact that I have to admit, Del, the manager of our local Coral's, could certainly back him up on.

I piped up. 'Any chance of seeing him go through his paces? Just to make sure, like.'

Sefton arranged for his stable jockey, Jimmy, to have the horse jump a couple of fences so we knew we weren't buying a wrong 'un.

Got to say the horse looked in good shape.

'You got a pub round here, mate?' Alf asked. 'I'm Hank Marvin, and I think we need to have a chat amongst ourselves, go over a few things, like.'

'Yeah, there's a pub a mile or two down the road,' Sefton replied. 'It's called The Albion, you'll get food in there. It's reasonable stuff.'

'Right then, we'll do that, have a bite to eat and get back to you in an hour or two,' I told him.

'Okay, but be back here or telephone me by four, starts getting dark then, and I need to lock up,' Sefton said.

'Sweet,' I said, and off we went to the van. Ten minutes later Gudge and I were sitting in the pub whilst the others were at the bar ordering drinks and food.

Gudge quietly turned to me and, with a quizzical expression, said, ''Ere, d'ya see that *Stars in Their Eyes* last week?'

'Not a programme I really bother with,' I told Gudge. I didn't add that the mood I'd been in of late, the last thing I needed to see was a bunch of plums imitating another bunch of plums.

'I said to Doll, fuck me, I didn't know that,' Gudge continued.

'What didn't you know, Gudge?' I enquired. I really should have known better than to ask.

'See, the way it works is that the guy doing the imitation has to give out clues as to who he's going to do. So this fella walks up to that long streak of piss who does the programme and says, "I was born in Argentina, was an original member of the Sex Pistols and wrote Princess Di's favourite song." Fuck me, I thought, who's this then?'

From the clues Gudge had given me, I didn't have a scooby.

'Doll didn't know either,' Gudge continued. 'Then Matthew Wassis Face says, "Well, who are you going to be?" And the fella says, "Tonight, Matthew, I'm gonna be Chris de Burgh ..."'

For a second there I thought Gudge had said Chris de Burgh. 'Yeah,' said Gudge, 'Chris de Burgh.'

'You what? Chris de Burgh?! You're having a laugh, mate.

How many Fosters you had? Chris de Burgh was never in the Sex Pistols!'

'What you talking about, that's what the fella said, I'm telling ya.'

This was classic Gudger, talking bollocks most of the time and putting people in stitches by doing so.

O'sh came towards us with a couple of pints.

'Oi! O'sh!' I shouted. 'Gudger here reckons Chris de Burgh was born in Argentina and was in the Sex Pistols!'

O'sh, who has known Gudge for ever, shook his head.

'You silly old twonk,' he said. 'To start with, Chris de Burgh is Irish and he was never, ever, without a shadow of a fucking doubt, in the fucking Sex Pistols!'

Gudge shook his head. 'You're talking out yer mouth, son. I'm telling you, that is what the fella said.'

O'sh and me sat there dumbfounded. It had been a long day. We had shlepped out to the middle of nowhere to look at a fucking horse, taken hours to get here, and now this silly old duffer was bending our ears with this nonsense.

God give me strength . . .

Alfie came over to the table with more drinks.

'Here Alf,' said Gudger, taking his glass. 'D'ya see *Stars in Their Eyes* last week?'

'Yeah,' Alf replied, without missing a beat, 'I didn't know that Chris de Burgh was an Argie and in them Sex Pistols . . .'

'See, told ya,' Gudger said triumphantly.

O'sh and I just buried our heads in our hands and shook them. I couldn't take much more. When we looked up, all the drinks and the scoff were in front of us, and the real talking could begin.

'I reckon, all things being equal,' said Dave, 'we offer him six large and pay seven, tops.'

'Six grand, I hope I ain't stood for something here,' sighed O'sh. 'I must be as mad as the Chris de Burgh fan club sitting over there.'

'Too late to back out now,' I reminded him. 'Got to see it through. All agreed then, we offer six, pay seven?'

Everyone looked at Gudge and he nodded. It was on. I walked over to the phone in the pub and dialled Sefton's number. A couple of rings and it was answered.

'Hello, Sefton, Mark 'ere, mate. We've had a chat and yeah, we're up for it, decided to offer six grand for the horse ...'

The answer was what I expected.

'It's eight grand.'

'Nah, can't do eight. Can't you move at all?' Silence.

'Seven five,' he said cautiously.

'Tell you what, we'll go to six five. Last offer, mate.'

Another silence. Then a negative reply came down the line. I looked over at everyone staring at me. I did a round circle of their faces with my eyes and saw the expectation.

'Okay, seven ... final offer,' I said.

Then I turned away from the boys and as I did, I heard Sefton say, 'Okay, yours, he's yours.'

'Lovely,' I said, 'lovely. We'll be over within the hour, shake hands on it.' I put down the phone.

I turned round and said, 'Get the drinks in, Freddie. Bleeding Chris de Burgh and Princess Di could have slept with every one of the Sex Pistols in Argentina, for all I care. We've just bought a fucking racehorse.'

5

A Job for Life

It was Gudge who came up with the question. As we travelled home through the dark night, he suddenly asked, ''Ere, what's the horse's name?'

We all looked at each other, apart from O'sh who was peering carefully out of the front window keeping his eyes on the road ahead. I hadn't given it a thought. No one had. To everyone, he was simply ... the horse.

'He ain't got one,' I said. 'Even Sefton calls him the horse.'

'We'll have to name it then, won't we?' Fred said.

'How about The Flying Dutchman?' laughed Dave.

'Blinding, or how about Two Warm Lights,' said O'sh.

'Ere,' said Alf, 'he'll have to have racing colours as well, won't he?'

'Got to be Millwall blue and white, ain't it?' Fred said.

'Oi! Whad'ya mean, Millwall blue and white,' said Alf, a West Ham fan man and boy. Alf had been born East End but married a girl from down our way.

'I'm 'aving the claret and blue, son,' he proudly stated.

'Bollocks! It's a south London horse, ain't it,' Gudge pointed out in his own inimitable manner.

This left Alf with a puzzled look on his face. The rest of us just laughed. After half an hour of banter back and forth, we settled on four possible names. The Camberwell Beauty, which is a name of the rarely seen local butterfly;

Two Warm Lights, in honour of my old man, this being his regular drink; The Flying Dutchman, our pub of choice of course; and The Mumper, a term we all used on regular occasions.

As it was getting late and had been a long day, it was decided we should meet at The Dutchman the next day, Sunday, and sort it out once and for all. As soon as that was agreed upon, the van went quiet. First Alf, then Gudge fell asleep. I went as well, falling into that nice sleep where you can't open your eyes but you are kind of aware of what's around you. Next thing I knew, I could see the horse running round and round Camberwell Green Park with my old man on its back, only he was aged about twenty and looked really young. His face was all smoothed out and he was smiling. No more pain, no more worry. It was a lovely sight.

They started jumping over the park benches, the old man whooping it up as they did so, the horse clearing one after the other. His shouting got louder, and as it did the horse started to accelerate. His strong legs began gathering speed, and my old man started gripping the reins even tighter as they raced on and on, until *wallop*, the horse hit a bench and the old man was sent flying through the air. He went up and up, and then started to descend, faster and faster, and just as he was about to hit the ground . . . I jumped awake.

'All right, son?' said the O'sh, looking over at me laughing.

'Yes, mate,' I said, getting my bearings back. Hardly surprising, I suppose, I should combine the horse and the old man in a dream. He would have loved today.

At twelve the next day, we were all safely gathered in The Dutchman, where we took our normal table with our normal drinks and got ready to christen the horse. Gudge had already decided how we were going to go about it.

'Right, the simplest way to do this,' he announced, 'is to put the four names in a pint pot and then get Brenda to draw one out and that's the name we'll have. No arguing, that's it. Same for the colours, save all this poncing about.'

No one argued, the Gudge Man had spoken. He turned to the bar. 'Brenda, you got a pen, sweetheart?'

Brenda nodded and came over with one of those small blue pens you get in a bookie's. Gudge took it and wrote a different name on four separate fag papers. The papers were then placed in a pint glass, which Gudge shook up and then handed back to Brenda.

'Do us a favour, girl,' he said nicely. 'Pick one of those out.' Brenda put her hand into the glass and pulled out a Rizla.

'Go on then, read it out, babe,' Fred said.

'Yeah, come on,' Gudge said.

'Shut up then,' she said good-naturedly and then with a voice that has launched a thousand raffles, she announced, 'The winner is ... The Mumper!'

'Get in there,' I cried. That was my suggestion. And for the uninitiated among you ...

Mumper /*Mump'er*/ *n* A beggar; a begging impostor. *Deceived by the tales of a Lincoln's Inn mumper.* –Macaulay.

I had first heard the word mumper when I started work in the Print. It was used by Bill Braithwaite, my old guv'nor, and for ages I had no idea what it meant, even though I had now begun to use it daily. One day I couldn't stand it any more, so I asked him for the definition.

'It's a word for a sort of ponce, son,' he explained. 'It's donkey's years old. My old gran would call my grandad a mumper, among many other things.'

'I like it,' said Gudge, 'good name that.'

'I preferred Two Warm Light Ales,' said O'sh. 'Now we've ended up with Mumper, the bleeding Jumper ...'

'Nothing wrong with that, son,' Gudge said. 'Anyway, it was all done fair and square, weren't it? No complaints, now.'

'What about the colours, Millwall or West Ham?' O'sh asked. As five of us were south London and only Alf was from the dark side, there was no contest really. Millwall it was.

'I thought you were going to draw them out of the glass?' complained Alf. 'You south Londoners are all the same. Where's Reggie and Ronnie when I need a bit of back-up ... fuck ya!'

The table laughed and then the drink began to flow.

The next morning, Monday, found me in mourning, mourning the fact that, as usual, I caned it yesterday and now had a hangover the size of the 45 bus I was taking to work. It's always the same of a Sunday, carnage, absolute carnage, and more so yesterday after the naming of our very own racehorse.

Our own racehorse. Who would have thought it?

Early morning London flashed past in grey as I travelled from finest Camberwell to Fleet Street and planned the day ahead. My main concern was, who would be on my shift today? I was hoping it was Mickey and Sagey. They were the same age as me and we had similar tastes, such as smart clothes, R 'n' B tunes and having a good time. The only thing we differed on was our football teams. The two boys were mad for Tottenham ... some people just have bad taste, I suppose, when it comes to the national game. As I said, I got this job at the Print through Gudge. When I left school, he put me on a kind of unofficial waiting list. It took a couple of years for my name to rise to the top, and while I waited, I did all kinds of things to make a dollar.

Throughout it all, I was desperate to get into the world

of the Print. Everyone knew the score: once in, you had a job for life. Then, a couple of years back, my old man came home and said, 'You need to get yourself to The Dutchman on Sunday. Gudger's got some news. All right?'

I didn't have to ask any questions. Come Sunday, I was the first punter in the pub. Soon after, my old man and Gudge bowled in. The usual verbals ensued, how their week had gone, how pony Millwall were, until finally the talk got round to why we were all there. Gudge went first.

'Spoke to Sid about you, boy. The man said he might find you a way in.'

Sid was the main charge hand on Gudger's night shift. He was the fella who paved the way for all of us looking to get on the Print. 'He wants to have a chat, no promises like, but he's the one in the know.'

'Worth looking after Sid as well,' my old man butted in. 'Gudge tells me he likes a drop of Scotch, so take a decent bottle with you, no rubbish, boy.'

As this man was about to change my life, it was the least I could do. Gudge said he had arranged for me to meet Sid in The Popinjay, a pub on Fleet Street, the next day at twelve.

'You can't miss him,' Gudge said. 'He's a big man. Mid-fifties, grey hair. When you walk into the pub he'll be sitting at the end of the bar. That's his spot.'

The next day I was up early. Spent hours getting ready. I wanted to look the part, impress the man. So out came the brown whistle, complemented with a nice crisp white and navy-blue check button-down and burgundy penny loafers. At twelve exact, I bowled into The Popinjay with my green Adidas bag in my hand and spotted a fella sat alone at the end of the bar with half a glass of dark liquid placed in front of him.

The pub was a quarter full. I walked over, introduced myself. "Allo son, Gudge has told me about ya, and of course I know your dad. Sit down, son, sit down.' I did as I was told and pulled a bottle of Scotch out of the bag and placed it on the table. It seemed the right thing to do.

'Thought you might like this,' I said.

'Ta, son,' he said, picking it up. He was smiling, and probably thinking *this boy's been schooled well*. 'One of my favourites, I'll look forward to a drop of that.'

Sid then started giving me the SP on the job, explaining that he would get me into an office, where I would bide my time. If I kept my nose clean, I could then move on to all the extras the world of the Print had to offer. But that was some way down the line. In the meantime, I would start work at a place called the National News Agency.

'It's a messenger's job,' he explained. 'You'll be given a three-month temporary contract. You start a week today. When you get there, ask for Jackie Mays. He'll show you the ropes.' And that was it. Simple as that. I had been waiting for that meeting for the past two years, and it was all over in a matter of ten minutes.

There's an old saying in life, it's not what you know, it's who you know. Never a truer word spoken. I walked out of the pub feeling ecstatic. I was on my way to securing a job for life. When I got home, my old man was chuffed to hear the news, as was the old lady. They could now see their eldest was settled in a well-paid job for the rest of his natural. All a parent could ask for, really.

On the following Monday, I pitched up at the National News Agency, located at number 64 Fleet Street. Standing outside the five-storey building I couldn't fail but be impressed. This was obviously a highly successful operation. I soon discovered that the NNA had started off life providing all the national papers with the latest breaking news. It had proved so efficient at doing this that everyone, from the Royal Family downwards, went there first. If the NNA was unaware of a news event, that was because it simply hadn't happened yet. It had become the country's official mouthpiece.

I walked in, glided across the marble floor to the reception desk and told the woman sitting there I was looking for a Jack Mays. She barely acknowledged me, just picked up a phone. A minute later the fella Jack came down, a tall man with a large moustache. He nodded in my direction.

'You the new boy, Baxter?' he asked.

'That's me,' I replied. As we walked to the lifts, I added, 'Nice to meet you, mate, here on a three-month contract.'

'Three-month, eh?' Jack said smiling, then out of the side of his mouth he quietly added, 'Don't worry 'bout that too much, son. Sid's had a word. Play your cards right and you'll be here much longer than three poxy months. Follow me: they've put you on the third floor.'

We got into a lift and went upwards. When we stepped out, I saw a sign above the door saying Sports Department. That'll do me, I thought. I love a bit of sport. My playing days were mostly behind me, vodka and cigars had won me over, but I could watch football, boxing, golf and horse racing all day long if needs be. Loved all of them. The office was full and noisy. About twenty-five men with white shirts, ties and beer guts sat at desks, furiously smoking fags, attacking big old typewriters with huge gusto, the phones ringing constantly. A shout of 'Copy!' would suddenly go up and an old guy, shabbily dressed with a bandage on his head, carpet slippers and a stained jumper with holes in the elbows would struggle up from his chair, walk over to a journalist, take the copy and shuffle off. That same man now walked right past us and Jack stopped him.

'Wally, Wally, come here,' he said. 'This is Mark, and he'll be working with you for a while.'

Wally looked me up and down a bit and grunted a sort of reply. As he did, a rancid smell of urine and alcohol rose off his body and hit my nostrils. I stepped back a little.

'You're all his,' Jack said to me, smiling and walked off.

Fuck me, so this is the glamorous world of the Print, I thought as I stood looking at the old bloke in front of me. I would later discover that Wally was incontinent, and after a lunchtime session down the pub would often wet his strides. Hence the aroma. Lovely.

'Come with me, son,' Wally slowly said.

'What happened to your nut?' I said, trying to make friendly talk.

'Fell asleep, didn't I?' he replied as we got to the table where he had been sitting. 'Fell a kip and banged me head on here,' pointing to the table. 'Claret all over the place.'

I couldn't believe what I was hearing.

'Anyway, get that chair over there, sit down and then I'll go through what's what.'

I pulled over an orange moulded plastic chair, sat down and then watched in amazement as Wally's eyes now slowly closed, his head nodded, his body sagged and he fell asleep. Right in front of me! I sat there feeling like a right lemon, not knowing what to do. I looked around for some help but if anyone had noticed what was happening, they didn't appear to be bothered. Suddenly, someone shouted 'Copy!' and without warning, Wally's eyes opened.

'C'mon, son,' he said and slowly got to his feet. 'I'll show you what to do.'

I got up and followed him. We walked over to a desk

where a piece of paper lay in a tray. Wally picked up the paper and placed it in another tray on a desk next to it. Then he turned and walked back to where we had been sitting. That was it. That was my job. Taking a bit of paper from one tray and putting it into another.

'You think you can handle that M ... Mat ... Matthew,' Wally said, getting my name wrong. I couldn't see the point of correcting him.

'Yeah,' I replied, 'yeah, I believe I can manage that.'

We sat down and again Wally closed his eyes and fell asleep. Around me, dozens of men typed away, people coming and going, and in the middle of it all there was Wally fast a kip. I couldn't help but smile to myself. I had been there an hour or so, and had now done a couple of solo runs without his aid, when all of a sudden an overwhelming smell of stale perfume hit me. I looked up and saw a little fat fella staring at me. His very sparse barnet was piled on top of his head like a ragged bird's nest, and his eyebrows looked like they were painted on. On closer inspection, it turned out they were.

'Oooh, hello, who are you?' he said in a very effeminate voice.

'Mark, I'm Mark, I'm helping Wally out,' I replied, a little bit startled. The fella looked over at Wally and an obvious look of disgust crossed his face.

'He's a drunk, he is. Absolute piss artist. Yes.'

He held out his hand and said, 'My name's Trevor, Trevor Oxford. I work here too. Yes.'

It turned out that Wally and Trevor shared this job, one on the early run, hours seven 'til three-thirty, the other doing the twelve 'til eight-thirty shift. It was quickly apparent that they badly despised each other. Wally, on hearing voices around him, woke up again and rubbed his eyes.

Clocking Trevor, he said, 'Right, I'm getting me dinner,' and he ambled off.

Trevor took his vacant chair. 'Piss head,' he muttered. 'And tight, so tight. If he ever dropped a fiver it would hit him in the back of the head on its way to the floor, love. He once got thrown out of Kennedy's 'cos he moaned they were charging him for the greaseproof paper as well as the quarter of ham he was buying; he said the scales weighed the paper and that affected the price, can you believe that? Horrible man.'

I smiled at Trevor's patter. At least he was more talkative than Wally. Well, he was awake for a start. For the next hour I sat there and listened as he gave me his view on life, the universe and everything. Yes. Women were gold-diggers, yes. Never trust them, yes. They are horrible creatures, yes. You'll like this job, yes. It began to drive me potty. Yes?

I sat there, transfixed. In a strange, road-crash kind of way, Trevor was absolutely fascinating. A lavender, no doubt, but a fascinating lavender. At just after one, Wally came stumbling back from his lunch and took his chair. He stank of beer. Trevor shot him another nasty glance and announced, 'Well, I am off to eat. Yes.'

Wally took no notice. He just mumbled something and closed his eyes. I had this job sussed already, so I took it upon myself to get busy. Every time someone shouted, 'Copy!' I would walk over before Wally could stir and take the sheets of paper being offered.

'All right, mate,' I said to a few of the journalists, being friendly. Nothing doing. They all blanked me. Except the ones who looked at me with expressions of, 'How dare you speak to me?' I hadn't encountered anything like this before. In my walk of life, to say hello to someone and get a response was natural. Not here, though. Obviously I was expected to know my place. Okay, if that's how you want to play it, I thought to myself, arseholes to the lot of ya ...

After an hour of me moving bits of paper from one tray to another, Trevor returned from his lunch and woke Wally up.

Wally stretched out, looked at me and said, 'Right Matthew, off ya go, son, see ya tomorrow.'

It was two in the afternoon. I had been there just four hours. I looked at him in disbelief.

'What?'

'Go home, son, you're making the room look untidy.'

'But ... I've only just got here,' I pointed out. I had expected to go on lunch, not to be sent home.

'Bill, our guv'nor, told me you were only to do a couple of hours for the first couple of days, break yourself in, like. It's two o'clock, go on, piss off ... Trevor's here now. Three's a crowd, I'm done and so are you.'

I looked at Trevor for guidance, but he just smiled at me and nodded for me to go. I had no choice.

'Okay,' I said, 'if you say so, I'll go.'

I got up and walked out of the room. As I did so I thought, any minute now someone is going to stop me and ask where the fuck are you going? But I was wrong. No one said a dickie bird. I looked back, but no one was looking my way, so I carried on through the doors.

On the bus home, it hit me. It was a set-up between Wally and Trevor. When I go back in tomorrow, someone will want to know where the fuck I was and give me a right bollocking, maybe even the tin-tack. Furthermore, if they ask those two old nutters for evidence, God only knows what they'll say. I was well and truly fucked. I got home by three and walked through the back door into the kitchen.

My mum was there, cooking.

'What you doing home?' she demanded. 'You ain't lost that job already, have ya? Your dad will kill you. Gudge went through murders to get you that job.'

'Mum, shut up will ya? They let me go home. It got to two, and that was it, I wasn't wanted any more.'

'Don't you lie to me,' my mum said. 'What do you think I am? Stupid or something?'

'Leave it out, Mum. God's honest, they sent me home.'

I tried to explain but the old girl just wasn't having any of it, and who could blame her? Who would have believed the story I was coming out with? That I had spent the day with a piss head and a lavender, both of whom had told me to go home four hours into my shift. I went up to my room, shut the door and spent the rest of the afternoon listening to *Mexican Green* by Tubby Hayes, eyes shut and trying to ignore my mum, who came up every now and then to ask me if I was sure they let me go home and did I want to tell her something?

Thankfully, when the old man came home that evening, he was able to calm her down. 'That's the way of the Print,' I heard him tell her.

'It has its own way of doing things and it's best not to question it. If they told the boy to go home, then they told the boy to go home.' My mum eased up after that. Like my dad, she was a grafter, came from a world where you worked hard whatever the conditions. All of this was a bit alien to her. All she needed was my dad's reassurance, though, then she was fine. Truth is, I could always rely on the old fella. Don't get me wrong, we'd clashed heads a few times, but we were close. Always had been. I think that of all the things we had in common – music, clothes – it was our love of football that bound us together the most.

My old man loved the game, absolutely loved it. He would come home an hour late for his dinner because he had stopped to watch a bunch of kids kicking a ball about in a park. They tell me he wasn't a bad player himself, that his park team actually threw up a couple of lads who became professionals. One of them was a fella called Joey Wallace who signed for Wolves, a top side back in the fifties. Nearly did the Double in 1960 just before the Spurs cracked it, so my dad's mob must have been a decent standard. As soon as I was old enough, the old man took me down Millwall.

The date is burnt into my memory. My first game was against Sunderland on 26 September 1970. My sixth birthday had taken place on the 22nd, so this was a proper treat. I remember it to this day.

The old blokes in their grey overcoats and flat caps eating hot dogs, a few skinheads dotted about the terraces, the peanut-seller shouting about his Percy Daltons and the crowd throwing the bags of monkey nuts from the front to the back of the stands, and everyone drinking cups of steaming Bovril, holding on to the cups in the cold night air like their lives depended on it. Me and the old man sat in the seats (I was too small then for the terracing), and I remember him shouting on his favourite player, the full-back Harry Cripps. When 'Arry Boy brought the Sunderland winger crashing to the ground through one of his enthusiastic but clumsy challenges, the crowd erupted. The noise startled me badly. I looked round in fright but some bloke behind me saw my face and winked, as if to say, 'It's all right, mate, welcome to The Den.' After that, despite my first game ending up a drab 0–0, I was hooked. Every week, I asked my old man if we could go to the game, and bless him, he did his best to get me there. I can never forget his habit of taking a small transistor radio to every game, so he could listen to all the Saturday-afternoon results on the walk to the bus home. He was like the Pied Piper of New Cross, a trail of other supporters following him asking how Chelsea, the Spurs, or whoever, had got on. He *needed* to know the scores, it was almost a matter of life and death. My favourites, though, were the night games at The Den. The players blowing out holy air under floodlights, the ball making a *schussshing* sound as it zipped over the turf, the whole pitch bathed in a glorious muted colour under the floodlights.

The fact that Millwall didn't win anything but the odd game here and there didn't seem to matter; it was live, professional football and I absolutely loved it. As I got older, my mates and me started going to games on our own, although if I knew the old man was going, I would always meet up with him at some stage, the pair of us laughing or moaning depending on how they had done. Funnily enough, it rubbed off on my old girl as well.

At home, she watched as much football as we did on the telly, and actually became very tactically aware. Every now and then, she'd look up from her knitting and say, 'That left-back wants to get forward more, there's plenty of space for him there.'

Once I started work, I saw less of the old man. You grow up and move on, dont'cha? I was well into my music by this point, especially the jazz gear, and I was hardly going to take him to the Electric Ballroom on a Friday night for a spot of Paul Murphy's DJing, was I?

That's why the drink with him and Gudge, Fred, Dave and the others on Sundays sat right with me. Many of my mates thought their old fellas were tossers and ignored them. I thought the complete opposite. My old man was one of my best mates, and the others he sat with weren't far behind. They all had something I could learn from.

The other passion my old man had was singing in pub talent nights. Even though he was essentially a shy man, he was good, very good. When I reached thirteen or fourteen, I began touring around with him in the south London area, visiting pubs in places like Peckham, Walworth and the Elephant. I would plot up at a table and he would clamber onstage and stand with his back almost to the crowd. Then he would start singing. I know he's my old man, and you can accuse me of looking through red misty specs when I talk about him, but once he started singing I swear the whole pub would go quiet and everyone would stand and listen.

'I tell you, son,' Gudge would always say to me at those moments, 'your dad can't half chant.'

He always started with the same three numbers. First up, 'Roses of Picardy', which was an old World War One tune covered by the likes of Perry Como. Then he went into 'I Left My Heart In San Francisco', the Tony Bennett standard and finally, 'Any Time', by his favourite singer Eddie Fisher, or Eddie Fishcakes as he called him. If there was a competition on, invariably he would win, but he always put his prize money back in the whip, so everyone would end up having a drink on him. Of course, I'd be given a Coke with a straw poking out of it, but that wouldn't stop me sneakily drinking someone else's pint by the end of the session. When I made a move for a second pint, my old man would suddenly bark, 'Oi! No more, son. School in the morning, and your mother will have my bollocks for earrings if you go home rolling.'

I didn't see a lot of him during the week as I got older. He often worked late and I was out with the lads, but you know what, even if I had been on the piss on a Friday night and rolled in at four in the morning, he would be knocking on my bedroom door at ten to twelve on the Saturday, shouting, 'C'mon son, liven up. *Grandstand* starts in ten minutes.'

I would crawl out of my pit and struggle downstairs to find two ham and tomato rolls and a cup of coffee waiting on a tray in the front room. It meant I didn't have to fuck about in the kitchen looking for something to eat. I could just sit down and watch the sport with him. A looked-after kid or what, eh?

Despite my old man's explanation about my first day on the Print, and the reassurances to my old girl, I was shitting myself going back to work the next day. I was absolutely sure that as soon as I walked in I would be given a major bollocking. And you know what? It never happened. I walked in, and the first thing I saw was Wally sitting in his usual seat, head going like a nodding dog, struggling to stay awake.

He glanced up at me.

'All right Matthew,' he said. 'Come back for more, then?'

I just laughed. 'Yeah, thought I might as well. After all, ain't got much else on.'

I later realised that in all the time I worked with him, he never once got my name right. It didn't seem to matter after a while.

Later on that day, Trevor came and took over from Wally. 'Hello,' he said in his high voice, 'come back to old Trevor, have we? Yes.'

He was looking me straight in the eyes, and I smiled a little nervously at him. Trevor giggled. Yes. Sorry, mate. No!

The morning wore on and I began to relax. My old man had been right. This world, the world of the Print, was a law unto itself. I settled down in my chair, waiting for the shout of 'Copy!' to push me into action.

'You Mark?' demanded a booming, cockney voice whose vocal cords had been soaked in nicotine.

The question woke me from my daydream. I looked up, startled, to see a tall, imposing middle-aged fella. I nodded.

'Thought as much. Hello son, Bill, Bill Braithwaite, I'm in charge of all the messengers here.'

I shook Bill's hand, which was like a bunch of bananas. Wally and Trevor had mentioned a Bill yesterday.

'Thought I'd come up and introduce myself. How's Wally and Trevor treating ya, okay?'

'Yeah, they're fine,' I said, lying.

'Good,' he said. 'You got a minute? Come over here.'

Bill put his arm round my shoulder and steered me away from the sleepy Wally.

'Look, son, as you have probably sussed, a lot of the men here are getting on a bit. That means the firm is looking for a couple of bright lads to come in and eventually take over, know what I mean? Now, I know this isn't the most exciting work in the world, but just wanted to tell ya, keep that,' he said, tapping my nose, 'clean, and, well, you never know how far you can go, son.'

Straight away, I liked Bill. He reminded me of the fellas in The Dutchman. Decent geezers with kind hearts and coronets.

'Okay,' I found myself saying.

'Sid tells me you're from south of the river. That right?' he asked.

'Yeah, Camberwell. Know it?'

'Yeah, I know it, son, 'er indoors gets her wet fish from a stall down at East Lane every Thursday.'

He was local, or used to be. Could be sweet here.

'All right, son, stick this for a couple of months and we'll see what's about after that.'

Then his voice changed.

'You get away early yesterday?' he demanded to know.

Fuck, and it was going so well. Now it was here, the big bollocking. I thought I had got away with it.

'I didn't want to go,' I said, 'I kind of, sort of . . .'

'All right boy,' Bill said jokily, 'settle down, don't lose your bottle. It's all right, I told that old mumper to let you have an easy one on your first day. Thought you should settle yourself in gently, no need to rush about on your first day, is there? Anyone says anything to ya, tell them Bill said it was okay, all right?'

I smiled. I was starting to like it here.

After a couple of weeks I was beginning to get used to Trevor and Wally's 'ways'. They were obviously, in their own manner, a pair of first-class nutters, but I was warming to them. Still, that didn't stop me branching out a bit and talking to some of the younger faces I kept seeing about, all in different departments. The other lads in the office were like me, young, working-class boys who had been recommended to the firm by relatives already in the Print. Bobby and Danny were the two I got on particularly well with. I think one of the things that got us talking (apart from the fact that we all wore Farah trousers) was our mutual amazement at how many old boys were employed in this gaff, and how they got away with doing as little as possible. Bobby's old man had told him that the old 'uns were untouchable. If the firm decided to 'let them go', the unions would create havoc. The fact that most of these geezers were so far over the retirement age they were about to hit year one and start all over again didn't seem to matter at all.

One day, Danny began telling me about this guy Ted, who worked in his section. Ted was in his eighties and as far as Danny could tell, his only job was to make tea for the editorial staff. This, Danny pointed out, made Ted the oldest tea boy in the country.

'Don't say anything but here he comes now,' Danny said.

I looked up to see this little old bloke coming towards us. He had a face like a bulldog, with a jutting jaw and the bandiest legs I have ever seen.

'All right my old cunt ... tree,' he said to Danny as he walked past carrying a kettle.

'What did he just call ya?' I asked. Danny just laughed.

'Heard that, did ya? All day yesterday, I thought he was calling me and everybody else a cunt. I was getting well wound up until I noticed that after a little pause he said the word tree as well. As in, "Hello my Old Country".'

We all shook our heads.

'They are fucking lunatics, the lot of them,' I noted.

'I know,' Danny replied, 'but lunatics you can't help liking. Still, better get your fill of them, as I hear the firm is looking to get rid of 'em.'

'How do you mean?' I asked.

'The company wants to put this conveyor-belt system in. Instead of all these old guys moving bits of paper around, the journos will just whack it on a belt and that will take it to the subs and the editors.'

'When's all this happening?' I asked.

'Fuck knows,' Danny said. 'They wanted to do it back in 1981 but the union has been stalling them ever since, claiming it's new technology and will cause redundancies.'

'A conveyor belt?' I said. 'New technology?'

'It's the Print, mate, you know the score. Law unto itself. Everyone's at it, trying to keep the gravy train going. You up for a sherbet after work?'

I certainly was. Actually, I was up for a sherbet before, during and after work. There were two pubs that everyone from our offices generally used. The Red Lion, at the back of where we worked, and The Dog and Duck, which was on Fleet Street itself.

The Red Lion was where our switchboard called first, if they were looking for someone who should have been working. It was pretty usual to hear Mary, the Irish landlady, regularly calling out above the din of the pub, 'Which one of you fuckers is supposed to be on duty on the News Desk? . . . Phone!'

Over at The Dog and Duck, Joey, the landlord, was a great fella, also of Irish extraction. He had a way with words and a few sayings that fascinated me. For example, whenever you asked him the time, he'd say, 'Quarter past the freckle, halfway round the turd.' He also called everyone Skipper. That way he didn't have to remember any names. Trouble with Joey was that he liked his own supply just a little bit too much. He'd be speaking to you quite normally about the football or whatever and then, mid-sentence, he would stop talking and fall forward in the classic 'Timber!' style, out cold from the effects of the drink.

As our drinking was often interrupted by the firm's switchboard, we put into place our own system to counteract this irritating fact of life. One of us would stay behind at work, so if things got a little bit busy, that person could cover until we got back. We worked this system on a rota basis so everyone got a drink out of it. And believe me, those in our building liked a drink.

From the journos to the security guys to us, everyone would be in the pub at some stage during the day, necking the drink like it was going out of style. Yet despite this fondness for the sauce, and the bonhomie it created, the various groups didn't really mix that much. There were one or two exceptions, but in the main, you stuck to your immediate colleagues. Everyone else you treated with indifference or hostility. Especially those journos who would sit at their desk and shout to you, 'Boy! Copy!' I had to grit my teeth then. Boy, fucking boy. Who are you calling a boy, you university ponced-up ...

One day at work, the phone call I was waiting for from Bill Braithwaite came through. Luckily, I wasn't in the pub at the time.

Bill said, 'Sid wants to see you in the morning. Your three months are nearly up and ...' he paused for just a little bit too long before adding, 'you have been granted a union card.'

The loudest bells I have ever heard went off inside my head. I was in! I had cracked it. I was on the Print, and that meant one thing and one thing alone – I had a job for life. I could do what I wanted and no one could touch me. For the rest of my working days I would have regular bunce coming in and a lovely pension waiting for me at the end of it. You couldn't ask for any more at eighteen years of age. I went home that night and told my old man. He was so pleased for me.

'Well done, boy, nice one,' he said. 'Remember. You owe Gudge a large one for this.'

A large one? Gudge could have a drink from me every night for the rest of my life if he so wanted. That night, I went to sleep the happiest face in Camberwell. The next day, I went down to see Sid alone. No one else had been given a card. I asked about my mates, Bob and Danny, and it seemed that they had gone to the boozer just a little bit too often and had missed out this time around. Naturally, they were choked. But it wasn't the end of their world. As it turned out, they were taken on for a further three months and then given permanent work after that. Someone had obviously pulled more strings than the Thunderbirds on their behalf. Sid took me into his office.

'Well done, young Mark. Sign there, son.'

I scribbled my name and then he handed me my membership card. On it were printed the magical words – National Society of Operative Printers and Assistants, Graphical and Media Personnel, NATSOPA for short. I was smiling from ear to ear. From now on, that card would always get me a job somewhere within the Print. Which, of course, meant I would always have the opportunity to earn decent dough, and when you come from my manor there is no greater reward, apart from Millwall getting to a cup final, which is defined in the dictionary as a freak of nature …

When I came out of the office, Bill was waiting for me. 'Hello, boy, congratulations, son, well deserved. We are gonna start you in Despatch. I'll have a word with Personnel, get you a start date, that okay with you?'

The smile on my face faded a little. Despatch? All I had heard from everyone over the last three months was that the despatch boys were the biggest bunch of rude, miserable, horrible bastards anyone had ever met. I swallowed hard.

'Despatch?' I asked.

'Yeah, Despatch. Got a problem?' He seemed to sense my unease.

'No, Bill,' I said, quickly styling it out, 'not at all. I'll give it a go.'

'That's very decent of you,' Bill replied, smiling, 'to give it a go. Very decent.'

The news knocked me back a bit but then I thought, sod it. Who fancies a sherbet? The next day, as I lay in bed watching the ceiling spin one way, then the other, recovering from a lock-in at The Dog and Duck, I smiled to myself as I thought of the forthcoming Monday and the rest of my working life ...

'You Billy Sastard! ...'

'Bollocks! ...'

'What d'ya mean, bollocks? I saw ya cheat, you no-good shithouse ...'

'Bollocks! ...'

I was walking down a wooden staircase with Bill Braithwaite towards the despatch department on my first day, and a torrent of expletives was rushing up to greet me. Christ, I thought, what am I walking into? Sounds like a fight is about to break out. I looked at Bill for reassurance. He just looked at me, a small smile on his face.

'Don't worry 'bout them, boy, bark's worse than their bite.' Oh, that's all right then ...

'He's doing it again! Fucking 'ell, Bob, what are you doing? You cheating swine.'

'Bollocks, Len, you just don't like losing, mate.'

As I walked in with Bill, everyone suddenly stopped and turned. I scanned the room quickly. What a shithole. There were odd chairs on their last legs parked next to a table on top of which were old fag packets and sweet wrappers. Page three birds were sellotaped to the walls, in particular, Tory pin-up Samantha Fox. There were five old blokes sitting around the table, on which there was also a deck of cards and a wooden cribbage board. I realised that all the shouting and effing and blinding was over a game of crib!

'Len,' Bill admonished, 'we could hear you up those fucking stairs, keep the lord-mayoring down, mate, you never know who might fucking walk in here one day.'

'Leave it out I beg ya, Bill, who ever comes down here?'

Len then looked directly at me. Taking his cue, Bill said 'Lads, lads. This is young Mark, he'll be working with you lot as a messenger for the foreseeable. H., look after him, will ya?'

I was stunned. Lads? Bill thought these were lads? Every one of them was at least sixty. H. looked up and I had to say, I was impressed.

H., or Hal Taylor to give him his full title, was a good-looking bloke, nearly six feet tall I'd have said, and dressed in a neat Prince of Wales suit with a white shirt and navy-blue knitted tie. He looked at me, but didn't say anything, which after the verbals I had just heard, I saw as a result.

'Okay, Bill,' he said and looked back at his cards.

'All right, son,' Bill said to me, 'if you want to know anything, ask Hal Taylor.'

With that he walked off to his office, leaving me standing there. One by one, they all went back to their card game. I saw an empty chair, and went to sit down.

'That's Mick's chair, son,' one of 'em said without even looking at me. 'He'll be back in a minute.'

I made a move towards the only other available chair. 'And that's Al's . . .' someone else said.

I felt like a right plum standing there, but what could I do?

I went to pick up a copy of the *Sun* that had been left on the side.

'Do you mind, son? That's mine,' the one called Bob said. Lovely – no chair, no paper, no anything. The message was simple, stand in the corner and keep your trap shut.

Footsteps clattered down the wooden stairs. A younger fella walked in, dressed all in leather motorcycle gear.

'Who's this?' he said as he took off his crash helmet.

'New kid Bill just brought in. H. has got him.'

'What is he, twelve?'

That got a few chuckles. 'How old are ya?' the biker asked me.

'Eighteen, mate.' I said, my face going a little red but happy for some attention all the same.

The man quickly turned to face me.

'I ain't your mate, all right?' he said in a tone just short of really threatening.

'Leave it out, Crusher,' said H. (Crusher, he's called Crusher!) Crusher turned and went and sat down in 'Al's chair'.

He was about thirty and a big fucker, going a bit butter on top but a right lump. Definitely not someone to mess about with.

'Right, Len, over to the *Express*. Hal Taylor, you've got the *Telegraph*.'

The voice startled me. I realised it was coming from behind a glass partition, where I now saw a fella sitting at a desk. To my surprise, it was Jackie Mays, the fella who'd met me on my very first day at the NNA. Jack just looked at me and winked, not saying a word … as I said, it ain't what you know but who you know.

Behind Jack, there were six other geezers all working away at various jobs, in a room roughly twice the size of where I was standing. Because of my warm welcome, I hadn't noticed any of them.

'I'm taking the boy with me, all right Jack?' Jack didn't even look up at Hal Taylor, just nodded. 'C'mon, son,' H. said, 'let's go for a stroll.'

I still had my coat on, as I had been too frightened to take it off and hang it up, in case I used someone's peg!

I followed H. out of the building and onto the pavement. As we crossed over the road H. told me we'd be taking the racing results to the *Telegraph* and then we were going to the most important building in the job.

We went directly into the *Telegraph*, bang opposite our building. H. left the results at reception, gave the bird behind the jump a cheeky smile and then said to me, 'Right, son, now pay attention to where we are going. This is important.'

With that thought in my mind, we walked into Ye Olde Cheshire Cheese public house in Wine Office Court. It first opened in the sixteenth century. Dr Samuel Johnson and his biographer, Boswell, regularly drank in here. So did Dickens. So do many tourists.

H. and I made our way to the bar, where he got the very tidy barmaid's immediate attention.

'Usual please, Julie my darling, and a bottle of pop for the boy.'

A poxy bottle of pop!? I wasn't having that. 'Make that a vodka and diet please, love, and I'll get these … one for yourself?' I said.

My old man had taught me many rules. One of the most prominent was always: stand your round. It was a good lesson to learn, as Hal Taylor now looked at me a little bit differently.

'Cheers, son,' he said, as his pint was put in front of him. 'What's yer name again?'

I reminded him and the ice was broken. After a couple of sips, H. relaxed and started opening up.

'Don't take too much notice of the verbals you got back there,' he said reassuringly. 'Just a lot of noise, sounding you out really. Trouble you've got is that a lot of the young blokes they've been sending down to us have been right arrogant little bastards. They never talk to us 'cos they think we are just old boys, and they never buy a drink. Until you prove otherwise, you're getting tarred with the same brush. That's just the way it is, son.'

'Fair enough, H., I can handle it,' I told him.

I surveyed the pub. 'This your local, then?'

H. told me that he used this pub mainly because the tourists came here to soak up its history, and you could get a free light ale or two if you boxed clever.

He would often stand at the bar and, on hearing an American or Australian voice, introduce himself. Once acquainted, he would start telling the unsuspecting visitor stories about old London, the Blitz or anything else he thought might tickle their fancy.

As he rabbitted on, they would get him drink after drink, and he would eventually go home three parts pissed but never out of pocket. A couple of minutes later, I saw H. in action with my own eyes.

He was at the bar getting the next round in when an American came in and began taking a few photos of the wood-panelled interior of the pub. 'Vacationing?' H. asked him very casually.

'That's right, sir,' the septic cheerfully boomed back. 'I'm from Texas. What an amazing place this is.'

'Oh yeah,' says H., 'and very famous, yer know.' (I noted how the cockney accent suddenly got stronger at this point.)

'Really?' the Yank said, baited up and about to be reeled in.

'Save yourself a bit of film for that seat over there,' H. said helpfully, pointing to a wooden bench. 'See the leg on it, see how it's a bit chipped and battered?'

The Yank went over to the bench and rubbed it with his hand. 'That seat, sir,' H. continued, 'is where Bill Sykes himself used to sit.'

'*The* Bill Sykes?' the Texan replied, 'the one out of the film *Oliver*, right?'

'Well done, sir,' H. replied, not missing a beat. 'I see you know your history. Now you see all that chipped wood? Well, that is where his dog Bullseye used to gnaw away whilst Bill was attending to his business.'

'Sir,' the Texan said, 'would you do me the honour of standing and pointing to that wood while I take a photograph? Naturally, I'll be happy to make it worth your while.'

'Glad to oblige, sir,' H. said, 'very glad to oblige.'

I just stood there smiling, thinking of that American who bought London Bridge thinking he was getting Tower Bridge. I think I now know who sold it to him.

After a couple of weeks working in the despatch department, I felt like the rest of the chaps were gradually accepting me. Their bark was certainly worse than their bite, just as Bill had said. They were basically sounding me out back then. Was I going to be a flash little bastard, or show a little respect for my elders? Obviously, my background helped me in treating the old 'uns with a bit of respect. They liked that, and they even let me sit down after a week ...

The despatch department was often called 'The Holiday Camp', and let's be honest, that is exactly what it was. No one really gave a fuck. There was an overwhelming feeling that you were there for the rest of your working life, so you might as well enjoy it, so nearly every day there was a card school, a crib or domino competition on the go. As a kid of eighteen, I loved it. I was earning great dough and playing cards for the majority of the day. You couldn't complain, could you?

After a couple of months, I discovered I was actually looking forward to going to work. This was an astounding feeling, really. Before, on all the other jobs I had done, I dreaded Monday morning the most. Every Sunday night, I would have an extra couple of vodkas to try and kill off the horrible thought of going to work the next day.

Now I was still having the extra couple of drinks, but in celebration of the laughs about to come my way in the week ahead.

I liked my routine. It ran on the Print time. Say I was on the early shift, which meant a seven a.m. start and an official three-thirty p.m. finish. On arrival I would go up to the staff canteen and order a huge fry-up breakfast – egg, bacon, sausage, beans, the full bifta. If it was a Monday, the talk was of the weekend, how your team got on, tales of the Doris you had got hold of in The Dun Cow on the Old Kent Road, and how you rolled home off your trolley the night before. You know, stuff of a highbrow calibre.

Breakfast over, we would then creep down and start our shift.

Despatch's early shift was made up of a team of three clerks, three messengers and a multilith printer. The guys on the multiliths printed off stationery for the company, letter headings, invoices and so on as well as the horse, dog and football results for the national newspapers.

Working on the multiliths was the best-paid job in there, and there was a waiting list as long as your arm to get on those machines. I was already on that list.

Work would begin with a game of cards or a good read of the paper, taking in a lot of banter, and by one o'clock I was often finished for the day and out of the office, heading for home or the pub.

The National News Agency never shut. It operated twenty-four hours a day, three hundred and sixty-five days a year.

That meant we all had to do the odd shift at holiday times such as Christmas Day or New Year's Eve, although if you got stuck on one of those, you would usually find a moriarty going on somewhere in the building or at a local Fleet Street pub, where the drink flowed very nicely, thank you, and the switchboard girls looked that little bit nicer.

Occasionally, when you had spent the entire day drinking, playing cards, bantering with everyone like they were your best friends, you would think to yourself, surely this cannot last?

But then you remembered the mantra you had heard all your life, that once you got your union card you were there for life, and you shrugged your shoulders and carried on regardless.

This is why I had no financial worries when it came to The Mumper. I had a very settled job, with good money coming in every week. Whatever the price had been, I could have found a way to meet it. In fact, I already had my share of the horse sitting in a bank.

But when the words 'Wapping' and 'new technology'

started being heard in and around our pubs on a more regular basis, I should have paid a bit more attention and realised what the future was about to bring.

6

Fat Men and Raspberries

I spent the following week making plans for getting the syndicate money together and then getting it to Sefton. I told the lads at work the story of how we had bought the horse and called it The Mumper. They all laughed at the name, putting them in the minority of those who know the history and the origins of it.

'You might regret spending that money though, son,' said H. unexpectedly. 'That's if the rumours going around here are true.'

'What rumours?' I asked him.

'I'm hearing stories from Terry [Terry was our FOC, the Father of the Chapel, our union rep] that they'll be looking for redundancies here soon, the way things are going over at the *Sun*.'

'Leave it out, son,' I said dismissively, but H. was adamant on the subject. He explained that since Eddie Shah in Warrington had printed up his newspapers without union labour, word had it the rest of the nationals were planning something similar. If News International, which was all of the Murdoch titles – the *Sun*, the *News of the World*, *The Times* and the *Sunday Times* – moved out of Fleet Street down to Wapping, then a lot of firms would inevitably be laying staff off. Apparently, H. added, there were ongoing talks, but people he had spoken to felt it was a done deal. Murdoch had already built new premises down on the Highway. Now it was about who would work in them.

'Nah, that won't mean me, will it, it'll be all you old tossers first,' I said smiling.

'Don't be so sure, son,' said H. 'Don't be so sure.'

'That's all I'm short of, that is. Losing me wages?' Frankie said. 'Where the fuck am I going to get another job at my age, eh?'

'Worry 'bout it when it happens, mate,' said Mick, looking at the cards in his hand. 'C'mon, it's your lay ...'

I decided to ignore all of this. My job was for life. Everyone knew that. It was understood. All I was thinking about was getting down to Sefton and handing over the dough. Once that was done, the horse was ours.

After I had finished my shift, I had a swift one with Joey in The Dog and Duck. Being the landlord of a Fleet Street pub meant he was privy to all kinds of valuable info. Which boss was knocking off which bird secretary, who had a couple of shifts going at which paper, that kind of thing. But today Joey had gossip of another kind.

'Heard something is definitely in the wind on the Print front, skipper,' he said, finishing off the double Scotch he had just poured himself from the optic. 'And if old Rupert moves out of the Fleet, I'll be fucked. The loss of trade, well, it don't bear thinking about ...'

With that, he went quiet and looked into his drink.

This was all I needed. More rumours and Chinese whispers. I thanked Joey for the vodka and the information, and then made my way up to Guy's Hospital to see the old man. When I saw him it struck me hard just how tired he looked. They had stabilised him but he was looking very old, and losing weight rapidly.

'Hello, son,' he said weakly as he saw me walking towards

his bed. 'You just missed Gudge. He tells me you've agreed a price for that horse. That right?'

'That's right, Pop,' I confirmed in my most upbeat voice.

'Good boy, I've told yer mum to get a long 'un out of the bank and to give it to you, as my part of the whack.'

I couldn't help thinking that giving me this money was probably gonna be his last gesture, our last father-and-son act. I had to admit to myself then that the fella in front of me wasn't really my old man. Not really. He was just a poor version of him, know what I mean?

Yet there he lay, my old man, and this *was* real and no good running or blanking the situation out, which is what I wanted to do more than anything else. He *was* dying and I had to get used to that fact of life.

'Oi,' he said clocking my boat, 'I don't want to see no tears, mate, you hear me, I ain't having it, right?'

I just laughed at him through the sniffles. 'Bit of dirt in my eye, Pop, that's all.'

'Promise me you'll take the dough, it'll mean a lot to me,' he said.

''Course I'll take it. 'Course ... We've called it The Mumper by the way, gonna run him in Millwall colours, an' all.'

He laughed when he heard that, but quickly the laughing turned to a ferocious coughing, a terrible sound.

'The Mumper, eh? [cough] like it son, like it. G'won you Lions, eh ... [cough].'

Hearing the coughing, the nurse on the ward poked her head round the door. She saw me and smiled. I smiled back. I like a nurse. I love that rustling sound they make when they walk. My dad coughed again, and thoughts of what I could do with a rustling nurse instantly vanished. He leant his head back into the pillow. The effort of talking to me and then laughing, and then coughing, had worn him out. He closed his eyes.

'The Mumper . . . like it,' he whispered. I saw him squeeze on his morphine button, smiling as he did so, eyes still shut, and he drifted off.

I sat there for ten minutes, just watching him sleep. All around me was still, all around me so quiet except for the slow breath of life that drifted in and out of his open mouth.

Safe in the knowledge that he was comfortable, I left the hospital.

On the bus back home, I began thinking about the stuff H. and Joey had said about Murdoch and Wapping. I didn't need this hanging over me. I had given it the big 'un at work saying it didn't worry me, but the truth is, although my natural inclination was to dismiss the stories, I had heard the same scenario one too many times for comfort. In fact, I had heard the same story from Gudger at the pub last Sunday. I hadn't taken too much notice, figuring Gudger was pissed and getting the story arse about face, so I hadn't said anything to anyone at work. But now the alarm bells were starting to ring in my head. No smoke without fire they reckon, and something was definitely cooking . . . Nah, had this job for life, everyone knew that. I settled back in my seat and let London, sweet old London, flash past me.

On the Wednesday we all met in The Dutchy and everyone handed over their thousand-pound bundles to me. Mine was the money I was saving up for a deposit on a flat, but that was out of the question now. I had decided to stay at home at least another year. The old girl needed me now. Simple as that. I put all the money into a large envelope and took it home. In my bedroom I emptied the lot onto my bed and just looked at it. Fivers, twenties and tenners. Lot of dough, that, I thought. Could do a lot with dough like that . . .

Yeah, I thought, you could buy the bleeding racehorse with it!

I had a loose floorboard in my bedroom. Under there I kept my more advanced adult reading material. I lifted the board up and put the envelope into the gap. I dropped the board back into place and then went to bed. That night I couldn't sleep, my mind filled with thoughts of my dad, the horse, my job and even that lovely nurse. No matter how hard I tried I couldn't let go of consciousness and fall into slumber. The hours passed slowly.

Finally, I turned over and glanced at my alarm clock. Five o'clock. Fuck it. This was pointless. I got up, dressed in the dark and then got my old Adidas bag from the top of the wardrobe.

I retrieved the dough from under the floor, placed it carefully inside the bag, put a half-read copy of *Absolute Beginners* by Colin MacInnes and a Polaroid camera on top of it, and then crept downstairs and out into the brisk and cold morning air.

The day was fresh to say the least. I made my way to the bus stop and just after six I was at King's Cross Station. I bought several newspapers and a return ticket to Newmarket. Then I boarded the first train out, put my bag between my knees and didn't move for the whole journey. At Newmarket, I found a cabbie who knew where Sefton's stables were.

He dropped me off by the lane, and I cursed my stupidity for not bringing along a suitable pair of shoes. The memory of Fred and his suedes crossed my mind, and I smiled and cursed myself at the same time. I walked gingerly up the wet muddy path and found the stables in full swing. The noise of the horses walking around the yard gave off an elegant drumbeat which echoed off the brick walls in the courtyard. I could see the horses being brushed down, watered and fed as I entered the inner circle. Others were being saddled up in the yard and some were already out in the fields, racing along the horizon. I drew the sweet country air into my lungs, and then I saw Sefton about thirty yards away getting into a Land Rover. I shouted over to him. He stopped and I walked briskly towards him.

'Mark, isn't it?' he said. 'I wasn't expecting you today.'

'Hello, Sefton, got the day off work, mate, thought I'd drop the money down. Anywhere we can go?'

'Jump in,' he said. 'Just going to put a few of them through their paces, yours included. Not in a rush to get back, are you?'

I certainly wasn't. Despite the cold, it was glorious up there. A pale sun was breaking above, and the countryside around me looked mysterious and beautiful in the morning light. I got into the car.

'By the way,' Sefton asked as we pulled off, 'have you and the lads thought of a name for the horse?'

'Yeah, we have as it happens ... it's going to be called The Mumper.'

'The what!' he exclaimed.

I repeated the name and explained its origins. Sefton chuckled. It wasn't often London culture came into his orbit.

'Well, it's original, I'll give you that,' he said, smiling. 'Handy you have a name, though 'cos I'm entering him in a race in a couple of weeks' time, and now I know what to put down on the entry form.'

I smiled at him. 'Blinding, Sefton, blinding, the boys will be well chuffed, mate.'

Sefton then looked down at my mud-covered shoes.

'Brown shoes, eh? Someone once told me that you can always spot a south Londoner, 'cos they all wear brown shoes.'

Fuck knows what he was on about, but it made me smile.

We drove to a large piece of land and Sefton pointed out the newly named Mumper, who was going over a couple of jumps. When we had done the deal on our first visit, Sefton had taken him out, got him running so the boys could see we weren't buying a wrong 'un. But it was reassuring to see him again, to watch him perform so powerfully as he leapt over fences at speed, especially after laying out seven grand's worth of hay. I watched The Mumper be put through his paces for an hour or thereabouts. The jockey then brought him over to us. The Mumper was breathing heavily but there seemed a strange electricity coursing through his body. I took out my Polaroid, cracked off a few snaps. Then I stroked him and let him go back to rest in his stable.

Training over, Sefton invited me into his house for a drop of breakfast. As soon as he did, I realised how hungry I was. That country air soon opens up the stomach, I can tell ya. I don't think I can remember a better meal. It hit all the points. Afterwards, Sefton took me into his office and I handed over the loot. Fair play to the man, he didn't even bother to count it. Instead, he placed the dough in a drawer and then offered me a lift back to the train station.

I liked this man; he was considerate, and judging by the stables he ran, we were in business with a real pro, someone who would look after our interests. I started to relax a bit.

As soon as I got back to sunny Camberwell, I belled Fred at his shop.

'Frederico, thought I'd let you know I paid Sefton off this morning, and he told me he's sticking The Mumper into his first race, mate.'

'Really? That's blinding. Where's he running, then?'

'Not sure yet,' I told him. 'Sefton said he'll ring me in a couple of days to go over the details.'

'Got to have a bit of that, ain't we,' Fred said excitedly. 'I quite fancy dodging about with the rest of the owners.'

'I was thinking that as well,' I told Fred. 'Why don't I bell Georgie up and get him to sort us out some proper gear for the occasion? Suits, top hats, the full bifta, then we can swan around the owners' enclosure looking the bollocks.'

'Oh yes, blinding idea, Bax, put me down for one, son. George did me a lovely mohair suit the other month. The lining is so bright it would stop a bus!'

In our manor, Georgie was to suits what Fred was to shoes. Everyone in the area who wanted a bit of decent cloth went to George. He was the son of a Jamaican immigrant, himself a trouser-maker, and was raised and schooled in Peckham. George adored clothes, so as soon as he could, he entered the schmutter trade. It was a smart move.

George really had a talent for tailoring, and all of us had been through his door for a new whistle or a tickle up on an old one, at some point in our lives. It was George who had made me that brown mohair number I told you about, the one I sit looking at with such love.

'Okay, Fred, I'll bell Georgie,' I said. 'I'll sort out a price for the lot and get back to you.'

A couple of days later, Sefton called. The Mumper had been entered into a Maiden Hurdle at Fontwell Park on Saturday, 15 December.

'Don't expect too much for his first run, though,' he warned me. 'We'll just give him a little trot out over two miles, see how he copes with it. After all, it'll be his first proper race.'

'Okay, Sefton, it's your shout,' I told him. 'You do

whatever you think is right. Me and the boys are gonna come up for it though, cheer it on, like.'

'I should hope you will. I'll sort out some owners' passes for you, so you can get into the owners' enclosure and stands. It will be good to see everyone again. I take it you will want to go into the owners' enclosure?'

'Too right, Sefton mate. The suits are being sorted even as we speak.'

After we said our goodbyes, I got out a road map. Fontwell Park is located down in West Sussex, Brighton way. Naturally, I began thinking of making a weekend of it. I figured we could kick off in Brighton on the Friday night and then make our way down to the racecourse on the Saturday morning. All right, Brighton in the winter would be a touch fresh, but I didn't think we'd be spending too much time outdoors. We'd just find a nice warm boozer somewhere, plot up there and let the evening weave its magic.

Now I had the date sorted, I rang the chaps. All of them gave the beano idea, and grabbing new suits for the big day, the thumbs-up. My only regret about the whole thing was that the old man wouldn't be there to see the race. After seeing him in hospital over the past week, it had become pretty obvious that he had probably left his house for the last time. He was stabilised but they hadn't started the chemo, and every time I asked a doctor when they would start it, they just said soon, Mr Baxter, soon. But soon never came. My mum was hanging onto any hope, but me and my brother Glen now knew the score. There was no point giving him chemo. The cancer was too far advanced. It was just a matter of time.

Glen and I, however much we hated it, had to start making plans for a life without the old man. Our first priority was to work out what was best for Mum. On his last visit, we had started to work out the many possibles that lay in front of us.

'She'll have to move, mate,' I pointed out. 'That house is too big and full of memories, it'll kill her staying there.'

'Yeah I know, Blue, give her a couple of months and we'll sort something out. Maybe she can move down towards me? Quiet down there,' Glen replied.

'Can't see it, son. You know she's Camberwell through and through, she'll be lost out of the area.'

Which was true, except so was the fact that the house, every street and every shop would be a constant reminder of the old man. The pair of them had lived their whole lives in Camberwell. Grown up two streets apart and then joined together for ever. They had never really thought of moving out, although once the old man had this mad idea of moving to Rye down in Sussex, after spending a nice weekend down there.

'Lovely gaff that, nice and quiet. That would do me,' he said on his return. I wasn't convinced, nor was my mum.

'What happens if one of us dies, though?' she said. 'The other one is stuck down there all on their own, ain't they?'

'Die? Who's gonna die?'

My ma must have known something back then . . .

'Got to do something though, bruv, ain't we?' said Glen.

He, like me, was angry about the whole thing. He couldn't understand why a man who had worked hard all his life, protected his family and lived a life of honour should get the big C, whilst others walked away unscathed.

As he often said, 'All those fucking methers up the Green, totally off their boxes all day long, drinking God knows what, they somehow keeping breathing and here's the old man, worked his bollocks off all his life, knocking his pipe out day after day and . . . and . . .'

Glen couldn't finish the sentence, but he didn't have to say any more. I knew what he meant and he was right, life is hard sometimes, and so unfair. On our last visit, as we got ready to leave the hospital, with the old man sound asleep, I left the best photo of The Mumper that I had shot that day at the stables on his bedside cabinet. Next to it I put a note. It said, 'Dad, meet The Mumper.'

'Markie? That you?'

The voice on the other end of the telephone was instantly recognisable.

'Hello, Georgie, how's it going, son, how's trade?'

'Up and down like Tower Bridge, son, got a couple of whistles going through which will keep the taxman from my door, so no dramas. As my pal Jimmy has always said, 'Don't worry, George, us tailors will always have fat men and raspberries to make for!'

We both laughed. George was known for his way with lyrics. He was belling me now to arrange the fitting for our racing suits.

'I got six suits, various sizes, just waiting here,' he informed me. 'Get the chaps to come in and I'll tickle them up, they'll be 'andsome, son, believe me.'

George had got these suits off a bird he knew who did hire clobber. They were thirty snots each, and us being racehorse owners meant we had to go the full bifta, top hats and all.

'Lovely, George,' I said. 'I'll round them up for a visit to you on Saturday morning, have a bit of breakfast in the café next door first, eh? Say about ten o'clock, and then nut into you after?'

'Nice, I'll see you in there, mate. Be lucky, son.'

I then rang a couple of B&Bs in the Brighton area and

got us booked in. Not a lot of call for rooms in Brighton in December, as it turned out.

'Wonder if George can get us some long johns as well,' mused Alfie when I told him. 'I'm gonna freeze what's left of my bollocks off down there.'

As arranged, we gathered in the café next door to George's on the Walworth Road. As I sat down, I noticed Ronnie the builder sitting morosely at the table next to me, a couple of untouched Danish pastries and a cup of tea in front of him.

'How's tricks, Ronnie? Juggling?' I said to him.

He shook his head. 'Doing a big painting job for the council, but it ain't going well,' he explained. 'My mind is all over the place. I don't like what I'm coming up with at the moment. Nothing's flowing. Telling ya, my confidence is shot to pieces. I'll have to take up another career, Bax. This painting game is nearly up for me . . .'

'What's he on about?' asked Fred the Shoe from across our table.

'Leave him,' I replied, 'he's having a nightmare at the minute, that boy.'

After polishing off the eggs and bacon, the fried slice, and the what-have-yas, we all trooped next door into the shop. Gorgeous Georgie's is a tiny place, full of cloths and silks and patterns and threads. Like Fred's, his shop is also a social place, a place for people to gather and talk. Today was no exception. Sweet, a van driver mate of George's, was out back minding the shop when we marched in. Sweet is a big lad, well over six foot, built like a brick shithouse. Him and George went well back, back to their schooldays at Peckham Manor. Sweet was also a dresser of repute. Today he was in a brown and orange Gabicci knitted shirt, and a pair of black and white dog-tooth trousers. His shoes were snakeskin in a bronze colour, and the look was topped off with a matching dog-tooth cheese-cutter, worn at an angle. His accent, like George's, was mainly south London, heavy with a sprinkling of Jamaican patois. Sweet was so called because he said the word 'sweet' in every sentence he uttered.

'S., Polly put the kettle on Spar, these boys will be here for a while,' George shouted to his friend.

'Sweet, George, I'll make a sweet brew.'

We all acknowledged Sweet as we filed in behind George.

'Markie, stick the "Closed" sign up, mate, can't get no more punters in here today, what with you fat bastards inside,' said Georgie, cracking open his smile to reveal a set of nice white pearlers.

'Oi, I resemble that remark,' the O'sh perceptively replied.

We were each handed a suit on a hanger, and one by one we changed in to them.

'Fuck my old boots,' laughed Fred as he surveyed the scene in front of him. 'We look like a load of out-of-work bingo callers.'

When I looked up, I couldn't help but laugh. What a motley mob! Each of us had on black strides, a white wing-collared, ruffled shirt and a black tailcoat. We did look a sight.

'Now, I've got you stick-on bow ties for you to wear,' Georgie said, handing them out. 'Thought the real tie-up ones would be too difficult for you load of plums, especially you, Gudge, what with your minces,' laughed George.

'As it happens, you're talking out of your mouth, son,' said the Gudge.

'When have you ever done a bow tie up, Gudge?' Dave asked.

'Listen, mate, I had one once, wore it when I was courting Doll, it was one of my old man's, looked lovely.'

'I would have paid good money to see you then,' said the O'sh.

'I'm telling ya, Goldfish, I was a right bobby dazzler in my day. See all this clobber, a bit of me, this, mate, a bit of me.'

'You're going senile, Gudger,' laughed Fred.

'What you saying, chaps, how we doing?' asked George, tape measure round his neck.

'Me trousers are a bit long,' said Fred. With this man every detail had to be right.

'And mine,' said Dave.

'Easy enough to sort,' said George, 'you're only a couple of short-arses, I expected nothing else. Alf, I take it you ain't leaving on that flat cap, mate? Try on the topper you've got.'

'Nah, George, this is my lucky cap, don't go anywhere without it,' Alfie said, his hand unconsciously holding the front of his hat.

'Sweet Jesus,' sighed George.

'My jekylls are a bit tight, Georgie,' the O'sh said, tugging at his waistband.

'That's all that timber you're carrying around, son, ain't it time you dropped a couple of pounds of suet? I'll let them out a touch, all right? Right, come on lads, try on the titfers I got ya.'

We all took out the top hats from the boxes where they were resting.

'You look well,' I laughed, catching sight of O'sh with his hat on.

Apart from it being too small, his ginger mop of hair had spilled out from both sides.

'Don't know what you're laughing at, son, you seen you in yours?' he said.

I turned round and looked in the mirror. I had to admit, it wasn't too pretty.

'We're going to be a laughing stock at this race,' I exclaimed to the gang.

'What you talking about, we look well tasty,' said Gudge, moving me out of the way to gaze adoringly into the mirror.

'I look like a pox doctor's clerk ...' said Alf, taking the topper off and putting the brown checked flat cap back on.

'Boys,' George announced, 'you'll just have to swap the hats around 'til you find one that fits. Thing is, I got them in various sizes.'

'Here y'are boys, here's ya sweet tea ... Bladclart! Look at you in your suit and t'ing!'

George's mate Sweet had come out from the kitchen. He put down the tray and tried to control his laughter, his gold tooth glinting as he did so.

'Cha na man, that's the funniest thing I have seen in years mate, years ... Sssschhweeeeet!'

'Thanks, S.,' I said, 'you've made us feel a lot better.'

'Nah man, I'm not laughing at yous, yous look nice, sweet, gorgeous ... it's just I ... I ain't never seen anything like it,' and he was off again, cackling like a hyena.

I had to concede he had a point. Looking at us all standing there, he was right, we did look Sid Nicholas, but I sensed the boys didn't really care. Well, Gudger didn't, anyway.

'What's Sweet know, anyway?' said Gudge, sticking his chest out. 'Wrap them up, Georgie old son ... we'll take them.'

'Good boys,' George purred. The taxman was becoming less of a problem.

*

I managed to get a shift swap at work, and got the Saturday of the race off. Of course, I had the piss ripped out of me by nearly all my work colleagues when I explained where I was going.

'You've lost the plot, son, fucking lost it. Fancy spunking all that dough on a fucking donkey.' That was Crusher, one of many who couldn't wait to muller me.

'What d'ya mean, donkey,' I said, rising to the bait, despite my best efforts not to.

'The bloke is bound to have sold you a pup, ain't he? He won't have sold you anything decent. I'll bet ya right now on it.' Crusher was getting into his stride now. 'And you and your silly mates have gone for it. Been mugged off, the lot of ya.'

All around me the people I had down as my mates began laughing. Always the same. If you do anything different from the norm there's always somebody waiting to have a pop, try and bring you down a level. To be honest, though, this was something I was used to. Ever since I had started wearing the Mod clothing, I had faced a daily piss-take.

'Fuck me, son, my old man used to have that cardigan, he was wondering what had happened to it.'

That was just one of many lines I had heard over the past two or three years. I used to stand there and think, I don't want to be the same as you, don't you understand that concept? Judging by the stick I got, clearly not. Now they had extra ammunition to fire at me, the idea of me owning a racehorse obviously giving them enough ammo to keep on firing for years to come. Still, at least it diverted the chat away from the work situation, because even I was beginning to think serious moves were afoot. Whatever we said or did, the issue just wouldn't go away.

'I wouldn't be throwing your cash away so quickly,' Al

said. 'You're going to need it soon, son. The day of reckoning is coming, believe me, it's coming, my boy told me.'

Al's son worked for SOGAT up at The House, which was what the union office was known as.

'He told me,' Al revealed, 'that if the unions reject Murdoch's plans one more time, Murdoch will move out and sack everybody.'

'Fuck off,' said Len, 'he'll never do that. If he tried mass sackings it would be carnage, mate, carnage. Rupert won't risk it. He'll lose too much dough. Nah, they'll work something out, they always do.'

All of us nodded, all of us agreed, all of us thought, *I fucking hope so . . .*

At four o'clock on the afternoon of Friday, 14 December, the six of us met up outside The Dutchy in preparation for the trip down to Brighton. The sky was a heavy grey and it was so cold that the brass monkeys hadn't been seen all day. Once again the Goldfish had volunteered to do the driving, and once again he had 'borrowed' a Royal Mail van to get us down to the coast.

Each of the lads had an overnight bag with them. So did I, plus the six suits from George.

'C'mon on, then, let's be having ya,' said Fred as we clambered aboard.

'Doll's done some rolls, boys, so if you're peckish, let me know, plenty here for later,' Gudge said.

'What you got, Gudge? Ham salad?' asked Alf.

'Nah, a bit of ham, tomato, lettuce and cucumber,' Gudge revealed.

That was the thing about the man. You didn't know if he was cracking a joke or if he was serious.

'Oh, fuck ya,' said Alf, smiling.

'Lovely woman you've got there, Gudge ... sling us one over,' said O'sh.

'Fuck me, Goldfish, they were for the trip, you ain't started the van yet, you hungry bastard.'

O'sh just laughed. 'Lee Marvin, ain't I? Just finished an early turn, mate. Had nothing to eat yet since this morning, wasting away 'ere.'

'About time,' Dave said.

'Right,' said Fred, the last to get aboard. 'All settled in? Eh? Wagons roll, O'sh.'

Naturally, there was plenty of beer on board, and it wasn't long before one or two had started knocking them back. As we skirted around Croydon, the air suddenly turned somewhat rancid; straight away, Alf owned up.

'Sorry, boys,' he said.

'Fuck me, Alf, that thing's got teeth,' Fred said holding his nose. 'You want to check your strides there, mate.'

'Can't help it,' he replied. 'Lil did me a casserole last night, playing havoc with my darby.'

'Playing havoc with us as well, as it happens,' laughed Dave.

'Bloody hell,' Fred said, as the smell deepened, 'open that side window, Bax, let some air in, son! That thing's got me by the throat.'

'If I had known it was going to smell like that, I wouldn't have done it,' said Alf.

'You what?' Dave retorted. 'Who the fuck knows what an apple tart is going to smell like before they do one? Senile, mate, that's what you are.'

Alf just flicked him a quick two-finger salute. Everyone was in a good mood, and why not? Despite Alf's bowels, we were on to a blinding weekend. A couple of light ales and a night out down by the seaside, and then watch The Mumper run its first race. Lovely. I mean, what more do you want from life?

'Did I ever tell you lot about the first arrest at sea that the old bill ever did?' Alf suddenly exclaimed out of nowhere.

He was dressed in what can only be described as old bloke's clothing, which meant a pair of grey slacks with a pair of red braces that went over his Farah short-sleeved shirt. On top of that was a blue-ish Marks' cardigan with suede patches on it, and on top of that, a green car-coat type of thing. On his feet were a pair of blue boating pumps from Fred's and on his head, his ever-present checked flat cap.

'What?' said Fred.

'The first ever arrest on water,' Alf repeated. 'Big story that was, you must have heard about it.'

'Heard about it? How old do you think we are?' I said, smiling.

'Do you want to hear this or not?' Alf said, getting the hump.

'Might as well, it'll take our minds off worrying when you gonna next have a trouser cough,' said the O'sh.

'Fuck ya,' Alf said sulkily.

'Nah, go on, Alfie. Got me curious,' said Dave.

'Right. It was in 1910 ...'

'1910! Fucking hell, and you're surprised we haven't heard about it,' I shouted at him.

'It was in 1910,' he said, ignoring me, 'and there was this geezer called Dr Crippen. Him and his bird were making their escape on a boat across the channel. He had killed his missus, after she had found him having naughties with this fancy woman. Anyway, the police had searches at all the ports, but he and this bird had disguised themselves and slipped through the net. So he's making his escape on this boat, when he discovers the old bill are chasing him on one of their new motor launches. Well, he's shitting himself now, ain't he?'

'Bit like you earlier,' Fred said.

'Got nowhere to go,' continued Alf. 'Nowhere to hide. Eventually the police catch his boat and board it. They search all over but they can't find him. Finally, they find this khazi and bang on its door. 'Anyone in there?' they cry.

No answer. They bang again, 'You in there, Crippen?'

'No,' a voice shouts back, 'I'm in here crappin'!' With that, Alf and Gudge burst out laughing.

'Always gets 'em, that one,' Alf said, laughing, looking at our faces, well pleased with himself.

'Silly old duffer,' smiled Fred, 'that's twice you've stunk this van out today.' Fred now turned to me. 'Bax, what did Sefton say about The Mumper? He in good shape?'

'Yeah, he reckons he's fine, going to put that Jimmy on him. He works at the stables, knows the horse well. Seft said he'll do okay, but he also said don't expect a winner. Too early, and all that.'

'Gonna have a bet on him though, ain't we?' Fred said. 'Be rude not to.'

'Oh yeah, I'll have a couple of quid,' I said. 'Sporting bet really. After all, just stuck a long 'un on him, ain't I?'

'Too right, son,' said Gudge. 'Besides, Doll will slaughter me if I blow any more dough. She's already narked at me for putting the thousand down. My money, I told her, but all I got was the silent treatment.'

Up until that point I hadn't really thought about how the various missus would feel about their significant others splashing out. Me and the O'sh were okay, only had our pricks to keep, but the rest had others who had to be talked round.

'Didn't tell Sue,' Dave confessed. 'Just used the dough I've been putting away for my trip to Memphis.'

Memphis was where Stax Studios once operated, the place where Otis Redding and bands such as Booker T. and the MGs had recorded. The amount of fantastic music that had been made in that place was mind-boggling, and Dave had always wanted to go and pay his respects. Now his trip would have to wait a little longer.

'I must be fucking mad ...' he said, gazing out at the lights on the freezing-cold Brighton seafront, which we were heading rapidly towards. 'A racehorse over Otis, what am I thinking of ...?'

On seeing the sea in front of us, Gudge suddenly mentioned the planned Channel Tunnel that had been all over the news in the last few weeks.

'What do we want to join up with those French mare bags for, eh? They hate us and we hate them. I mean, we saved their arses in the last war, done them enough favours, mate.'

'Nah, Gudge, we ain't English no more, we're Europeans, son,' said Dave very slyly, on the gee-up.

'Never, not me, not as long as I've got a hole in my arse.'

Thank you so much Mr Foreign Secretary, I thought, so much for the Entente Cordiale ...

Within twenty minutes we were pulling up outside The Polar Bed and Breakfast in Sussex Gardens. The time was just before six p.m. We unloaded our bags from the van and made our way to reception. We were sharing rooms. I was in with the O'sh, Fred was with Dave and Gudge was in with Alfie.

'You'll need a gas mask if that casserole of his comes up again,' Fred said to Gudge as we signed in.

Gudge made a face as if to say, I know, I'm looking forward to that . . .

'Right, then,' I announced, 'quick spruce-up and then a few light ales in the nearest pub. Agreed?'

Nods all round.

'Okay, synchronise your watches, girls, see you all down here in say, forty-five minutes?'

Again, nods all round.

'Tonight,' I announced, 'Brighton meets The New Jolly Boys!' This time, it was cheers all round.

7

The Goldfish and the Stripper

At just after seven p.m. we were all in the TV lounge of the B&B, looking forward to the night ahead. All of us had scrubbed up well, even if I do say so myself, with a notable cloud of aftershave filling the room. Fred, Dave, Gudge and me were in suits (Fred and Dave adding peckhams to their look, Gudge and me going without). The Goldfish was in Fiorucci jeans, Lacoste polo, Burberry golf jacket and a pair of Gucci loafers, and ever the odd one out, Alf had managed to put on a clean shirt. Pity he didn't seem to realise that his jacket and strides were from different suits. Of all the groups down in Brighton that weekend, we had to be one of the strangest. Six blokes with an age range that started at twenty and stretched to seventy-three, with all the stops in between. To us this gathering was normal, but to the outside world ...

'Ah, it's nice to see a family on holiday together,' said the landlady, a Mrs Cooper, who was hovering around by the reception desk as we were getting ready to leave.

She was in her mid-sixties, Mrs Cooper, a very pale woman with a fag hanging out of her gob, the ash of which had fallen onto her tight jumper and then her slippers. Family! She thinks we're family!

'That's right, love, he's my twin,' said Fred, pointing to Gudger.

'Cheeky sod,' she replied. 'He's yer dad, isn't he?'

'No, love, he's his dad,' he said, pointing to the O'sh.

'Silly bleeder,' she said, smiling at the O'sh. 'You got yer keys? I won't get up to let you in if you're late, believe me.'

'Yeah, we're all keyed up, love, you get your beauty sleep, don't worry about us, mate,' said Dave, eager to get on the move. 'Right then, boys, fit?'

'Bit late for the beauty sleep I would have thought,' said Alf, quietly nodding in her direction.

'She likes you, Alf, you can tell, mate,' said O'sh, pulling his chain.

'She'd be wasting her time there. I can't raise a gallop any more, son, my leg-over days are well and truly over.'

'Is that why Lil's trying to poison yer with her dodgy casseroles, then? So she can get a toyboy in?'

Smiles all round, and within minutes we were walking towards the main part of Brighton.

'There's a chippy just down here,' Fred said, gesturing to the right. 'Why don't we have a sit-down, a warm-up and a bit of fish and 'taters, line the stomachs for later?'

'Yeah, could do with something meself,' I said. 'I'm a touch peckish.'

'Actually,' O'sh said, about to spring the biggest surprise of the night, 'I'd rather get a drink in. Stomach's a bit dicky, boys. Must have been the trip down.'

The five of us stopped. Dead. In our tracks.

'You don't want any grub?' I said in amazement.

'Don't want to risk it,' O'sh said. 'Rather get the lagers in.'

'Oh well,' put in Alfie, 'you know what they say. Ireland for the Irish and Peckham for the Peckish! Let's eat and O'sh can watch. If you're that way inclined ...'

Before too long, we had passed through the door of The Flying Fish chip shop and entered a world of plastic. Plastic chairs, plastic tablecloths and plastic menus. The food smelt good, though.

'Hello, gents, what can I do you for?' said the bloke behind the jump as we found a table.

'We'll have six – er five sit-down dinners, mate. Cod and chips all round. Okay, fellas?' Fred asked.

'Can't come down to the seaside and not have a bit of fish and chips, can ya?' said Gudge, sitting down. 'Tradition like, ain't it?'

There was no arguing with that, and no one else in the chippy to argue with even if we had wanted to, so our scoff came up pretty quick. 'Lovely,' said Dave, eyeing up his dinner, 'nice drop of t-las on this and that's that sorted.'

'Ain't O'sh gone quiet,' said Alf, as we all got stuck in and the banter subsided at our table. O'sh was sat looking out of the window as if to look at food would bring a curse on him.

'Just get a move on, you plums,' O'sh said, not even bothering to turn his head. You could see he was dying to get to the light ales.

'Nice bit of cod that, mate,' Dave shouted to the owner, and then added in a quieter tone, 'At least that ain't plastic.'

For the next ten minutes or so the only sound that could be heard was that of mouths furiously chewing, cutlery scraping china, mugs of tea hitting the table.

'Cor, that's better,' said Alf finally, wiping his mouth with a serviette. 'Right, I feel a light ale coming on.'

He must have read our minds. Or at least, O'sh's.

We paid our bill, bid the fryer goodbye and walked towards the pier. Just on the left-hand side of the road, we found a boozer that wasn't too loud or too quiet and dived in. Brown drinking vouchers in the whip, drinks order placed. And we were off.

'I brought Doll down here when we were courting. Took her on the tunnel of love,' Gudger recalled.

'What? And she still married yer?' said Dave.

'Had some blinding times down here myself,' I said. 'Came down here with some pals for a Jam gig a few years back. Boiling hot in the venue, it was. Took me coat off and left it with my mate Martin, while me and the others made our way down to the front. Martin was caning the spliff and he was wobbling badly, so we left him at the back of the hall. Anyway, I found him at the end of the gig sitting on the floor. 'Martin, where's me smother, mate?' He looked down into his arms, thinking it was still there, but it weren't. He'd only dropped the fucking thing somewhere, hadn't he? I was going off alarming. A thing of beauty, that coat. Three-quarter leather, original sixties and I had just got George to re-line it. Plus, it's got me return train ticket in it, the key to the B&B and all my salmons. I went fucking mental. Went up to the security geezer and asked him if he had seen anyone wearing it, but he just laughed. I grabbed Martin and both of us waited outside. Now, this is December, so it's like tonight, fucking freezing out. I said to Martin, 'Look out for some cheeky slag coming out of the gig, wearing my coat. If you see it, grab the fella.' We stood outside for ten minutes and then I hear Martin call, 'Bax, Bax, got it, son, got it.' I run over to him and he's got hold of some little kid wearing a Levi's jean jacket. 'Fuck me, Martin, that ain't it, is it,' I shout at him. 'It's a fucking three-quarter leather we're looking for, mate.' He turned to me and said, 'Is it? Then he lets go of the kid and pukes up all over the place. Fucking nightmare.'

By now the table was roaring with laughter.

'How d'ya get on then, soppy bollocks?' asks Fred.

'Gave up, didn't I? Had to. The security had called the

old bill and we were warned off. Made me way back to the B&B, banged on the door and the landlord let us in, moaning all the time, had fucking frostbite by the time I got into bed.'

After a few more tales, we had done most of the whip and a good drink was between and inside us.

'I might have to make a move in a minute,' said Alf, 'I'm buckling badly.'

'Leave it out, Alf, the night is still young,' O'sh said. He had noticeably picked up since landing in this boozer.

'Might be for you, Goldfish, but I've had enough and we've got a big day tomorrow,' Alf retorted.

'You ain't tired, mate. I know what you're up to. You want to get back and get old Ma Cooper to tuck you in, eh?' said Fred.

'Bollocks, told ya, me and Ivy are just of the same generation that's all, that's why she talked to me,' Alf continued.

'Oh, Ivy, is it!' said Fred. 'It's Mrs Cooper to the rest of us, mate, you sure you ain't slipped in there already?'

'Leave it out, son, I'm well past all of that,' Alf said, a cheeky smile dancing along his lips.

'Tell you what, Alf, I might come with ya,' said Gudge. 'I'm flagging an' all. You mob go on if you want. Goldfish, get the nurse to call us a cab, mate.'

O'sh went up to the barmaid and sorted Alf and Gudge a cab back to the B&B. While he was up there, I saw O'sh order a double shot of vodka which he downed in one before ordering up another round of drinks, which arrived just before the barmaid threw the towels up on the pumps and rang the bell.

'Hope you can remember where the key is,' Gudger said to Alf, as we waited for our final knockings.

'That was your job,' Alf replied.

'Nah, it wasn't. It was yours.'

'Gudge, I gave that job to you, son.'

'What the fuck you talking about?' Fred asked.

Alf and Gudge then told us the key to their room had a large piece of metal attached to it, with the room number stamped on it. Because it was too big to lug about, they had decided to put it above one of the ceiling tiles over the room door.

Only trouble was, after a couple of pints, they now realised they had both forgotten what tile it was.

'What are you two like, eh?' asked Dave. 'When we get back there'll be ceiling tiles all over the place! Perhaps we should get old scruffy bollocks Bob Geldof to set up Gudge and Alf Aid, you two need looking after.'

O'sh came back to the table carrying a tray of drinks. Just as he got close he nearly tripped over and set the glasses flying.

'Oi, careful, son,' I cried. 'Jesus, bit unsteady on your feet, ain'tcha. I thought you were Tom Dick.'

'Rocking now, mate,' O'sh said, settling the tray down. 'Here, bloke up there reckons there's a strip club round the corner. Fiver on the door, first drink for free. Fancy a bit of that?'

'Been a while has it, son?' said Dave.

'Bollocks, mate, I get my fair share, don't you worry 'bout that,' the O'sh said, his face as red as his hair, his words noticeably slurring now.

'You know what they say, mate, use it or you'll lose it,' Dave said. He wasn't letting go.

'You wouldn't want it on your eye as a wart, son,' O'sh shot back. He wasn't letting go, either.

'Nah, I just thought it would round the night off nicely. Couple for the road, eh?'

'Oh go on, then, I'll have a fiver's worth with ya,' I said, but did so only because I could see my boy had reached the point where he would definitely need looking after, especially in a strange town.

'Come on, finish these up and we'll all go,' said Fred winking at me, somehow telepathically catching my thoughts.

Couple of minutes later we had waved Alf and Gudge off to play hunt the room key and five minutes after that we were entering the Lucky Seven Strip Club. It was a dark hole of a place, but there was a fair crowd in, most of whom were sat at tables studying a ropey old stripper peeling off to the tune of 'Like a Virgin' by Madonna. I think that's what some might call irony.

Fred, Dave and I made our way to the bar, but O'sh had other plans. Without telling us, he went over to the front of the stage and stood there swaying from side to side, trying to keep his balance as he watched the stripper remove her bra. Luckily, he wasn't blocking anyone's view.

'Look at him, he's lagging,' said Dave.

'Empty stomach,' I pointed out. 'We'll have to keep an eye on him. It's going to be carnage otherwise, I just know it.'

'Leave the boy, mate, he's in love,' laughed Fred.

The bird now whipped off her g-string, flung her arms out wide, stood still for all of two seconds, got a small cheer and an even smaller round of applause and then scuttled off stage. The music stopped and a new girl came on stage. Not bad, actually. Dark-haired, nice body, reminded me of someone, in fact. A new song started up. 'Rio' by Duran Duran. I hate Duran Duran. That Simon Le Bon is a right ...

'Fuck me, what's he doing now,' said Fred, interrupting my unpleasant thoughts about Mr Le Bon.

Then it hit me. The girl on the stage looked like O'sh's last girlfriend, Lauren. It wasn't her, but if you were nine sheets to the wind . . .

Next thing we know, the O'sh is clambering on stage and starting to cavort with the new stripper.

'Go on, my son!' shouted Dave.

Remarkably, the bird waved away the bouncer as he rushed to investigate. Pissed as he was, even she knew she was in no danger with the O'sh. Perhaps it was Lauren, after all. The only problem was, she was starting to remove *his* clothing.

'I hope he's got clean pants on,' said Fred, laughing, as the bird started to undo his belt.

His Fioruccis fell to the ground and, fuck me, he only had a semi lob on . . .

Dave, Fred and I fell about laughing, as it was obvious our ginger friend was oblivious to that fact. The crowds were going mad by this stage, cheering him on, and even the stripper was laughing. The bouncer had seen enough. He got on stage, put his arm around the O'sh and beckoned him to scoop up his strides. O'sh did just that and was led gently off the stage to an enthusiastic round of applause. He came staggering over to us, his face beaming, his balance still very much in the balance.

'Nice one, O'sh my son, d'ya get her number?' I said, laughing.

'Leave it out,' he slurred. 'I was just being friendly. She didn't half look familiar, though . . .'

'I just hope those photos I took come out,' said Fred. The look on O'sh's face at that moment will stay with me for the rest of my life.

'He's only pulling your pisser,' I said. 'Just like that bird was about to do, as it happens . . . Come on, son, let's get you home. I just remembered, you're driving tomorrow.'

The O'sh didn't utter a word. He just nodded his head and we led him away like a boxer who'd been laid out by Mike Tyson.

Breakfast at The Polar was served every morning between seven and nine a.m. Alf and Gudge were first up. Fred, Dave and I finally got down to the breakfast area at ten minutes to nine. As we entered we heard Gudge telling Mrs Cooper, that no, they didn't know why there were ceiling tiles all over the floor outside their room.

'I take it you found your key, then,' I asked Gudge.

'Yes, boy, she was still up so let us in the main door. We gave it five minutes for her to settle down and then found our room key after five tiles. Problem was, we couldn't get the bloody things back in. Told her she must have squirrels in the roof and they knocked the tiles down.'

I just stood there, shaking my head with a knowing smile on my face. Laugh, I nearly handed my fags round.

'Oooh, you nearly missed it, boys, I was about to start packing away. Where's the ginger boy?' Mrs Cooper asked as she walked back into the room.

The three of us laughed knowingly.

'What you lot laughing at?' said Alf.

'Alf, it was a classic last night,' Fred said. 'I don't think he'll be eating any eggs and bacon this morning.'

The tale of the Goldfish and the Stripper was then recounted, and not a detail was left out.

Needless to say, the senior members of the party laughed like drains. 'Gutted I missed that, gutted,' said Gudge.

'I've left him snoring his head off,' I told the assembled. 'I shook him and told him grub's up, but he just groaned. You know he ain't right when he's off his food,' I said.

At that very moment, as if by magic, a very weak-looking O'sh crept into view.

'Oi oi, it's Ginger Rose Lee,' shouted Dave.

Then we all broke out into the classic stripper theme. 'Na, na, na nah ... na, na, na nah ...'

O'sh smiled at us. 'Tell me I didn't do what I think I did last night,' he said.

'O'sh, is there any chance of going back and doing it again tonight, only me and Gudge are gutted we missed it,' Alf said, as if he was asking the man to pass the ketchup.

'Oh, my head, someone put something in my drink last night,' said the O'sh.

'What was that then?' said Fred, looking slightly concerned.

'Alcohol,' said the O'sh, 'bloody alcohol.'

I laughed and then saw Alfie yawning his head off.

'What's up, Alf? Ivy have you on her nest all night, mate?' I asked.

'Bollocks ... nah, it was this plonker,' he said, nodding towards Gudger. 'He had his nebuliser going all night. The noise that thing makes, it sounded like someone was digging the road up, right outside our room.'

'Was that what that was?' said Dave. 'What a bleeding noise.'

Gudger's asthma had been bad lately, hence the need for some help with his breathing. Mind you, the nebuliser hadn't been prescribed by a doctor. Too easy, that. No, Gudger had bought it from an advert at the back of the *News of the World*.

'I can't fucking help it, can I?' implored Gudge. 'It's me tubes.'

'I wouldn't mind, mate,' said Alf, 'but he has one puff on the nebuliser and then two drags on a fag, another puff on the thingy and then back on the oily rags ...'

There really is only one Gudger.

We settled up the bill, bade farewell to Mrs Cooper and then loaded the van up.

'I'll drive to Fontwell, I think,' said Dave, looking at the paler than usual O'sh. 'Don't think you're up to it, son.'

O'sh put up no argument whatsoever. In fact, he settled back into his seat and within a minute he was snoring. Like a very loud baby.

'Look at him, his mum would kill me if she could see him,' I said.

'Would have cut him in two if she had seen him with that bird last night,' Fred pointed out.

With that, Dave started up the engine and we were off to see The Mumper. Fred was navigating. He reckoned it was about twenty-odd miles to the racecourse.

The Mumper was running in the half-past-two race, a race packed with first-timers. It was now ten-thirty, so we had plenty of time. I was actually feeling really nervous. Had butterflies flying all over the place and, no, it wasn't the previous night's vodka playing up. After all, The Mumper was my horse, our horse, and all of a sudden I was feeling the weight of seven grand on my shoulders. My old man had lobbed in his grand, and he was back in London dying. I badly wanted, no, I badly needed this horse to justify the dough we had put down.

'You know what?' Fred said, 'I actually feel quite nervous.'

Thank fuck I wasn't the only one. The drive to Fontwell was quiet. We would normally be ripping the piss out of each other, or listening to Gudger's evacuation stories or Alf's stupid pre-war jokes. But today we were all strangely quiet.

We arrived at Fontwell at about midday. Our first move

was to see if we could find Sefton. We left the O'sh in the van. He was snoring strong enough to make the van's windows a health and safety concern. Once inside the main gates, we made our way to the back of the grandstand and took in the compelling view in front of us. Got to say there was a real buzz in the air, with at least a couple of thousand people milling about in front of us, their voices all clashing together to make that sound which is like no other on earth.

Sellers of fish and chips and beefburgers were doing a roaring trade, and the bookies were stood at their stands, wildly gesturing. Beyond them, acres and acres of every shade of green you can imagine stretched out, with the racecourse itself set in the middle of it all. It was a beautiful sight. Dave had wandered off and found the way to the parade ring, where the horses in the first race were walking around. He shouted out to us to follow him over there. We walked over to the enclosure and stood and watched the horses as they sauntered past, tails swishing. This close, you could really see the conditioning of the animals, their muscles rippling as they walked. Colours of blackish-blues and browns of every hue flashed past us. What was even stranger is that horses never seem to betray any emotion. You never know if they are happy, sad, bored or indifferent. Yet their physical presence alone is awe-inspiring. Experiencing all this only increased the butterflies in my stomach.

After ten minutes of watching, we jogged on and finally found the stable area. I walked up to the fella on the gate and explained I was an owner, that I was looking for Sefton, my trainer. When I formed those words, it felt really strange. What the hell was I talking about ... an owner ... my trainer ... but that was reality for me now. Never thought I'd see the day.

'Sefton!' shouted the gatekeeper towards the stable block, 'some fellas are here to see ya.'

Sefton appeared from behind a horse and smiled as he came towards us.

'Hello, boys, glad you could make it. The Mumper is in fine shape, very pleased with him.'

'Hello, Sefton, how you doing?' Fred asked him, as we all approached and shook the man's hand.

'Me? Bit nervous, chaps, I have to say,' admitted Sefton, 'first run and all that, but I reckon he'll do okay.'

'Mate, we've all got faith in you, we know you've done your best,' Fred reassured him.

'Ta, lads, happy to hear that.'

'Seft,' I said, 'we'll leave you to it, we'll get a bite to eat and settle ourselves in.' I could see he was a bit distracted by us buzzing around him.

'Before you go, boys, here's your badges. Put them through your buttonholes on your suits, then the stewards will know who you are.'

I collected the seven badges from Sefton and put one in my pocket. I would give that to my old man later. A steward had overheard us say we were owners, and directed us to the owners' enclosure over to our right.

'Right, boys,' I said. 'Time to get the whistles on, eh?'

We went back to the van and I woke up the O'sh. He looked dog-rough.

'C'mon, son, get your whistle on, we're here.'

'I feel fucking terrible, and these fucking suits ain't gonna help, are they,' he replied.

'C'mon, mate,' I said. 'You're used to taking your clothes off in public, ain't ya?'

'All right, all right, I'm with ya,' he said, giving me a *fuck right off, you* look.

We got changed into the suits in the van. It was a real squeeze, with legs and arms bumping into each other and plenty of blue words flying around. Finally, one by one we were all ready, and after sorting out each other's cuffs and ties, we locked up the van and made our way back to the track.

'What they fucking looking at?' said Gudge, nodding towards the onlookers as we walked towards the crowd.

It was only then that I noticed that no one else had dressed up anything like us. Everyone was in normal suits and overcoats. Us? We looked like a bunch of overdressed waiters on a day off at the racecourse.

'Bollocks to 'em,' said Alf as he puffed out his chest and strode on.

I noticed a burger van parked up not far from the owners' enclosure. 'I'm Hank, mate, need a bit of stodge,' I said.

'I can't eat,' said Dave, 'I'm a bag of nerves.'

'Well, I need something,' I said, marching over to the van. 'Need to settle myself down a touch.'

''Allo, mate,' I said to the burger fella, 'give me a week-off-work burger ...'

He looked at me like I was mad.

'Sorry, mate,' I said, seeing his confused face. 'I thought I was down Millwall for a minute,' I explained. 'That's what we call the burgers down there, a "week-off-work burger". Have two and you get a fortnight,' I laughed.

The fella didn't even raise a smile as he handed over the bun, and nor did I when tasted the burger.

'C'mon, Bax, he'll be out in a minute,' Dave shouted.

With our owner's badges on our lapels, and our top hats on our heads, except Alf, who couldn't be parted from his flat cap, we made our way towards the owners' enclosure.

The other people in the ring looked at us as if we were Martians.

'Who are these people?' I heard one woman say.

Cobblers to you, love, I thought. We're The Jolly Boys. Who the hell are you? We stood in the middle of the lush green parade ring, all wondering how the bleeding hell we had got here. Mind you, I noticed we were all smiling, even the under-the-weather Goldfish. Then we saw The Mumper. He was being led around the ring by one of Sefton's stable girls, and I got to say, he looked fantastic. Our smiles got bigger and bigger as he walked round.

'Look at him,' said Gudge. 'Just look at him . . .'

'Ain't he 'andsome, mate,' said Fred.

'He looks a picture,' said Alf. 'I hardly recognised him.'

Fifteen minutes before race time Sefton appeared with Jimmy, the jockey who was riding The Mumper today. Jimmy was in the Millwall blue-and-white silks we'd chosen as our colours, and he looked the bollocks.

'Hello,' Gudge said, 'How ya doing, mate?'

'I'm well boys, well,' Jimmy confidently replied, in a soft Irish accent. 'How are you guys?'

We all nodded and said we were fine.

Sefton then said, 'Boys, it's close to race time, need a few words with Jim here.' We backed off, giving them room to talk. 'Now, Jim, here is the plan. Listen and listen closely. I want you to take it steady at the start, get him round safe and sound on the first lap and then let's see what he is capable of on the second. You got that?'

'I have, boss,' Jimmy replied. 'I have.' One by one we all shook the jockey by the hand.

Personally, I just hoped he got round without any dramas. The jockey and the trainer said their goodbyes, then went off to join The Mumper.

'Good luck, son,' Alf said. 'Fucking hell, I ain't half nervous. Look at me, I'm seventy-three and I'm shaking like a baby.'

'He'll be fine,' said Dave reassuringly, 'he'll be fine. They know what they're doing.'

We made our way back out of the enclosure and stood looking towards the racetrack.

A couple of minutes later The Mumper went past us, Jimmy pulling at the reins, struggling to keep a hold of him on their way down to the start line. This was the signal for all of us to make our way over to the on-course bookmakers to make our bets. I walked up and down the line, checking the odds on offer as the tic-tac men waved their white-gloved hands around in a blur, signalling to each other the changes in prices. The bookies are constantly changing the odds on their boards, standing under brightly coloured umbrellas on which they have their names printed. 'Jolly Joe', 'Paddy Campbell', 'Mr Squire'. We just had time to stick a few bob on our horse, a tenner here, a fiver there, at odds of thirty-three to one.

My money went to Paddy Campbell. I held the ticket I was given like my life depended on it, and I took a deep breath, trying to calm down a bit. We walked back up to the owners' stand, arriving just in time to hear the on-course announcer say . . .

'And they're off in the two-thirty.'

We had found ourselves a little corner with a good view, but none of us had binoculars so we couldn't see too well where The Mumper was in the pack of ten runners.

''Scuse me, darling,' Dave said to a bit of posh totty who had rested her binoculars on the ledge, 'can I borrow those? Want to see if my horse is still standing, know what I mean?'

The bird looked at Dave like he had just dressed in a

dinner suit to come and collect the bins. She nodded yes, but more out of fright than politeness.

'Go on, my son,' Dave suddenly shouted as he scoured the field through the looking-glasses.

'Where is he, Dave?' Gudger said excitedly.

'He's in the middle, doing all right, jumping well.'

'Go on The Mumper, go on,' Gudge shouted as he struggled to pick out the blue-and-white colours.

Unlike Gudge, I could see The Mumper was going well, keeping up with the field. On the second circuit of the race we all picked up where he was.

He was doing well, in about fifth place, and then all of a sudden he seemed to be going backwards, like he had hit a brick wall or something. The other horses were beginning to run away from him.

'Go on, son,' I shouted, hoping that he would produce a last-minute run and take them all by surprise, but ...

'Go on ... son ...' our words trailed off as we watched The Mumper go further back ... sixth, seventh ... he was now eighth, ninth and then stone last.

The Mumper had faded badly. Dave put the binoculars back on the ledge as it dawned on us all that the horse was done for the day. Me, the O'sh, Gudge, Dave, Fred and Alf stood in silence. I felt exhausted, totally drained from watching it. I felt as if I had been watching seven grand in money being scattered by the wind in seven thousand different directions.

'What we done, eh? We've spunked our dough, ain't we?' said the O'sh.

I was thinking, 'Hold your bottle, son,' but even I couldn't put up an argument on the evidence of what we had just seen.

'We'll have a word with Seft, see what he reckons,' I said,

feeling them all looking at me as if to say, this is your fucking fault, Baxter, fancy getting us involved in all this bollocks.

We walked back out towards the stable area and found Sefton and Jimmy talking.

'What you saying, Sefton, mate?' I asked.

He could see we had all had a knock, but to our surprise, he was smiling.

'Don't get down, boys, he did well. He got round the fences, and Jimmy said he was as honest and brave as they come, kept going even though he had run his race. I did say not to expect too much at this stage, didn't I? Get some more training under his belt and he'll only come on stronger, believe me. I'll ring you in a day or two, let you know the plans for the future.'

As we made our way back to the van, we told each other he would improve, to have faith and all that . . . but I know they were all thinking they had done their money.

And to be honest, so was I.

Thank the good Lord above I had that job for life, eh?

8

Going Through the Curtains

One night, after a late shift, I was taken to a little drinking club called The Printers, which was by Pemberton Row, near to Dr Johnson's house. This was a private club, a tiny place. Its official name was something like The National Media and General Workers Club, and it was packed most nights with print workers taking advantage of the subsidised bar. The gaff was so tucked away you would have walked right past it unless someone had pointed it out to you.

I found myself down there being introduced to this fella known as Big Gary. No great mystery as to how he got that name: he must have been six-foot-four tall and gangly, with his blond hair cut into a wedge and pear-drop style glasses rounding off the effect. It turned out that, like me, he was also from the Deep South. Big Gary was a good five years older than me and had entered the Print through his old man who worked on the *Mirror*. His dad worked as a casual on the vans, delivering from the wholesalers to the newsagents.

We hit it off pretty much straight away. He was also a fellow Millwall sufferer, and after a couple of beers he said he'd show me how to get a bit of extra dough. Turned out he was true to his word. He started to ring me in the afternoons and tell me that he had heard there was a night on the *Sun* available, or at the *Telegraph*, or over at the *Mail*. These jobs landed you about thirty quid a night in the week, and seventy-odd for a Saturday night, all of it in your hand, tucked nicely in a little brown envelope. Remember, this was on top of your regular wages, which were good for my age in the first place. As you can imagine, I filled my boots and took everything going. Taxman? Who?

As a new face among all the old sweats who had worked in this system for years, it was tradition that you were basically ignored from the off when you turned up in their offices. Big Gary had warned me to expect this.

'Miserable old fuckers, most of them, don't want to hand down any crumbs to the likes of me and you. Fuck 'em, though, we're entitled,' he'd say.

'They actually hate you for being young. Bitter and twisted most of 'em, like Arsenal fans.'

On a shift you ended up working in a three-man team. On my first job in the week, the other two 'regulars' talked around me, discussing their timeshare in the Algarve or their situations at home, as if I wasn't even there.

The first Saturday I worked on the *Daily Mail*, I was put to work on the benches, bundling up the papers with a load of old boys who were collectively known as 'Dad's Army'. That was because none of them was below sixty-five. To a man, they shuffled around doing as little as possible and wore carpet slippers! I burst out laughing when I first saw them. I found it ridiculous, but no one else batted an eyelid.

When it came to getting something at the *Sun*, even though you had been given a call to say shifts were available, you had to queue up on arrival. The scam there was that if you knew someone who worked where the *Sun* was housed in Bouverie Street, you would ring them and they would go down and put your name on the work sheet. Then it became a case of 'first up, best dressed' – translated, first name down got the best jobs.

Everyone else would be issued a number on arrival, which placed you well down the pecking order and meant all that was left was the shit work. You were also given a time to come back, which could be hours later.

To kill the time, we would go and drink in The Printers. Only trouble was, we'd spend as much in there as we were going to be earning for that night. Then we would turn up for work ever so slightly Brahms, to put it mildly. It was in the club that Big Gary told me it was only a matter of time before all this would come to an end.

'You've joined at the wrong time, mate, you've missed the gravy boat, son. That Eddie Shah started it, getting in scab labour up at his gaffs in Warrington, and now Murdoch is going to finish it.'

Gary, it turned out, was well savvy and a bit of a political animal on the quiet. He was well read and spouted forth on lots of issues. I was listening most of the time, but as usual, not really hearing him. The best I could respond with was a shrug of my shoulders.

'What's up with ya?' he'd say, getting the hump with my apparent lack of interest. 'Don't you know anything, mate? Murdoch's been building a new gaff down in Wapping for ages now, gonna move lock, stock and barrel down there. They're all going, the *Sun*, *The Times* and the *News of*, and bollocks to the NGA and SOGAT. I mean, we have this reputation of being really militant, but old Rupert ain't gonna spend all that dough and then leave it empty, is he? If the unions don't like it, they can lump it.'

I had heard the story of the new building down the Highway in and around the boozers, although its real purpose had been obscured by gossip.

'That building is for a new evening paper,' I said, having been sold a dummy and, to Gary, talking like one.

'Nah,' he said, waving me away, 'that's all bollocks, and it's soppy fuckers like you believing that, which is letting him get away with it.'

'Be fair, Gary,' I said trying to defend myself. 'When I came into this game, I was promised a job for life, and, yeah, I believed it. Still do.'

'Yeah, we were all fed that line, mate, and it was fair comment back a few years, but you won't be hearing that much longer, son, the way this is going.'

You know something? I should have seen it coming. In all honesty, we had got lazy with the job, started to take things for granted. We turned up every day, played around, had a laugh. No stress, nice and easy. I mean, who wants a job with responsibility? We wanted to go home and forget about the day's work, not take it there with us. So we did the bare minimum and then went down the pub. The thing was, we knew we had the backing of a powerful union behind us. Those boys could shut a newspaper down in half an hour if there was something they didn't like going on. The bosses knew that and they were, frankly, running scared. Fact was, the unions had management over a barrel.

Let's say five million copies of the *Sun* had been printed up. For the bosses to get their money, the newspapers had to hit the shops. But what if the delivery-van drivers took umbrage at some little minor matter and refused to take the papers to the wholesalers or to the newsagents?

That would mean there were no sales that day, but the management still had millions of papers on their hands and bills to pay. It was a no-win situation for the guv'nors. But it was a situation that Rupert Murdoch and Eddie Shah, and a few others, were not going to tolerate for much longer. Of course we didn't see it like that. We thought it was our right to have that secured job and when you start thinking like that, you get cocky, arrogant even. So while we fiddled …

Gary had hit it right on the button. Over the next couple of months, in the lead-up to Christmas 1985, the threat of a mass walkout looked more and more likely, as negotiations between Murdoch and the unions dragged on and on with neither side budging an inch. The leader of SOGAT '82 was Brenda Dean. She reminded me of Maggie Thatcher, funnily enough, all blonde highlights and pearls round her neck. Brenda may have made all the right noises about fighting the injustice coming our way, but she had become known amongst some of the printers as Brenda Deal. Some of the printers felt that she was always looking to sort a deal out with the newspaper owners instead of taking them on.

To be honest, what with the old man being rough at the same time, I wasn't really concentrating like I should have been, and I was still hanging onto the thought that I would survive and if anyone went, it would be the older ones.

Then it came. The bolt out of the blue.

The NNA announced they were looking for voluntary redundancies.

Us youngsters couldn't believe it. This wasn't in the brochure when I signed on. Got to say, though, the firm was offering good redundancy money. Figures of forty thousand pounds and over for twenty-five years' service were on the table, and you could see a lot of the older faces getting tempted by that sizeable carrot dangling in their face.

I was in the canteen one morning having a breakfast with Bernie 'the Gnome' Edwards, who, as the nickname suggests, was a little fella who looked as if he should have been sitting in your garden with a red pointy hat on and a fishing rod in his hand. The Gnome told me he had put in to take the money.

The stunned look on my face prompted him to explain why.

'This game's dead, son. I mean I'm forty-five, going butter on top with an expanding waistline. I'm getting old. And they're offering me over forty large to piss off? Who else is going to offer me that kind of dough, eh? Besides that, the Print's changing, all this Wapping stuff is only going to end in tears. I've been here since I was sixteen. I've done me bit, it's time to get out, son, for me anyway.'

I sat and listened to him and heard a sound in the distance. It was the sound of the beginning of the end.

And as if that wasn't enough . . .

Four days before Christmas, Tubby Hayes was playing 'Dear Johnny B' in my bedroom when the phone started ringing its head off. I took the needle off the record and picked it up.

'Hello, is that Mark Baxter?'

'Who's that?'

'Mark, this is Sister Jenkins at Guy's Hospital. Can you get here as soon as you can? I'm afraid it's your father. He's had a turn for the worse. We'll explain in depth at the hospital, okay?'

The phone was put down at the other end. It took me a minute to unscramble my thoughts. Turn for the worse? He has incurable cancer, how can that turn worse? A voice in my head suddenly blurted out, 'He's on his last, you mug, sort yourself out and get lively.'

But I just stood there. The thoughts that were going round my head had literally frozen me to the spot. B-rr-iing, b-rr-iing. The noise of the phone made me refocus. I picked it up.

'Hello,' I said tentatively.

'Blue, you had a call?' It was my brother, Glen. 'Er, yeah . . . they rung you and all, then?'

'It don't sound too clever, mate. See you up there, yeah … You all right?' Glen sensed I wasn't really listening.

'Er, yeah … yeah, I'll see ya there.'

The enormity of what was now occurring in this very minute was beginning to dawn on me. I left the house and ran up to the top of my road where I jumped in a black cab. On the journey to Guy's, I sat there in silence as the cabbie rabbitted on. Cliché, I know, but then that's why they are clichés. They happen all the time.

'Changed round 'ere, mate, ain't it, gawd help us, state of it … you ever thought of getting out?'

I ignored him, I was lost in a world of thought.

The cabbie looked at me through his rear-view mirror. He could see he was wasting his time here, and thankfully he didn't say another word.

On arriving at the hospital doors, I threw a score at the cabbie and belted up to the ward. I was met at the reception desk by a senior nurse who turned out to be the same one I had spoken to on the dog.

'Mark, is it?' she said. I nodded.

'Mark, it's bad news, I'm afraid. Your father is slipping away. Your mum is in there …'

I let her say that much and then I was past her and through the door. I saw my dad sound asleep, his pyjama jacket wide open, and a slow-release morphine drip just above his heart. It meant he was on his way. It meant it was all over. My mum was sitting down, holding the old man's hand and staring at him. On seeing me, she got up and we hugged. Her eyes were moist with tears.

'You all right, Mum?' I asked and felt so stupid in doing so. She didn't even answer me.

I leant over my dad and whispered in his ear that I loved him. I stood up, and in that very moment I felt as if my chest was going to explode. Please, not in front of my mum.

Without a word, I made for the room's khazi. I locked the door, sat down and the moment I did the tears exploded out of my eyes. I mean, I bawled like a fucking baby. Streams of hot, painful tears trickled down my cheek.

It was as if all the past months had finally caught up with me and had burst through. Finally, I composed myself as best I could and dried my eyes. I unlocked the door, stepped back into the room.

Now it was my mum's turn to discover just how ineffective words are when life bites its hardest.

'You all right, Mark?'

I gave her a weak smile of assurance.

A couple of minutes later, Glen and my uncle Bob arrived. My uncle Bob was my mum's youngest brother, only ten years older than me, and more like an older brother to me than an uncle. He was prematurely grey, to which he'd say, 'Don't care what colour it goes, mate, as long as it stays on my head!' He was a stocky bloke, married now, with three kids of his own. He was also extremely loyal, always there if my mum or dad were in any trouble. As he entered the room with Glen and saw the old man lying there, his face crumbled. Like me, they were stunned by what they saw.

'Oh, fuck me,' he cried, 'what's happening here?'

It was a reasonable question, and one that had been troubling me since that phone call. After all, the old fella had been in pretty good spirits the night before, and the hospital had told us that, with the right medication, he should have a decent six to nine months left to live. The sister had followed the boys into the room. Before I could say a word, she began explaining that the doctor had seen my dad that morning, told him that they wouldn't be starting the chemo after all. There was no point. His cancer was so far advanced, it was in his lungs now. They had suggested putting him into an hospice. She said the old man nodded at her and sort of smiled resignedly.

Within an hour he had collapsed in his room and fell into this coma-like state.

When I heard her mention the hospice, I knew straight away what had happened. Ever since I was a boy, my old man had always said to me that whatever happened to him, I had to promise never to put him in an old people's home. He detested the idea of that. I'm sure he would have equated the hospice with being put into a home and then given up the game.

If my old man was one thing in life, it was bastard stubborn. Once he made his mind up, that was it. I know that might sound strange, but if he knew there was no hope, he would have just decided to turn it in and not put him, us or the old girl through any more dramas. This morning, all on his own, he had made his last ever decision.

'He hated seeing Connie in that home,' my mum said to no one in particular. Mum had worked it out as well.

Connie, his mum, my gran, had been put in a home up at Hither Green. The old 'uns just sat there, being spoon-fed and having their arses wiped when necessary. It was grim in there. My overriding memory of the place was the smell of stale piss and boiled greens.

'I'm never going into one of them, never,' he always said when we walked away from another grey visit. 'I'd rather top myself. Hate them places, I ain't gonna be one of those poor old fuckers, that's for sure.'

Now his wish had been granted. We all sat in the hospital room, looking at Dad, and then at each other, not really sure what to say or do. The silence was broken by the consultant, a Mr Miller, entering the room.

'Hello, Mrs Baxter,' he said softly, recognising Mum. 'Very sorry it's come to this. We really thought he would be with us well into the New Year, but I'm afraid we are near the end.'

Mum put her head down onto the bed, still holding my old man's hand. His fingers never looked so small.

Mr Miller looked at his watch.

'It's nearly seven o'clock. I would think we have another six hours at the most.' He then told us to stay as long as we liked and to give the nurse a call if we needed anything.

'I'm staying,' said Glen quietly. 'I'm staying.'

'Yeah, Doc, I think if it's all right with you, we'll all stay to the end,' Bob said.

'Absolutely,' he said sympathetically. 'A nurse will pop in every half-hour or so just to make sure all's under control.'

He shook all our hands. 'I'm so terribly sorry,' he said, and left the room looking genuinely upset.

'I need a smoke,' I said, looking at Bob. 'Coming, son?'

He nodded and we ended up outside the back entrance of the hospital, puffing like a couple of beagles.

'Well, this is ending quicker than I thought,' Bob sighed. 'Your dad was only saying the other night he was looking forward to the New Year and watching that soppy horse of yours run.'

I smiled at his little wind-up attempt to lighten the mood.

'One thing is for certain, there'll be no Christmas in my house this year,' I announced. 'Fuck all that tinsel and turkey, can't get my nut round all of that. Nah, my priority is to see the old girl is okay, cobblers to everything else.'

Bob just nodded. He had his own family to look after and celebrate with, even though his heart wouldn't be in it.

'Gonna be tough, Markie boy, gonna be tough,' he sighed.

We stood in silence, still trying to gauge the enormity of what was about to happen.

After finishing a couple of smokes each, we went back into the room and waited. And waited. The hours dragged. Every fifteen minutes I looked at my watch, expecting an hour to have passed.

Occasionally the old man would make a moaning noise and then go all quiet. We all turned to look at him each time he did, hoping, praying he would wake up. Once in a while, a nurse would quietly enter the room, take his readings, write them up on the board at the end of his bed and then leave. It was unbearable.

I was sitting in an armchair with a blanket barely covering me, drifting in and out of light sleep, when it happened. Bob shook me gently to wake me. My dad had slipped away. It was all very peaceful, his pain controlled by the morphine drip on his chest. No noise, no fuss, he just remained in the sleep he had been in for the past twelve hours or so. Funnily enough, I just sat there smiling. Strange reaction really, but there would be no more tears from me and no more pain for the old man. He was well out of it. I just sat there remembering all the nice things we had done together, the laughs, the good times. Going to Millwall for the first time, the Boxing Day piss-ups with the family, the holidays in a caravan down at Leysdown and him singing 'Roses of Picardy' on stage.

He was a great father, and there is no better accolade to lay upon a man's shoulders. Mum looked absolutely knackered and was obviously very distraught. She had hated seeing the old man suffering, but now it was all over, you could see the reality of the situation facing her, etched all over her face. She changed from my mum to an old lady right in front of my eyes.

As one, we all got up and hugged and comforted each other. We stayed half an hour and then said our goodbyes to the old man, finally leaving the old girl in the room on her own, giving her a chance to say farewell to her partner of more than twenty-five years.

We waited outside in that soulless corridor, and I remembered him not so long ago banging his fists against the wall, imploring me to look after his wife, my mother. No way would I let him down.

Glen decided to drive us all back to our house and stay the night. Bob came along and decided to stay as well.

Not long after getting home, Mum and Glen turned in for the night, but me and Bob cracked open a bottle of vodka and saw in the dawn, talking about the old man. Bob revealed he was only a kid when he was taken to the pubs where my dad and Gudger would give a song. He sat there laughing as he remembered the times, later on, when he used to play in the same darts teams. He said Gudger 'was lethal with a set of arrers in his hands, what with his eyesight being so bad'.

I couldn't help but chuckle.

Eventually we fell asleep in the chairs we sat in.

I was woken by daylight streaming through the blinds, and looked at my watch. It was seven a.m. As I rubbed my eyes, I thought of the day ahead and felt a black cloud settle on my shoulders.

The doorbell went. I staggered up and opened the door. My mum's sister Shirley was standing there, pools of water in her eyes about to spill. I hugged her and guided her towards the kitchen. I put the kettle on and told her to stay there. As I did so, my mum appeared at the kitchen door and they fell into each other's arms.

I livened Bob up and told him we should get going.

Glen, Bob and I had to go to the hospital to pick up my dad's belongings and then go and make the funeral arrangements. Bob nutted into the kitchen, said hello to Shirl. Shirley was my mum's closest sister, five years younger, but she looked old that morning, all hunched over and fragile, her face etched with lines. I reckoned she'd had no sleep last night. I had to make a couple of calls before I left, one being to Gudge.

I took a deep breath as I dialled the number. Understandably he was shocked at what I told him.

'No ...' he said as I told him the news. 'No, mate ... I thought he had a bit longer, Markie.'

'Yeah, so did we, but, well, it all caught up with him, Gudge, he's well out of it now, mate.'

I was choking as I tried to talk to him, the words from my heart tending to get stuck in my throat. I was struggling, badly.

'Gudge, got to go, mate. Got to make plans. Do me a favour and ring the others for me, let 'em know, yeah?'

'Sure, son, you look after Mum, and look after yourself. If you fancy a chat or a drink, bell me, you listening?'

'Will do, Gudge, will do ...'

We drove to the hospital, then to the funeral director's, and then on to register the death. With each stop, the day got harder. The three of us tried our best to keep our spirits up, but it was impossible. We finally ended up in The Flying Dutchman. The place was virtually empty when we walked in. The only face I recognised was old Wavy Davy.

'Hello, mate, how's your dad?' he asked with concern.

I just shook my head at him, and he got the message. He looked down at the bar, and into his pint. Brenda behind the bar saw my shake of the head and realised what had happened.

'Mark, I'm so sorry.'

I nodded back at her, and we ordered up our drinks. I walked to the pub phone and belled Gudge to tell him we were in there. We sank our drinks in silence. Gudge was with us within ten minutes. On arriving, he kissed me and Glen on our cheeks and shook Bob's hand. He plotted up, shaking his head.

After a suitable round of condolences, Gudge took my arm.

'Markie, there's something I have never told you about your dad, mate, and, well, with what has happened here, well, I think now's the time.'

He had the table's undivided attention.

'We had a chat round here three years back, after your dad was offered early retirement. The bank told him since he had put in twenty-five years he was entitled to apply for it. He belled me up and asked me to meet him to talk it over.

'John,' I said, 'take it, mate, enjoy your days, no more getting up at five in the morning in the freezing fucking cold.

'But your dad couldn't see it. He told me he felt he had to keep working, he had to provide for Jeannie and you boys. He was a worker and told me he would have felt guilty if he turned it in. Believe me, boys, I tried to talk him into it, but he weren't having it. Now this has happened . . .'

'Fuck me,' was all I could utter.

If only he had taken retirement, him and the old dear could have had three solid years to do as they had pleased. What had happened was truly tragic, no other way of looking at it. The table fell silent as we all took in what Gudger had just told us. After a minute or so, I raised my glass up in the air and saluted the old man, my dad, John Frederick Baxter.

It seemed the only thing to do.

I decided to spend that Christmas at home, keeping an eye on my mum. I pulled the ladder up and I blanked the parties I had planned to go to, my heart just wasn't in it. We had a few family visitors, and Glen and Tracey stayed Christmas Eve night. My mum made all of them welcome, but they could see she was struggling. Needless to say, Christmas Day and New Year's Eve 1985 didn't happen in that house, we all just got through it, just survived it.

I went back to work in the first week of January. Talk about back to work with a bang. The place was full of stories of how the negotiations between the bosses of News International and the print unions were struggling, and a strike now looked a certainty.

That afternoon, Terry, our SOGAT FOC, called a meeting that he insisted all attend. Most of us youngsters hated going to union meetings, they were so boring. But there was a feeling this one was going to be different. When I arrived, the room was packed and Terry was up and talking. Everyone was listening to him. He told us how Murdoch was insisting on flexible working, a no-strike clause, new technology and the abandonment of the closed shop at the new premises. Obviously this was a non-starter for the unions, and so talks had come to a stalemate. He warned us that the six thousand workers at News International were now likely to strike, and he would urge us all to support the strike by not working on the titles affected and by not buying any of them. He also hoped we would all go on the planned marches to the new building in Wapping. A big shout of approval went up on that one: the boys were spoiling for a fight.

Old H. now stood up.

'Terry, I can't speak for all present here today, but I'm sure the boys will get behind it, if this thing escalates. One question though, Terry. If the News International lot are out on strike, who will be doing the work at the new plant, mate?'

There was a murmur of discontent as Terry began to answer. 'Too early to say, Hal Taylor, but there are rumours that the electricians' union has done a deal with Murdoch, and they'll be stepping up.'

The shouting from the crowd in there became deafening. 'Bastards, scabs, nicking the bread from our mouths!'

'All right boys, calm down ... calm down.' Terry was struggling to control the assembled crowd. The mood in there was ugly. 'As I said, it was only a rumour ...' but the rest of what he was saying was lost in the noise of the crowd.

They, the crowd, declared the meeting over and everyone began to leave, anger etched on the many faces. As we made our way back to our office, the talk was of one thing: our determination to get behind any action.

'Those capitalist bastards,' Bob said, 'they are taking the right piss ...' and just as he was about to get out his orange box and spout forth, he was rudely interrupted by Jackie Mays.

'Bax, you had a call when you were out. Some geezer called Sefton ...'

The way my luck was lately, what with the old man and now the job wobbling, I half expected him to tell me the fucking horse had broken his fucking leg and had been put down.

I reached for the phone.

'Hello, Seft, you looking for me, mate?'

'Hello, Mark,' Sefton said, and God bless him. He sounded all cheery and full of good spirits.

'Mark, I've got The Mumper into another race. He's running at Folkestone, next Wednesday. Hope you can be there.'

As Wednesday was the day before my dad's funeral, that would be a no from me. I could get there and back, I supposed, but I had other priorities and loads on my mind. I told Sefton that would be fine, but that I wouldn't be making the race. I explained the situation and he was full of heartfelt condolences. I told him I would arrange for Fred and the others to be there on the day, though.

To be honest, I was choked that I was going to miss the race. I really could do with a day out with the chaps, take my mind off all that was going on, have a laugh and drown out the horrors in a sea of Smirnoff. But I couldn't do it. I was the eldest son, and therefore had to accept the responsibility of making the day of the cremation go as well as it could. I knew I could rely on Glen to do his bit, but I kept hearing my dad's voice in my head telling me to look after my mum, and that was what I was going to do. She was my main concern at the minute. Once that day was finished, I could get on with the rest of my life.

I rang Fred and Gudge and they told me they would get to Folkestone, and then belt back for the funeral the next day.

'Leave it to us, boy, we'll take care of everything. You look after Mum.' Gudge knew my mum well and knew she would be suffering badly. 'She needs you to be strong, son, know what I mean?'

'I do, Gudge, mate, I do.'

The funeral arrangements had all been made, as had the seventy-odd phone calls to all the relatives, friends and work colleagues. A mixture of shock and sadness came back to me down the phone lines. They were hard calls to make but made easier in some ways by hearing how popular the old man was.

On the day of the race itself, I didn't hear anything from the chaps. Understandable, I suppose. But I couldn't help but wonder how The Mumper had got on. I planned to ring Sefton later that evening, but after seeing my mum, and the state she was in with *that* day in front of her, the thought went out of my head.

On the morning of the funeral I awoke around four a.m. with dread in my belly. I lay in my bed contemplating the day ahead. I would rather be anywhere today but here, but I also knew that there was nothing else for it, that I had to get up and get on with this blackest of black days. We had a steady stream of people arriving at the house from nine-ish. Along with the people, hundreds of flowers of every shape and colour also arrived. I greeted everybody as best I could. A lot of the neighbours had come out onto the street, to wish me and Glen all the best. Nice touch, that.

My mum was in the front room, sat on her favourite armchair, head bowed, her hands being wrung into knots. There was the occasional snuffle and a cough as people tried hard to keep their emotions in check. Me, I just kept shaking hands and making small talk, smiling and putting a brave face on it until finally the cars arrived, my dad's coffin in one of them. I swallowed hard when I saw that. I helped load up the flowers from the immediate family into the main car. There were loads of blue and white flowers and ribbons, signifying my dad's love of Millwall, and I could only smile when I saw Gudger's bouquet. It was in the shape of a light ale bottle.

Funny thing was, I couldn't see Fred, Gudge or any of

the chaps anywhere. Knowing them, I thought, they probably got pissed up and are struggling to get here in time. The thought made me chuckle. Good luck to 'em. Me and Glen had a struggle to get my mum into the car. She really didn't want to go and wouldn't even look up.

'Come on, Mum,' Glen said, 'sooner we go, sooner it will be all over, mate.'

'Come on, Jeannie,' Shirley said through the tears, 'we're all here for you ...' In the end, we virtually carried her towards the car. She was gone, totally lost.

There was total silence in the car as it made its way to Nunhead cemetery, apart from the noise of the purring engine and the small groans of heart pain. At the church, the funeral directors lifted the coffin out of the back of the car and walked it up a small flight of stairs towards the chapel. We followed close behind, with me and Glen either side of the old girl. The voice of Nat King Cole singing 'Roses of Picardy' guided us towards the vicar. The tune was so familiar to me, I found myself mouthing the words along to it as I walked to the first row of pews, holding Mum by the elbows to stop her from collapsing. We sat down and soon after the vicar got up and started talking. But I heard none of it. I was lost in a fog of memories, some sad, some happy. Occasionally my mum would howl, and me and Glen had to hold her up on the pew.

Hymns were sung, kind words were spoken and then the coffin went through the curtains. I heard a lot of crying behind me, but I didn't look round. My face didn't crack and I didn't feel like crying, I just felt an overwhelming, crippling sadness. Then the sound of Eddie Fisher singing 'Anytime' filled the church. This was my dad's favourite singer singing his favourite song, and it sounded amazing. It was then my mum just went. She must have heard the old man sing that song hundreds of times, around the home, in holiday-camp talent competitions and in countless pubs. I bet she never thought she would hear it in a church and he not be by her side.

God, it hurt to hear it today.

The song signalled the end of the service. I stood up to walk my mum out of the church. She, we, had had enough.

As I turned round, I was met by a sea of faces, hundreds of them. In the fog of the day, I just hadn't realised how many people had made their way to pay their last respects.

The place was packed full of family, both immediate and distant, plus Mum and Dad's friends from over the years, his work colleagues from Barclays, over seventy of them, and even Sagey and Jerry from my office representing the rest of the lads. I nodded towards them as I walked past, still not crying. Truth be told, I had no tears left. As we entered the shock of daylight, the first people I saw were Gudge and Fred, and in between the two of them was The Mumper, surrounded by Alfie, O'sh, Sefton and Dave ... They had brought the horse to the funeral, complete with a black sash around its neck. People smiled when they saw the sight before them, even my mum. I walked up and hugged every one of the syndicate, and as I did so, Gudge whispered in my ear that the horse had come fourth at Folkestone.

'He run blinding, son, blinding, as game as a pebble he was,' and then he turned his head away, weeping and wiping his eyes.

Once again I smiled. Sefton had agreed for them to bring The Mumper to the church, and I was so grateful to him for doing so. What a touch. Meant a lot to me, that. Me and Glen spent the next half an hour shaking hands and expressing our thanks to all who had come. It's fair to say that no one really knew what to say to us. Which was fine. Their tears spoke for them.

Most of the funeral party ended up at The Dutchman for a drink and a sandwich. The pub was quiet, and quiet didn't suit The Dutchman. I asked Eric to put on one of his old tapes, one that had a few of the tunes that the old man and Gudge had sung over the years. Before long, The Dutchman sounded right. We all sat there for a couple of hours talking about the old times, the strokes they had all pulled, the laughs they had had. It was a bit surreal, laughing on that day of all days. But I decided it was better than crying, and there had been plenty of that already.

Finally, I ended up back at home. I had had a good drink but it hadn't had any effect on me, nothing, it was as if the alcohol had given up trying to soak up my pain. I was exhausted. Mum was already up in bed, and the majority of people had now made their way home. It was only Glen, Bob and me left sitting downstairs. Still, we somehow found the inclination to unscrew and finish off a bottle of vodka between us, in the hope it would at least have the kindness to knock us out. Thankfully, it did.

I fell asleep in the chair I sat in, still with my black tie around my neck, and I dreamt of a tomorrow that could only get better ...

9

Rupert Gets His Revenge

On 24 January 1986, unable to agree a settlement with the News International management to move its workforce down to a new building in Wapping, east London, the print unions called a strike that would prove historic. Six thousand members who worked on Rupert Murdoch's titles walked out and immediately News International issued dismissal notices to all of them. One of the nastiest, most notorious industrial fights of recent times had started in earnest. It would be for ever known as the 'Wapping Dispute'.

It's important to remember here that it wasn't just the printers who got their P45s, it was also the cleaners, the secretaries, the accounts people, normal Joes who had got caught in the crossfire. Their jobs were taken by coachloads of men and women who were bussed in from unemployment black spots all round England. Maggie T.'s policies had created sky-high unemployment, forming an army of dispossessed that the bosses could call upon for scab work. Members of the electricians' union, the EETPU, were bussed in as well, arriving in coaches with grilles up at the windows, part of a plan that had already been developed over the preceding months as it became obvious that an agreement was unlikely. So Murdoch printed on, with *The Times*, the *Sunday Times*, the *Sun* and the *News of the World* all moving down to the new plant off Virginia Street, not that far from Tower Bridge.

The immediate effect on me personally was negligible. My job was still okay at the NAA, and I carried on as normal. Sure, the bit of bunce at Bouverie Street had stopped but there was still a couple of quid to be nicked at other newspapers that were not Murdoch's.

Terry, our FOC, had put the call out for us to support the strike the best we could, and the most effective way of doing this was to go on the marches and demonstrations.

The strike was the talk of the country as well as the table in The Dutchman. Even though he was now in his sixties, Gudger had discovered that his militant streak had not dimmed with old age.

Against all orders, he had been going down to the picket lines on a regular basis.

That gave him the perfect excuse to come over all Churchillian every time we got together. 'The chaps are great down there, the old Dunkirk spirit lives on, over the top, boys and all that, know what I mean? Loads of old faces there. I know we're getting slaughtered in the press, but that's all loaded one way, ain't it? Fucking Murdoch. He's made bundles off the back of us, and now he's trying to squash us like bugs. Bollocks to him.'

'Hark at him, he'll be getting out the hammer and sickle in a minute!' laughed Dave.

'Keep the Red Flag flying high, is it, Gudge?' said the O'sh.

'Look, I ain't no commie, but people like Thatcher and old Rupert are shitting on the working classes, mate, from a great height and I, for one, have had enough,' Gudge stated firmly, getting into his stride.

'You going down much, Bax?' asked Alfie.

'Yes, mate, been down a few times, plenty of support

there, as it happens. Fair to say there's a lot of strong feeling amongst the people.'

'Any bother so far?' asked the O'sh.

'Nothing too bad, bit of huffing and puffing. The tit-headed old bill are taking the piss down there, though, bang out of order they are, actually laughing at us they are, the slags,' I replied.

'Well, that's the gavvers for ya, ain't it?' said Alfie.

'How's your job looking, boy?' Fred asked.

'Safe, mate, my firm has had a bit of voluntary redundancy going, taken care of getting rid of a few, so that's all over now. I'll be sweet.'

'Glad to hear it, son,' said Dave.

I was still sticking to that line, as nothing had been said to my face to make me think otherwise. In all honesty, I had had enough of the rabbit about 'Wapping'. I heard it all week at work and at home, where it made the old girl worry. I didn't want that. Now it was beginning to invade my weekends. It was beginning to get on my tits, people going over and over it. I needed to lighten the mood. I noticed that O'sh had got paint all over his hands. I asked him what he had been up to.

'Don't talk to me about that,' he said, getting the hump instantly.

'Why?' I laughed.

'Why? Fucking why? 'Cos of that nebbish, Ronnie the builder, that's why!'

'What's he done?' said Fred, realising a chuckle was on.

'It's not so much what he's done as what he ain't done,' said O'sh, looking all needled.

'Tell us more, Goldfish,' said Gudge.

'Well, I rang Ronnie and got him to quote my old lady a price on doing her kitchen up. Took for ever to get him to call back. Finally, he came round and said he would start last Monday. "Bish, bash, bosh," he said, "soon have that sorted." So I got all the paint in and left him to it. Only, I get a call at work on Monday afternoon. It's my old girl. "Mark," she says, "yer man has scarpered, saying something about not being quite right and leaving me with a quarter-painted kitchen!"'

I start to laugh, sensing I might know the rest of this story.

'Turns out,' the O'sh continues, 'that the colour of the paint she had chosen, had, and I quote, "started to unnerve him" when he began, and he felt unable to finish the bleeding job. I rung him and got through to his missus. She told me he was in bed, suffering with his nerves and was waiting for a doctor. I ask ya, what sort of poxy painter is that?'

'It's a painter with painter's block,' I said smiling, which made the whole affair worse for the O'sh.

'But why have you got paint all over ya?' Alf said.

''Cos my mother is now driving me garrity! I'm having to finish off the bloody job myself, you dozy old twonk! Old Ronnie is having an artistic crisis and I'm bloody paying for it.'

With that, the entire table fell about laughing as O'sh carried on cursing Ronnie.

Back home, both Dave and Fred rung me separately. Neither had said a thing at the table, but they were worried about Gudge getting too involved at the picket lines. The papers were full of how it got pretty tasty down there sometimes, with all the pushing and shoving and jostling going on, and that's without mentioning the contemptuous way the police were treating the men and women on the picket line.

They had decided to come down and support me and Gudge, and that way they could keep an eye on him if things got silly.

'Can't let you two plums get bashed up, can we? Doll and your mum would never forgive us. Besides, that Murdoch's a right ponce. Spat you out and told you to walk, ain't he?'

I couldn't argue with them. Well, I could, but there would be very little point. They had spoken, and that was very much that.

I had arranged to meet Big Gary in The Dog and Duck on the night of the next march. All go together, safety in numbers and all that.

I travelled down to Fleet Street with Fred, Dave and Gudge on a 45 bus, same route I did day after day. We were all in a good mood, but there was apprehension in the air at the same time. The banter flowed, but I couldn't help noting it was a little stilted. Crossing Blackfriars Bridge going into the City is the part of the journey I liked best. It always felt like I was entering a different world, a world where anything could happen.

Tonight that feeling was heightened.

On walking into the Victorian green-and-cream-tiled splendour that was The Dog and Duck, we were hit straight away by an atmosphere I can only describe as one of great expectations. Something was about to go off tonight, that was for sure.

I had had this feeling before down The Den, when one of the big clubs were in town, and you walked past a welcoming committee of Millwall's finest getting ready to 'greet' them.

I walked up to the long wooden bar and winked at Joey, the landlord.

'Hello, son,' he said, clocking my slight nervousness, 'you look like you could do with a large one.'

I nodded gratefully and put in the order. I sipped a bit of my vodka and diet as I waited on Joey to get the rest of the drinks, and the alcohol tasted so much sweeter than usual, as if it was trying to do its bit for the strike as well. Walking back to the table the others had plotted up at, I noticed loads of faces from my firm, and other bods I knew through my work. Big turnout tonight, that was for sure. Up at the other end of the bar, animatedly pointing this way and that, Big Gary was holding court, his voice the loudest in the gaff by a long mile. I nodded to him and motioned that we would meet him outside when the time came. He was too busy saving the world for me to make introductions to Gudge and Co., so I left him to it.

Gudge had spotted him, though.

'Your mate loves the sound of his own voice, don't he?' he smiled, nodding in Gary's direction and gulping down his first drop of lager.

'Know what you mean, Gudge,' I replied. 'He called this spot-on, though, got to say that for him. He saw what was coming and he told us, but no one was listening. He's a good lad, really. Just full of frustration at the plums who've ignored him over the past six months ... plums like me.'

'Big 'un, though, ain't he?' said Dave. 'With Fred on my shoulders, we would only come up to his belt.'

Fred laughed. 'Fuck standing behind him at Millwall, wouldn't see cough all,' he said.

The banter, as intended by its creators, relaxed us a touch. Dave now nudged Gudge on the arm.

'Thought Doll would have sent you out with a few cheese rolls for the trip, like,' he said. 'Personally, I could eat The Mumper and chase the jockey, right now!'

'Liberty, mate, I know. I'll have to have a word with her for next time, Dave,' Gudge said, raising his eyebrows, playing along with him.

As he said it, Fred turned his head and looked around the pub. I noticed what had caught his attention. A few of the chaps had started sinking their pints, others were putting their smothers on, all preparing for the trip down to Wapping.

'Come on then, lively,' said Fred, 'looks like we're under starter's orders.'

We polished off our drinks and went outside where the Big 'Un was waiting for us by his van. I finally made the introductions, and smiled at the sight of Gary standing next to Fred and Dave. I couldn't help thinking: whatever happened to Snow White and the other five dwarves ...

'What are ya, mate,' asked Dave, 'eight foot?'

'Something like that, fella,' Gary grunted back. He obviously didn't like the attention his size brought him. As was evident by his question back to Dave.

'Heavy smoker are ya then, mate?'

'What?' asked Dave.

'Well, something's stunted your growth, ain't it?' Gary smirked.

Dave looked at me and then Fred. 'Cheeky mug,' he uttered under his breath. Fair to say, these two wouldn't be exchanging Christmas cards in the near future.

We piled into Gary's van and we were off. It was quiet in there, no one quite sure what the night held in store for us. Before too long, we hit a bit of traffic.

'Loads of the boys out tonight,' Gary pointed out. 'Bollocks to it, I might as well park up here and we can walk the rest of the way with the mob, eh?'

We all agreed. I could do with a drop of air anyway.

Gary parked up round the back of Tower Hill tube station and we walked down and joined the march, which numbered thousands already. In no time at all we had picked up the pace, with numerous big colourful silk union banners being thrust into the air, and the holders of them shouting anti-Thatcher and Murdoch chants out loud. Amongst those nearest to me, one banner belonged to the London Central Branch of SOGAT and was at least six foot by six foot, mainly bright red in colour with golden scrolls all over it. It was held aloft by four burly fellas, two on each side.

Another one was bright yellow and had the words '*Daily Express* Night Machine Chapel' printed on it in big bold black letters. Around these banners were hundreds and hundreds of faces, young and old, all wrapped up against the cold night air.

Nylon blue parka rubbed up against sheepskin coat. A brown woollen beanie hat bounced along next to a tartan peaked cap, all voices shouting for old Rupert's head. The air of excited anticipation was intoxicating. The vast majority of the crowd were card-carrying union members, but word was now going round that the march had been infiltrated by a sort of rent-a-mob, who were there to stir up the crowd.

Within thirty minutes of us joining the march, we had reached the main line of old bill. They stood there motionless, holding their riot shields. Behind them stood another row of police, only they were on horseback, whilst behind them lay rolls and rolls of barbed wire. What a sight.

Although we all felt strongly about what was happening, none of us felt the need to take on the old bill. Odds like that, there was only one winner. Besides that, Dave, Fred and I were keeping an eye on Gudge. Big Gary pressed on and we let him go. I think he liked the idea of having a pop at the gavvers who seemed to love the thought of taking on the unions, just as they had with the miners last year. Jesus, they had waded into them with Thatcher's blessing. It was sick how they had clobbered not only the men but their women and children, too. More than that, it was unforgivable. You don't say you're civilised and then treat people like animals, whatever your thoughts concerning them. I held Thatcher responsible, her actions had set an ugly tone that pervaded the whole country. People starved whilst others laughed at them. And it wasn't just her, it was her smirking allies, the Tebbits, the Aitkens, all of them up to their neck in hatred and bitterness. No compassion, no understanding.

I hated the lot of them for their power-crazed ways, especially Maggie. In fact, I knew people who were already planning street celebrations the day she goes.

The majority of the roads around the plant were closed, all except those on which the vans going in and out of Wapping were travelling. It was the law who ensured that the plant could operate effectively. The drivers of these scab vans that drove the papers out of Wapping and down to the newsagents and the wholesalers were obvious targets for the crowd. Word had it that a lot of them had come up from a couple of boozers in the Portsmouth area which had a reputation for doing stuff like this in the past. I really couldn't understand how they could do it. It was all alien to me. You just wouldn't take another man's job in these circumstances.

Would you? I don't know, I suppose desperate people do desperate things. Or was I being naive – was it just simple greed on their behalf? A lot of printers were going out of their way to identify these geezers, and God knows what they would have done if they had got their hands on them.

As the night drew on, the crowd gradually dispersed and

we started to walk away from the area. We found a boozer and plotted up for a brandy each to keep the cold from getting any further into our bones and then headed home, all of us tired out by the night's events.

The next day at work, I heard stories of how the old bill had charged the last groups of stragglers left on the picket lines late last night. They were knocked all over the place.

Apparently, so the story goes, as the police drove away in their coaches after their shift had finished, they waved their overtime pay packets at the strikers, along with copies of the *Sun*.

Nice, eh?

A couple of nights later, I was indoors watching the telly and the editor of *The Times*, Andrew Neil, came on defending what News International was doing. He said the papers were held to ransom by the unions. New technology had to be introduced. That it was crazy that, despite the widespread use of the offset litho printing process elsewhere, the Murdoch papers, in common with the rest of Fleet Street, continued to be produced by the hot-metal and labour-intensive linotype method.

He also said it was crazy that his journalists compiled their stories on old-fashioned typewriters, and that only NGA staff could then transfer their copy to the newspapers using typesetting keyboards.

Neil conceded that News International probably deserved some criticism for the way the whole thing had been handled. He claimed they had tried negotiation but that had failed. In the end, they felt they had no alternative but to sack the workers and bring in a new workforce.

I sat there thinking that anyone watching this, who knew nothing about the dispute, would think the owners had the right to do what they liked with their workforce, although

I had to concede that some of the points he raised were valid.

Some of the old working practices were really outdated, and of course new technology had to come in. That was the future. Yet I had also seen with my own eyes how the print workers had been treated down at Wapping on the picket lines, and that had just made me want to dig in deeper and fight him and News International all the way.

It wasn't so much what they had done, more about the way they were doing it.

I was now sporting a 'Don't Buy the *Sun*!' badge to work, worn as I walked around the floors dropping mail off to various departments. As I did so, I found I was getting a few dodgy looks, mainly from the journalists who disliked the fact I was openly supporting the strike. Bollocks to 'em, I thought.

There had never been a lot of love lost between the general print worker and the journos.

Of course there were always some exceptions to that rule, but they were few and far between. One of the good guys was a writer called John Chamberlain. John was a youngish guy who worked on the sports pages.

We had got on well when I first worked up there in my early days, and it had been good to see John rise through the ranks at the NNA. John was now a deputy editor. We still met up for a beer or three, if we found ourselves on the same shifts.

One night we were in The Dog and Duck, laughing at Joey the landlord as he attempted to run the bar whilst being three parts pissed. John, who was a smallish guy, with jet-black hair and a 'Fleet Street belly' on the go, began to tell me about his mate Barry, who had worked on *The Times* sports desk.

He told me Barry was put under a lot of pressure to cave in and move to Wapping, but he really didn't feel comfortable with the idea. Or with going through the picket line to get there.

Next thing you know, Barry had received word that a letter which told him to go to Wapping or be fired, was coming his way. That plan was scuppered when someone 'leaked' these letters to the press and there was a huge outcry.

But it showed that Murdoch would do anything and take on anybody to get what he wanted.

'So what did he do then, John?' I asked.

'He turned it in, Markie, resigned,' John replied.

'Good boy,' I said. I admired this Barry's principles.

'Yeah. He's even been down on the marches a couple of times, standing alongside your mob, got right into it he has.'

'Good old Barry, here's to ya,' I said, as I drained the contents of my glass.

That story summed up the way the dispute was beginning to divide people. Even in my office there was a bit of tension.

Since my old guv'nor Bill Braithwaite had retired a year back, a bird called Glenda Smith had taken charge. She was a little fat bird, around her mid-fifties, all beehive hairdo, with a boxer's nose. That's a boxer dog as opposed to a prize fighter. She always wore white blouses covered in bits of ash and splashes of tea, and her shoes were falling apart. A right scruffy old sort she was.

Glenda had been Bill's secretary, but had still taken part in all the card schools over the years. But as soon as she had got control of the office, she began cracking the whip. There was a lot of resentment about her behaviour from the rest of us, but gradually she got her way.

As it happens, I was never a big lover of the bird in the first place. She was a right mouth on a stick, thinking her words gospel. She was also a Tory voter, loved her 'sister' Thatcher and was naturally against the strike. Needless to say, my 'Don't Buy the *Sun!*' badge hadn't gone down too well.

'Mark, not sure about you wearing that badge, especially round the floors,' she said. 'Typical of you. You've got a right chip on your shoulder, you have.'

'Got that wrong, Glenda darling!' I said, walking off. 'I'm actually well balanced. I've got a chip on both shoulders.' She hated being fronted up, which of course I couldn't resist doing.

Make me take it off, you mug, I thought, and I'll bring Terry the FOC in here quicker than you can say *I love you, Maggie.*

It's fair to say we didn't get on, which wasn't really healthy for me in the long run. I should have played the game with her but I'm one of those people who, if I don't like something or someone, I let them know. Can't help myself. All or nothing, me, as the great Steve Marriott once sang.

A lot of the old faces were also getting pissed off with Glenda and her arrogant new ways, her silly new rules.

'What makes me laugh,' Bob pointed out, 'is that she was the first one out with the cribbage board and the cards when Bill was in charge. Now, it's "Sorry, chaps, can you put that away? There's work to be done." She's a wrong 'un, mate,' he added, 'a fucking wrong 'un.'

Old Bob spoke for us all there. We fell silent, all of us thinking about this woman, and it was then I noticed how the joking had dried up over the past couple of months, how Glenda was poisoning the gaff just by her presence.

It was now the end of March, and there was no end in

sight for the dispute. It was getting more militant on the picket line as people began to suffer badly. Mortgages weren't getting paid, marriages were beginning to crack and I even heard of a suicide as the hardship began to bite.

It was a Friday, about nine-thirty in the morning. I was on a late shift, so I was at home and John Coltrane was in my bedroom about to perform his album, *A Love Supreme*, when I got a call from Glenda at home.

'Hello, Mark, can you come in a bit early today, please? There is a meeting for some of the Despatch staff at twelve, and I need you to attend,' she said.

Immediately, the alarm bells went off in my head. 'What's it all about?' I asked.

'Erm ... can't go into too much detail at this stage, so if you can get in for the meet, that'll be great.'

I didn't like the sound of that.

I arrived in Fleet Street at eleven-thirty that morning, so had time for a quick livener in the Old Bell. I found Sagey, Jerry and Martin in there.

'Hello, Bax, wet the bed, have ya?' said Martin, noticing I was in early.

'Nah, that slag Glenda rang me indoors, told me to get up here for a meeting at twelve.'

'Yeah, I had one of them,' said Jerry. 'Wonder what's up?'

'I reckon she's going to bounce the old 'uns, and get some under-fives in to do the graft,' I said.

'Wouldn't surprise me,' he said. 'Probably getting a back-hander to do the dirty work.'

Jerry hated her as much as the rest of us.

'You're probably right, but what's she want you two in there for, though?' said Sagey.

'She'll give us the kids to look after, won't she?' I said.

'Make sure they learn the ropes. She won't do fuck-all work sorting them out, but she'll take all the credit.'

We supped up and walked the familiar route to the NNA. When we got there, we found old Bob and Johnny Mak who worked on the multilith machines also waiting for the meeting to start. We winked at the boys and they said they thought the same as us, that Glenda was going to bounce all the old 'uns.

'Told ya, didn't I, she's a wrong 'un,' Bob stated.

We made our way into the boardroom and found Glenda and a fella called Wayne Perkins sitting there. Perkins was from Personnel, and he was a prize tit.

He was a right slippery-looking geezer, all hair gel and too much aftershave. We sat down around a table and Glenda coughed, looking really uncomfortable.

'Hello, gents, thanks for coming in early. There's no real easy way of saying this ...'

I looked at Jerry, and he glanced a puzzled look back at me.

'I'm afraid, due to the ongoing dispute, and other factors, the NNA are going to make you all redundant ...'

Fucking hell, did I hear that right? No, I couldn't have done. 'What? What are you talking about?' I blurted out.

'Sorry, Mark. As I said, this isn't easy. I'm afraid in ...'

I wouldn't let her continue. 'It ain't a bundle of laughs on this side of the table either, love.'

'As I was saying, I'm afraid in the present economic climate, the NNA have decided to make a few changes, and that means you are all being made redundant.'

'This is bollocks!' Jerry shouted out. 'What other factors? What are you talking about, Glenda?'

Then realisation broke like an egg over Jerry's head. I should have seen it as well.

'Wouldn't by any chance be the NNA taking advantage of the strike situation, would it?' Jerry asked in the most sarcastic manner possible.

'I can categorically deny that.' It was Perkins's turn to pipe up now. 'The National News Agency has been looking at the staffing levels in the Despatch for over six months, pre-dating the current dispute, and we feel we cannot continue at the current levels.'

'That's bollocks,' Bob said, 'and you fucking know it.'

Perkins interrupted him. 'Please try and keep this as civilised as possible.'

'Oi, you,' I said, 'let the fella speak. You ain't been here five minutes, and already you're playing with people's lives? Bob's been here for years, never late, never sick, he deserves better than this and you both know that.'

'Yeah, same goes for Johnny here,' said Jerry, pointing to John, who just sat there with a stunned look on his face.

The atmosphere in there was getting very edgy. Glenda was squirming in her seat. Literally.

Perkins now piped up, 'Mark, Jerry, I must ask you to keep your voices down. I know this has come as a shock to you both, but I'm afraid the decision has been made. You will work a four-week notice period, and we'll have the paperwork ready in a day or two.'

This Perkins mush was beginning to get right on my nipple ends. He was only a couple of years older than me, but it was like listening to an old bloke speak. Everything he said was out of a manual. He had no soul, the fella.

As for Glenda, well, in my eyes she had shat on her own doorstep, crossed the line. Me and her was finished.

'We done?' Jerry demanded.

'Yes, Jerry, we are,' said Wayne.

'Right, come on, boys, pub!'

We all got up and made our way out of the room. Going down in the lift, the knowledge that I was effectively out of work hadn't yet sunk in. All I knew was that I needed a vodka. A very large vodka. We made our way to The Dog and Duck and drank the next couple of hours away. In no time, I was lagging, and lagging badly. A couple of the lads from the office came to find us, as we hadn't arrived for our shifts. The news of what had happened had already gone round the building.

'Bax, Glenda is looking for you, mate,' Sagey said.

'Sagey, she can fuck off, the bird, I've had enough,' I slurred towards him.

'Son, I understand that, but you don't want to get sacked, do you, and lose out on your redundo?'

Hearing that slightly sobered me up. Fuck that, they ain't getting my dough off me as well, the fuckers.

I got up and staggered back to my office. I was all over the place, but Sagey, good lad that he is, held me upright. As soon as I entered my office I saw Glenda standing by a desk to the right of me. She saw me and looked quickly at the floor.

'WHORE!' I shouted right at her, and I would have carried on with a few more choice words but Sagey and Martin got me out of the room.

'Bax, this is no good, mate,' Sagey said, sitting me down on a chair. For a moment there the floor zoomed up towards me like a crocodile leaping out of the river to sink its teeth into some poor unsuspecting animal.

'Let's get you out of here,' Sagey said.

I was led out of a nearby back door, and sat on a little wall in the courtyard. The fresh air hit me like a jolt of electricity. Within a couple of minutes, Val had appeared.

Val was a middle-aged, well-dressed bird who also worked

in the Personnel department. I knew her well, she came from my manor but had worked her way up into a high-ranking position in Personnel.

If she knew this was going to happen today, she had kept the secret well.

'Mark, I'm really sorry, mate.'

'Val, straight up, did you know, girl?'

'No, of course not. Perkins and Glenda cooked this one up. But, Mark, you've got to be careful, they will sack you if you carry on abusing them. Glenda's already rung me about what you called her earlier.'

I looked at her and we both chuckled. 'Fuck her, Val, I'm gonna have her,' I said.

'Oi! You listen to me,' Val demanded, as her south London instincts reared into life. 'You've got nine grand coming, I've checked. Now think about it. Can you afford to lose that kind of dough over a slag like Glenda?'

Hearing that was the best hangover cure you could get. I had worked there for just over three years, and nine grand was not a bad return for my graft. I could do a lot with nine grand, I was thinking.

'Right, now I've got your attention, think about it, mate, you know Glenda would love to deprive you of that, so don't let her. Get your head down, see your days out and walk out with what you deserve. Don't let an idiot like that fuck you up. All right?'

I stood up and kissed Val on the cheek, and didn't say another word. I walked through the building, out of the front door, hailed a black cab and made my way home.

I slept like a log when I got in. My body and soul were exhausted. I woke up and that was when it hit me – I was out of a job. A wave of fear went right through me. What was I going to do? How was I going to survive without regular dough in my sky? And not only that – the people I worked with weren't just colleagues or work mates, they were friends and, in some cases, like brothers. I was going to miss 'em badly.

Another punch hit me inside. Fuck. What was I going to tell my old girl? She was slowly getting back on her feet after the funeral. This would be a bad knock for her, one she could do without.

I decided to leave my news unspoken for a couple of days. I looked at the clock and it read eight a.m. I must have been asleep for near on twelve hours. I decided to get up and go to work. I wasn't due to be working that weekend, but I had the overriding need to go to Fleet Street. It was like a magnet was drawing me in. It being a Saturday, none of the managers were in, just a couple of the lads. I settled down for a cup of tea and a chat.

They told me how Glenda had kept a low profile for the rest of the day after I left. I told them that I wouldn't talk to the arsehole any more. I'd do the shifts, do my notice period, but I wouldn't talk to her.

I was on earlies the next Monday, and as I lay in bed I thought about throwing a sickie. They didn't give a fuck about me, so why should I . . .

Then it struck me – that's exactly what she'd be expecting. Bunking off work would give her the perfect chance to sack me and save nine grand. I wouldn't give her the satisfaction. So in I went. The atmosphere was really subdued in the Despatch. Four of us in total had lost our jobs. Furthermore, we had lost that which bound us together. The card table would stay unused and the jokes would no longer fly.

A couple of days later, I got my redundancy paperwork and Val was right, I had nine grand coming. I decided not to look for another job straight away.

I'd give work a swerve for a while. Instead, I decided to give Sefton a call. I told him to get The Mumper into a race as soon as he could, I fancied a bit of a bet. Already, that nine grand was starting to burn a hole in my pocket . . .

10

The Pie and Liquor

I found that I was waking up in the early hours of the morning and just lying there, staring at the ceiling, wondering what the hell had happened to me. I mean, six months ago I was bouncing along so nicely. I had dough in my bin, a smile on the way into work and a job to see me through to the end. My old man was busy making plans for his early retirement, and my mum was never happier.

Now the old girl was in bits and the two things I thought would be in my life for ever, my old fella and the job, had both dropped off the radar within months of each other.

The old man situation spoke for itself. I'd get used to it, no doubt. But I'd never get over it. I was surprised, though, about how losing my job affected me.

It was the people more than anything – I missed 'em. I missed the banter, the drinking, the social life. I didn't know what to do with myself. I'd lost the purpose of my day, lost the routine. The only bright side was the redundo dough, which meant that I was in no rush to get back on the treadmill. I'd take it easy for a couple of months, see what turned up. In the meantime, a lesson has been learnt by yours truly and it was this: don't take anything for granted, and when an opportunity falls in your lap, grab the bastard as hard as you can and hang on for the ride. It's all you can do.

As I lay on my bed, suddenly The Mumper ran (grin)

through my thoughts, and I realised that what started out as a bit of fun had now turned into the one stable (another grin) thing in my life. I thanked God I'd got the syndicate together. I really needed them boys now. And they wouldn't let me down, I knew that for a fact. When word of my dismissal hit the local airwaves, they all rang within the day.

Gudger was really cut up over it, saying he felt guilty that the job hadn't worked out as expected. I told him not to worry. Times were changing, and the old way of doing things was no more. In Maggie's hands no one was safe any more. Most of the country seemed to be suffering, whilst those left standing were having the time of their lives. 'We will bring harmony,' she said on the day she was elected. Must have meant the hairspray, eh? Not that the very real concern of my friends stopped them laying into me at the earliest opportunity they got.

At my first Dutchman session after the redundancy, I was absolutely slaughtered.

'Oi, oi, here he comes, the Giro Kid,' Fred shouted when I walked in the boozer. 'Do you want me to stick a tenner for you in the whip, son? It'll be coming out of my pocket eventually in your dole money, anyway. Might as well cut out the middle man!'

Fred's banter had the table in stitches. Half the pub, as well.

''Allo, Fred,' I said, trying my hardest not to rise to the bait. 'How's your week been?'

'Same old, same old, mind you, you've got to have a week to have a weekend, eh?' More laughter.

Dave picked up the redundancy thread. 'Nah, seriously, Baxie boy, gutted for you, although I think you should do Gudger on a trades description charge. Job for life he told you, didn't he?'

'Oi, shut yer cake'ole, don't drag me into it, it's Thatcher and her mob of monkeys that have ruined all of that,' Gudge said. He wasn't happy today.

'Oh, leave it out, mate, all you greedy old bastard printers bled poor Rupert dry over the years. No wonder there's nothing left in the pot for the boy,' Fred said, on a roll.

'He's got a fair point there, Gudge,' said the O'sh with a grin.

'I need you, don't I?' said an exasperated Gudger. 'Anyways, changing the subject . . .' he suddenly announced.

'Hang on tight boys, I feel a Gudger special coming up,' Fred said, rubbing his hands together.

'You seen that kid who plays in goal for Birmingham? Big lump, David . . . Sea . . . what's his bleeding name, Sea . . . Seaman, that's it. Filth, he is.'

This was classic Gudger, dropping a story in that had no relation whatsoever to anything else that was being said at the time.

'Why's that then?' Fred asked, eager to know why Gudger should be so against a footballer he had never met.

''Cos he's the spitting image of that bastard Customs bloke who done me for all those fags at Lanzarote airport a couple of years back. Got to be related, I tell ya!'

I was sitting there with tears in my eyes, but they were tears of laughter and not despair. Only this mob could rip me to bits like this and then launch into some surreal story that linked a professional footballer with an incident at Customs and Excise years ago. Thank fuck they were around me, that's all I can say.

A week into my enforced 'holiday', I began going into The Dutchman of a lunchtime. I couldn't think of what else to do. Got to say, it was a real strange experience, like meeting a friend who has changed everything about themselves for the day. For example, the only face I recognised when I went in was Wavy Davy's, and true to form he was still rocking and rolling on his stool. On this particular day, he had one of those Rubik's cubes in his hands, whilst trying to remain on his seat. That was hard enough for Davy, let alone getting all the colours in the right order. The other punters there I didn't recognise. It was either local office bods, eating a cheese and tomato roll and having a swift one before going back to nod off at their desks, or dirt-stained geezers off a local building site, or a bunch of Southwark Council road sweepers who had finished for the day.

Even the barmaid was different. Kate does the lunchtime week shifts. She's in her mid to late fifties and always well turned out, as it happens.

'Hello, Mark, you back again, mate?' she asked brightly.

'You got it, Kate,' I replied. 'You all right, girl?'

'Vodka and diet, is it?' she asked.

I nodded and handed over a tenner. 'Yes, please, babe, and one for yourself.'

Kate smiled. 'Aah, ta, boy,' and turned around and put a baby glass under the vodka optic, poured in a drop of diet coke and then did herself a Pernod and black.

The usual table was available, so I plotted up there. I think Gudger must have set up an exclusion zone around this table, because I had never seen anyone sit here, not even during these hours.

I opened up the copy of the *Standard* I had in my back sky and I scanned the job pages. Although I was in no rush to get back to work, I was curious to see what was out there. The problem I had was my years in the education system. They were hardly what anyone would call productive. In fact, the only thing I left school with (apart from an aversion to school), was an 'O' level in Art, and even that was a poor grade. Any jobs going that required qualifications were pretty much out for me. That left working on the Royal Mail, or the dust, or maybe BT.

Problem was ... those jobs didn't really appeal to me, to be honest. *I suppose I could get a job in an office, maybe work in a postroom, or perhaps I could* ... I closed the paper, sat back and took a sip of my drink. Fuck work. I'd get on it tomorrow. Today, I'd have off.

Lovely.

I scanned The Dutchman. A lot of the office mob had now made their way back to work, and they'd left behind the flotsam and jetsam that perpetually resided in this corner of south London. That meant the pub was populated mainly by blokes on their own, middle-aged, shabbily dressed, drinking quickly and staring blankly into space. Wavy Davy was the only exception to this rule, but although he might have nodded in your direction, he said very little, seemingly lost in a world of his own. Occasionally he smiled to himself, as something unspoken struck him as funny, but more often than not, it was quickly replaced by a grimace as he nearly lost his balance and fell to the floor. Without warning, the horrible thought that this might be me in a couple of years flashed up in my mind's eye. I saw myself sitting at a table, v and d in front of me, staring blankly into the void until eventually I, not Wavy Davy, crashed to the floor.

Fuck, if I didn't pull my finger out soon and get a job ...

Kate came over to empty the ashtray and wipe the table down. 'Same again, son?' she asked.

I glanced up at Wavy Davy and saw he had resorted to picking off the coloured stickers from his Rubik's cube and rearranging them, so all the colours matched. I looked around at the other desperate wasters filling the room with gloom, and before I knew it found myself saying, 'Nah, Kate, think I'll leave it today, love.'

I got up and headed for the exit door. Fuck me, I thought to myself, I only came round here to cheer myself up!

Once back indoors, I decided to bell Sefton, see if he felt the time was right for The Mumper to run again.

We were getting near to the end of the jump season, and another race would help me focus on something a bit livelier and more interesting than my life at that moment.

Sefton answered the phone, and after the usual pleasantries, told me The Mumper was really well, and that he had had exactly the same idea: there was a race at Newbury he could get the horse into in a couple of weeks' time. Perfect, I thought. I thanked him, put the phone down and it was then that it suddenly occurred to me: perhaps we could organise a coach for the day and take the old man's friends and family to the race, hold a Johnny Baxter Memorial Day sort of thing, where we could remember the old man and have a blowout at the same time. Excited, I went down to the kitchen and suggested the idea to the old lady. For the first time in ages I saw a slight smile cross her lips.

'Your dad would like that, son,' she said. She still spoke of him in the present tense, as though any minute now he would walk through the door and life as we knew it would start up again.

I told her to leave all the organisation to me. Then I ran back upstairs and began ringing round everyone I could think of. I got a great response. Everyone thought it would be a fitting tribute to the old man. After that, I got out a pen and some paper and wrote down the details.

A couple of days later, I went back to The Dutchy and stuck a couple of hand-drawn posters up on Eric's noticeboard. They read:

**Thimble Baxter Memorial Racing Day –
22 March 1986, at Newbury Racecourse.
Come and celebrate and remember the life of Johnny
'Thimble' Baxter and cheer on The Mumper.
Tickets £15, includes sandwiches and lager.
To book your seat on the coach, see Eric behind the bar.**

I left Eric my home number and told him to call me when we had enough punters. Then I could get on the case and book a coach.

I met up with the chaps the next Sunday. As I sat down, Dave said, 'You look tired, Gudge. What you been up to, mate?' Gudge was seriously yawning.

'I was up all night last looking for that Haley's Comet, weren't I? I didn't see a bleeding thing, waste of poxy time.'

'I saw that mentioned in the paper,' said Fred. 'But you can only see it during the day, can't ya?'

'Now he tells me,' exclaimed Gudge. 'I was out on my balcony for hours last night. Doll had to wake me up at four in the morning, bring me back inside.'

'You old plum . . .' laughed Fred.

'Does anyone know anyone who has seen that comet?' I asked. 'Do you know anyone? I don't. I have never met one person who has seen Haley's Comet. Every now and then you get the same thing in the newspapers. Look out the window at this time and you will see the great comet. We all do and we all see nada, but no one says a dickie. Then a year or so later we do the same thing all over again. Crazy, if you ask me.'

'Here, I saw the Fat Man the other night,' Alf said, putting his glass down on the table.

The Fat Man (never did catch his real name, as he never

179

dropped it) owned a minicab firm called 'A 2 B', just off the Walworth Road. He was known as the Fat Man on account of him being so skinny and the fact that no one had ever seen him eat. They call that irony. 'Guinness is like a roast dinner to me, cocker,' he'd say. Rumour had it that his belt went round him twice.

We all used the Fat Man's cabs to get from, well, A to B.

''Ere, O'sh,' Fred said, 'did you know that Fat was an actor years ago and went up for an audition for that film *Bridge Over the River Kwai*?'

'Didn't know that,' replied the O'sh, looking amazed. 'How'd he get on?'

'Well, he went in to meet the director, who looked at the state of Fat and said, "I'm sorry, mate, but the Japanese were never that cruel!"'

'You wanker,' said O'sh, embarrassed that after all these years at the table he could still be baited up and reeled in.

'What's this I hear about Fat tucking you up the other week?' Dave now said to Alf.

'Little stronzo,' Alf stated. 'You know what he was doing? He was going around collecting money for old Herbie Glynn. Told me Herbie had pegged out a couple of weeks earlier. I handed over a fiver, there and then.'

'Well?' asked Dave.

'Well? I'll give you fucking well. The fella's a complete Joe Loss,' Alf spluttered, his face going redder and redder. 'I'm in The World Upside Down a couple of days later and fuck me, who walks in, none other than old Herbie! All right, Herbie, son, I shout to him. I thought you were dead, mate. Herbie looked at me strangely, which was understandable in the circumstances. "You know what, Alf," he says. "You're the fifth person to say that to me this week. Is there something I should know?"

'It turns out the Fat Man has been going round all the boozers telling people the same as he told me, that Herbie had died from a heart attack, collecting deep-sea divers as he went. When I challenged Fat the other night about it, he just said yeah, sorry about that, he had been given some bum information!'

'What about your fiver?' I asked.

'Fuck knows, it probably fell at the first ...' Alf said smiling.

'Right then,' I said, putting an end to the banter. 'Newbury ...'

'Yep,' said Dave, 'I reckon we'll fill a sixty-seater coach, easy.' It was nice how he emphasised the last word. It showed what my old man meant round this part of the world.

'I have news for you, my son,' I replied. 'Me and Eric are up to fifty names already, going to be a sell-out.'

'Absalastic fantoutley,' said Dave. 'I suppose what with you shirking from work, you've had a lot of time to sort all that out, eh?'

'Yeah, you're turning into a right soapy dole-scrounger,' said Fred, pulling my pisser. 'It's the likes of me, paying my taxes, that is keeping you going, mate, and don't you forget it.'

'Really?' I shot back. 'I'll remember that when I turn over in bed Monday morning, as the rest of you plums get up for work.'

The truth was, I would have rather have been getting up for work myself – I wasn't cut out for this dodging work caper. I had already begun thinking of maybe going back on the stalls. Summer was approaching, and at least by working for myself I wouldn't have some no-good ponce of a guv'nor like that Smith on my back. The only trouble was, I had got used to the wage slip. When you're self-employed you don't know if you are going to have a fiver or five hundred in your bin at the end of the day. Still, all of that could wait for now. Priority number one was to get The Mumper race done and dusted, and see where that left us.

The next day I belled round a few coach companies and got one sorted in no time. The fella on the phone told me it was a good clean coach, and the driver not only had a clean driving licence but help from above. I didn't have a clue as to what he was talking about with that last comment, but just said, 'Okay, mate,' and gave him the address of The Dutchman, which was to be the pick-up point.

Then I called my brother, Glen.

'How's Gudger, by the way?' he asked, after exchanging the usual pleasantries.

Like me, Glen had grown up with Gudger in his life from a very young age and loved him to bits.

'He's all right,' I replied. 'You know Gudge, he don't change. He's still on forty Benson a day. I reckon he'll see us all out in the end.'

'Still as blind as a bat though, ain't he?' Glen said kindly. 'I saw him in the street the other day. "Oi, Gudge," I shouted, "How you doing?" "Who's that?" he replied. Even though we were only ten feet away from each other, he couldn't work out who I was, what with his dodgy minces. "It's Thimble's boy," I shouted back to him. "Which one?" he said.'

We both laughed down the phone.

Glen said him and Tracey were up for the race day and looking forward to it. My mum would be so pleased.

She would want her family around her on that day. I set about ringing round the names I had on my list to give them the details. The coach was booked to pick us up at the pub at nine in the morning, leaving us with plenty of time to get to the racecourse for the first race, which was at twelve-thirty, with The Mumper racing in the two-thirty. As I picked up the phone and looked at the first name to call, then the second, then the third, I couldn't help but think to myself that I was living in a south London version of a Damon Runyan story.

From the top we had: Old Shut Eyes, followed by Harry Gossamer, then Titch Crawley, Old Mutton Eye, Alfie Apple, Dickie Tin Ear, Big Les, CID Sid, Harry the Milkman, Nil Sauce, the Fat Man, Mr Patel the Piano Man, Dixie, Naked, Jumbo, the Long 'Un, Champagne Colin and Ricardo Spaghetti. The list just went on and on. Throw in Gudger, the O'sh and Fred the Shoe, and things just looked, well, silly.

The night before the big day I went out for a meal with my mum. I took her to La Luna on the Walworth Road, the local Italian we always used for family dos. Nino and his staff looked after us there, and the food was always tip-top. I tried to keep the conversation light, but within minutes of sitting down the talk turned to my dad.

Seated so close to her, I could really see how painful life had become for her. She confessed freely that she couldn't accept he had gone. She told me, and told me as if it was a secret, that on a couple of occasions she had actually seen him in the street, even calling out his name once. She told me that her only enjoyment was going to bed and sleeping, because it was only in dreams that they were joined together again. As it should be. The only thing was, the whole time they were together, he had his back to her. Even when he spoke, he never turned round to face her. Naturally, she asked him to turn round, but he never did. One day he will, my mum said, and that, I realised, was what was keeping her going.

I reached across the table and held her hand. I told her that me and Glen would always be there for her. We knew we couldn't take the place of the old fella, but we were a part of him come to life, and the best seconds she could ever have.

She smiled and said, 'I know, I know.'

We drank a red-wine toast to the old man, and then Nino came over and said how sorry he was about our loss.

My mother looked him straight in the eye and said, 'Thank you, Nino.'

Then we both rose as one and made our way slowly back home. All the way there, I held my mother's hand.

I was up early the next day. It was a cool crisp March day, but thankfully dry. Sefton had told me in the week that The Mumper was looking great in training, and that he and Jimmy the jockey hoped for a good dry surface, as that suited the horse. Well, Seft, old son, I thought, looks like you've got the weather you wanted. I might just have to have that big bet I had promised myself.

I was round The Dutchman at eight-thirty, and it was a relief to see the coach already there. One less problem to worry about. I could see the back of the driver, wiping the headlights down with a wet cloth, so I went over to introduce myself.

''Allo, mate,' I said, 'my name's Bax and ...' My voice tailed off as the fella turned round.

Our coach driver was dressed as a vicar.

'Hello,' he said, 'my name is Vincent, Vinny, if you like. How's your luck?'

I didn't speak, but just looked at the dog collar he was wearing.

'I see you've noticed the outfit, then ...' Vinny said brightly as if it was the most natural thing in the world.

'Yeah,' I said, 'Yeah ... you know today ain't fancy dress, don't you, mate? I asked him.

'No, no,' he laughed, 'I'm a curate for St Peter's in Kennington. I'm actually an ex-black-cab driver, but I found the Lord over four years ago now. I drive for the coach firm occasionally, taking the parish pensioners or the local looked-after kids to the seaside. Yesterday, I had a call from Brian at the office, telling me he had a lot of bookings for this weekend and was short of drivers. Could I take a party to Newbury racecourse? So, here I am.'

I stood there for ten seconds, waiting for Dave or O'sh to jump out of the coach and tell me it was a wind-up. But they didn't.

Fuck me, we've got a pie and liquor as the driver of our coach. I just hoped he wouldn't need any help from the Man above before the day was out ...

II

All Fours and Sevens

Eric came staggering out of The Dutchman holding a crate of lagers. He sat them on the floor and motioned towards me to help him. Then he caught sight of Vincent sitting in the driver's seat.

'Here, what's all that about, Markie?'

'What?' I replied, on the gee-up.

'Stone me! What do you mean, what? You've got a God-botherer in the driving seat of the coach, son.'

'Oh him, that's Vinny the Vicar,' I said, and then carried on loading up the crates into the hold of the coach as if a man of the cloth driving a coach was an everyday occurrence.

Eric took a long drag on his salmon. After shaking his head, he went back into the pub, deciding better than to make any further comment. I just stood chuckling to myself. I could see this becoming a blinding wind-up day . . .

I turned round and saw the first few of the coach party coming my way. First up was my mum with Glen and Tracey, leading the way, naturally. I gave my mum and Tracey a little kiss on the cheek each and shook my brother's hand.

'All right, Mum? You're nice and early,' I said.

'Didn't want to be late for your dad's big day, did I, son?' she replied.

I just smiled at her. Together, we boarded the coach and were welcomed by Vinny.

'Morning each,' he said in his best sermon voice.

'All right mate … er, Father,' said my brother, doing a classic double-take.

My old girl then looked at me, puzzled, but took her seat without comment. Next up was Gudger and his missus, Doll. As he climbed the stairs onto the coach, Gudge caught sight of our driver and instinctively made the sign of the cross.

Then he whispered to me. 'Here, Markie, you've got a vicar driving the coach, mate,' as if I hadn't noticed.

I gave Doll a kiss on the cheek and said, 'He ain't a vicar.'

'What d'ya mean, he ain't a vicar, he's got a back-to-front collar and everything,' Gudge replied. 'I mean, I know me eyes are a bit …'

'He's a curate,' I said.

'You having a go, you cow, son?'

'Gudge!' Doll commanded. 'Sit down, you're being a right pain in the how's-yer-father. Look at you, getting in everyone's way …'

Gudge did as he was told and freed up the aisle on the coach. 'Here, Doll,' I heard him say behind me, 'what's a curate?'

'Flaming hell, how should I know, why?'

'The boy has got one driving the bleeding coach, that's why!' Doll ignored him and got her knitting out.

Slowly but surely, the coach filled up. You could tell everyone was in a good mood and looking forward to the day. Well, everyone but the O'sh, it seemed.

I noticed him hanging about outside the coach, looking very nervous indeed.

'Oi,' I shouted at him, banging on the window as I did so.

He turned round to look at me and then urgently beckoned me to get off the coach.

'What's up with you?' I asked as I got to the bottom of the stairs.

'What you playing at?' he demanded.

'What?'

'You've put me on a right dodgy one here, ain'tcha?'

'O'sh, what the fuck are you on about?'

'Only you would have a vicar driving the fucking coach.'

'He's not a vicar,' I replied, 'he is a curate and he comes as part of the package. What's the drama?'

'It's all right for you, son, ain't it? You ain't a bleeding Catholic … not like me,' he said, eyeing the driver warily.

'Oh fuck off, O'sh, you are not what I – or indeed the rest of the world – would call a practising Catholic, mate, are ya? You're like the rest of us, weddings and funerals only.'

'I know, I know, but being raised among all that, well, those things stay with ya, don't they? I mean, I'm going to break all their rules today, ain't I. I'm going to blaspheme, have a bet, get pissed and you never know, I might even get my leg over if all the stars align in the right place tonight, and thanks to you, you nebbish, I'm going to have a pie and liquor watching me do it all! Talk about giving me a touch of the guilts …'

'Oh, shut up you tart,' I shot back. 'He don't even play for your side, does he? He's from our mob. Besides, he's a nice fella. He couldn't give a monkey's what you get up to today, believe me. Now get aboard, you blouse, we've got to crack on and get going.'

The ginger one sulkily got on board, almost curtseying as he walked past Vinny. It looked like we were nearly full, but as I looked back I spotted Dave and Fred in the pub, having a cheeky half. I jumped off the coach steps and ran in.

'Oi, bit early, ain't it?' I said.

'Hair of the dog, son,' Fred said conspiratorially. 'We were on it last night, down at The Corrib. Blinding night, but my head ain't agreeing with that statement this morning, I can tell you.'

'Noticed you've got a sky pilot driving the bus then,' laughed Dave.

'Yeah, he came with the coach. Nice fella, ex-cab driver, although I ain't told many that. Thought I'd keep that to myself for the wind-up.'

'Ex-cabbie, eh? Each to their own,' said Dave.

'Yeah, he told me he found the Lord a couple of years back,' I said.

'What, in the back of his cab?' Fred joked. 'Can you imagine him in one of those old green huts having a breakfast and telling the other cabbies: guess who I had in the back of my of cab last night?'

We all laughed, which must have been painful for those two with the hangovers they were tending. I looked at my watch, and Mickey Mouse's right hand said it was twenty-up.

'Talking of the coach, boys, we better jog on, we're already running late.'

The chaps drained their glasses and we made our way back. As Fred and Dave boarded they both said, 'Ace, King, Queen, Jack,' and crossed themselves as they passed by Vinny.

'And may the Lord bless you as well,' Vinny said, good-naturedly.

Fair play to the curate, he took it all in good part. I actually think he was enjoying all the attention.

'Right,' I shouted to the assembled beano party who sat before me. 'If you are not here, put your hand up, 'cos we're off.'

Everyone cheered and I nodded to Vinny for the wagons to roll. He kicked it into gear and we were on our way to the M4 and to Newbury racecourse. Within ten minutes, the beer and the grub were out.

'Bon AppeTIT,' said Ronnie the Builder, with the emphasis on the word tit, as he crammed in a couple of jam doughnuts.

'Feeling better now, Ronnie?' I said.

'Yes, ta, mate,' he said. 'My doctor sorted me out some counselling. It's calmed me right down. Built a brick wall last week, went up a treat, it all just flowed lovely. My counsellor told me it was all there in me, I just had to unlock the door, so to speak. "A crisis of confidence", he called it. Told me I was the first builder he'd seen with it, though. Funny that, eh?'

I doubt if the O'sh would find it that funny, I thought to myself. Towards the back of the coach, card schools were formed and a couple of songs were getting an airing. The Millwall song 'Let 'em Come' was sung the most. As you might have guessed, we had many Millwall sufferers on board. A few of the old ballads from my dad's singing days also got an airing, but with somewhat different words. 'Strangers in the Night' became 'Strangers up Your Kite', and 'Sing As You Go!' became 'Sit On My Face!'

Funny how quickly they had forgotten we had a person of the cloth driving, but I could see Vinny's face in the rear-view mirror and he was smiling away, obviously enjoying himself. As was I. There was a lovely vibe on that coach, and everyone was catching it. I saw my mum talking to Doll and Alf's Lil. Both women had been good to her since my dad died, ringing her on regular occasions, making sure she was okay. It was as though they had become her family, but family you wanted to be with, as opposed to being forced to be with. Most of her in-laws hadn't been near her since the funeral, but that didn't matter when you had such lovely, warm people around you.

Suddenly I heard my mum shout, 'Oh, Doll, I'd forgotten all about that! Weren't that funny?'

'What was, Jean?' asked Glen's Tracey, who was sitting behind her.

'Oh, Trace, haven't I told you that story about the time Johnny rung Gudger pretending to be from British Telecom? I must have done.'

Tracey shook her head. She obviously didn't know that my old man often rang Gudge on a wind-up. One week he'd be the gas board, another week, he'd be from the water people, and so on. This particular week he was the phone company.

'Yeah, he rung up Gudge and covered the phone with a hanky to disguise his voice,' my mum explained. 'He said, "Hello, is that Mr John Ginnaw?"

'"Yes, boy," replied Gudge, "who's this?"

'"Hello, Mr Ginnaw, I'm ringing from BT," replied Johnny. "There seems to be some sort of discrepancy with the length of telephone cable you've got in your house."

'"Oh, yeah," said Gudge, "I don't know nothing about that, boy." "Yes, well, what we propose to do is give it a tug at this end ..." "You what?" said Gudge.

'Now as you can imagine,' my mum explained, 'I'm creasing up in the kitchen hearing all this.

'"What are you talking about, boy?" said Gudge.

'"We need to adjust the cable to the permitted length, otherwise you'll incur extra charges. So we are going to tug it from this end and sort the problem out."

'"Bollocks to that," said Gudge, "I pay enough as it is."'

By now our part of the coach was enthralled by the story,

and it was hard for my old girl to tell it and not burst out in a mixture of laughter and tears.

'"Exactly," said Johnny, "this way, you will save money. So when you see the cable move, Mr Ginnaw, let me know and then we'll get you to measure what's left, okay?"

'"Okay, boy," said Gudge grudgingly, "pull away."

'Johnny then made some straining noises down the phone and asked Gudge if there had been any movement.

'"Not yet, boy, have another go," he replied. Johnny started to make the straining noises again, but burst out laughing in the middle of them. You could have heard the penny drop in Gudger's head a hundred foot away,' my mum said with contagious excitement.

'"That you, Thimble?!" shouted Gudge, realising he'd been done hook, line and sinker. "You're a shithouse, Baxter!"

'By now Johnny was laughing so hard down the phone, he could hardly speak. He finally came clean, "Sorry, Gudge, mate, couldn't resist it."'

'He was always doing that, he was a right git with all that,' laughed Gudger.

My mum was laughing really hard by now, and that was great to see. Doll stepped into the conversation.

'I said to Gudge last night, the closest I've been to going racing was watching *Black Beauty* on the telly.'

'Yeah,' said Gudge interrupting her, 'and every week when she saw that Black Beauty was in trouble,' she said, "He's gonna die, Gudge, he's gonna die." I said to the dozy mare, "He can't die, can he? The programme is back on next week!"'

Once again the coach rocked with laughter.

A little while later I heard my mum say, 'It's like the old days, being on this coach, like when we used to go down hopping.'

To see her smile like this was worth every penny I had paid for The Mumper alone.

At the back of the coach, Georgie the Tailor and the Fat Man were studying *Sporting Life* and the races at Newbury.

'Oi, Bax,' Georgie shouted across. 'I see The Mumper is down at 33–1 for his race. What's the inside info, son?'

'Put your business on him, Georgie, he's gonna skate home,' I said laughing.

'Fuck that. Mrs George won't be too happy if it don't do the honours. What you sticking on, Fat?'

The Fat Man dragged on his fag and coughed. 'Lend me a score and I'll stick that on.'

We both laughed. 'I'll have a tenner on his nose, got to believe these boys when they say he's improving, ain'tcha?' said Georgie.

I smiled to myself. Little did anyone know but I had nearly six large in my pocket, and I was in danger of sticking it all on our boy. The very thought brought a bead of sweat to my brow.

Halfway down the M4, I heard Mr Patel ask Vinny if there was much further to go. Vinny had trouble understanding Mr Patel's Indian/cockney accent.

'I'm sorry?' Vinny said.

'Further, Father?' said Mr Patel.

Vinny's response was to move the coach over to a turn-off for the services, taking Mr Patel's intervention as a sign to take a break, so all could stretch their legs and whatnot.

I got off the coach, went over to its side boot and took out the suits I had placed there earlier. My idea was for us to get togged up now and wear them on the coach, so we arrived in style at the course. I put the idea to the syndicate boys and there was agreement – well, apart from the O'sh.

'This mob are going to rip the eternal piss out of us when they see us in them suits, ain't they?' the O'sh gloomily pointed out. Catholic guilt was still very much evident in the boy's eyes.

'Not half, my son, not half,' smiled Fred.

'Bollocks . . .' sighed the O'sh. 'Give it here, then.'

Ten minutes later, we emerged from the Little Chef khazi in full view of our coach party.

'Oi, oi, look at that mob!' shouted Harry Gossamer, 'bit overdressed for a Little Chef breakfast, ain'tcha?!'

Everyone was creasing up with laughter. Even I had a little smile on my boat. But you know what, I didn't really care.

'Oi, Doll,' said Gudge to his wife of over forty years, 'I could do without you laughing at me, girl!'

'Sorry, Gudge, you look lovely, really, mate . . . it's just like looking at Fred Astaire in his prime,' she said, struggling to keep a straight face.

'More like Freddie Starr,' laughed Harry.

We had the entire service station looking and pointing at us as we made our way back to the coach, and we hadn't even put the bleeding top hats on yet!

'You look very smart, chaps,' said Vinny as we passed him on the way back to the coach, an opinion not shared by my brother Glen.

'Look at him, will ya . . . Mother, have a word with your eldest, for God's sake.'

My mum turned round and her eyes lit up. Then her mouth broke into a wide and lovely smile as she watched us coming towards her.

'You all look lovely, especially you, Gudge,' she said.

'Your mum always did have good taste, son,' the Gudge said, cooing and prancing about.

'Come on, Cary Grant, we've got a race to get to,' I said.

We were soon back on the road and bombing onwards. Just over half an hour later, we were pulling into the on-course car park.

Going to the races is a lot like going to football. No matter how good the TV coverage might be, you can't beat seeing the action unfold in front of your eyes. You could feel the anticipation and excitement in the party people as they queued up to pay their fiver to get on the course. Except us, of course, who went through the owners' and trainers' entrance, waving our hands like the Queen to the coach party on the way in. Most of them returned a slightly different hand gesture in our direction.

We had got there with twenty minutes to go before the first race at twelve-thirty, giving us enough time to buy a race card and then have a flutter.

A couple of our mob looked like they were already three parts pissed as they disembarked from the coach, and once in, they of course headed straight for the beer tent. These boys were getting 'on it' today.

A day away from the wife and the screaming kids didn't come along too often, so it had to be taken advantage of. It was why I liked racing. Everyone, rich or poor, let their hair down for the day. We all stood together, a microcosm of society, side by side, drink in hand, all joined as one by the sport of kings. With that kind of mix, anything can happen. It's why there was a lovely carnival-type atmosphere to breathe in that could dictate how you wanted your day to go. Nice and relaxed or bordering on the manic, didn't matter either way, everyone was on the same mission.

The sun was out, summer was in sniffing distance, the food vendors were busy, the beer tent heaving and the bookies taking notes by the score. It's at times like these you have to drop all your baggage and just live in the moment. You're a fool, otherwise.

I had already marked down on my *Sporting Life* the horses I was going to have a flutter on, so I went in search of a bookie to take my fiver. As I continued to walk along and check the ever-changing odds, I bumped into Johnny the Housewife's Choice at the end of a queue of punters.

'All right, Housewife, checking the odds, son?'

'Sort of, Bax, this geezer seems the best, but got to be honest, I'm mainly checking out the skirt on offer. Some tasty fillies out here today.'

You will have noted, no doubt, how Johnny Boy's nickname strongly alluded to the fact he had a roving eye and was somewhat popular with the female gender.

'You know,' he continued, 'I often wonder what birds see in us blokes … I mean, on the whole, blokes are overweight, bald and badly dressed, ain't they? Whereas the female of the species look lovely, smell sweet and dress nice … Yet still they go for us. You have to put it down to hormones, I s'pose, as to how we get together, no other way to understand it, mate … Anyway, what d'ya fancy in this one?'

His little speech had left me transfixed. There was me thinking Johnny was a shallow sort of fella, but no, he had obviously thought the whole male–female relations issue through to a stunning conclusion.

I looked hurriedly down at my race card, scanning its pages to try and find a horse with the words bird, blokes or hormones in its name, taking what the Housewife's Choice had said as a sign. Betting on the gee-gees encourages all kinds of nonsense.

'I'm going for The Tender Trap here, Johnny,' I said, thinking that was close enough.

He looked at me and smiled. 'Like it, son, like it.'

I still hadn't mentioned to anyone my plan to have a large bet on The Mumper. My old girl would have gone off alarming if she found out, and no doubt the likes of the Gudge and Alfie would try and talk me out of it. Just thinking about what I was going to do made my heart pound so hard it felt like it was going to come through my shirt any minute now. I took some deep breaths to calm myself down.

'What's up, son?' Alf asked, hearing me gulp. Little bastard had crept up behind me, caught me unawares.

'Getting nervous about the race, Alf, funny how it affects you, ain't it?'

'Got to say, I've got sweaty palms myself, son,' he replied.

We looked at each other, fifty years between us and smiled, both thinking, How the fuck did we end up with all this?, but also thinking, I wouldn't have missed it for the world.

If anything, the whole Mumper escapade had brought the six of us closer together, and I always thought you couldn't have got a fag paper between us in the first place. As I waited for our race to come round, I stuck to having tenners and fivers on all the other races and picked up a couple of quid with an each-way second in the two o'clock race.

By now, all of us were standing together, time heavy on our shoulders as the clock ticked down towards The Mumper's race.

''Bout time we had a quick chat with old Sefton, ain't it, boys?' said Fred. 'Getting close to race time now.'

He tried to sound jolly, but all of us could hear the little tinge of worry in the voice.

'Got to give The Mumper a pat for good luck and all that,' he explained to no one in particular.

'He'll be out in a minute, won't he?' O'sh said, 'give him a parade round the ring and all that malarkey.'

'Spot on, Goldfish,' Alf said in a fake upper-class accent. 'By rights we should make our way to the owners' enclosure ... coming?'

With that, we walked off towards the parade ring, joining the other owners. I was glad to note that we didn't look quite so out of place this time. The other connections also had their finery on. I actually felt like I should be there, like I belonged.

A line of stable boys and girls then appeared before us, leading out the rest of the field. According to the *Life*, there were twelve runners in total, with The Mumper numbered seven. When I read that, I recalled the Lucky Number Seven strip club in Brighton and took it as an omen. I just hoped that this time the Goldfish kept his kit on if the horse won!

Alfie spotted Sefton first, and he gave us a wink as he came towards us. Handshakes all around as we greeted Seft warmly, as all of us had a lot of time for this man.

''Allo, boys,' he said, 'decided to come along, then.'

'Yeah,' said Fred laughing. 'We were in the area, so thought we might as well pop in.'

'Glad you did,' Sefton said, his voice dropping down to a serious note. 'The horse has been a bit special in training.'

'Special? How special?' asked Gudge, his lugs pricking up like a cocker spaniel.

'Well, put it this way, I never as a rule bet on my own horse, bad luck and all that. But if there was one race I would change that rule for ...'

'Now don't fucking nause it for us Seft,' Gudge said.

'We've brought a coach party of sixty-odd south Londoners with us, and all of 'em will be putting something on the old Mumper, so I could do without you killing the whole thing stone dead, mate.'

'I hear you, Gudger, my old darling,' laughed Sefton, adopting our vernacular. 'I hear you.'

That was all I needed to hear. The big bet was on. Fuck it, the five and a half grand was burning a hole the size of Peckham in my strides. I was going to do it. I was going to stick the bleeding lot on The Mumper, and sod the consequences.

As I made the decision, I involuntarily gulped.

'He's off gulping again,' said Alf. 'You sure you're okay, boy?'

'I'm fine, Alf, fine. Listen,' I said to the seven people in front of me, who had backed me all the way on this adventure. 'I've got an idea. As Gudger was closest to my old man, why don't we let him have the honour of putting our bet on The Mumper?'

There were nods all round from the others. 'Ta boy,' Gudge said, 'that would mean a lot.'

'Yeah, got to be done, ain't it?' said Alf, 'that would be a nice touch, that.'

O'sh now piped up. 'Boys, I'm gonna find a few of our mob that are still standing and tell them what Seft said about The Mumper, make sure they get on him, know what I mean?'

'Right, well lively then, Goldfish,' said Dave, "cos we need to get our dough all together and give this doddery old fucker,' nodding in Gudger's direction, 'time to get up to the bookie's.'

The five of us went into a little corner to count out our dough. Fred stuck in two hundred, Dave three hundred.

Alfie gave up one hundred and fifty. 'Don't tell Lil if it loses, will ya, she'll murder me,' he said as he handed it over.

Gudge brought forward another two hundred. They counted out the extra wedge to pay the tax, and handed that over too. Now it was my turn. I reached into the inside sky rocket of my jacket and pulled out three grand. I then extracted two and a half grand from the opposite pocket.

'What's all that?' said Fred, pointing to the two large rolls of notes held together by a brown elastic band.

'It's my stake,' I said, as calm as I could.

'What! All that? How much is there?' Fred demanded.

'Five and a half large,' I said.

'Five fucking large! You gone stupid, boy?' cried Gudger. 'You can't do that, son, your mum will go spare.'

'Fuck me, Bax, that's serious poppy, son,' said Dave, looking concerned.

'I know, boys, I know … look, the old girl ain't got to know, has she, and if the horse comes in, well, what's the problem?'

'Yeah, but what if he don't, you plum, what then? You'd have spunked your future away, won't ya?'

Gudger gripped me by the arm. Tight.

'Mark,' he said, 'I want you to think very seriously about what you are doing, son. I don't want to bring your dad into it on this day of all days, but I want you to think what exactly he would say right now if he knew what you were up to.'

I knew he was serious. He had called me Mark.

'Gudge,' I replied, 'out of you and my old man, who loved a bet more?'

'Your old man, I know, point taken, son, and I can't stop you doing whatever you want to do. You're big and ugly enough to make your own way. But I would never forgive myself if I didn't say something to you before you make any move. For a kick-off, your old girl would clip me so hard around the ear I wouldn't be able to hear for the rest of my life. As for your old man . . .'

His words trailed away, and he looked me in the eye just as the O'sh came back. 'What's up with you mob? Look like you've won the pools but lost the coupon.'

'Tell him,' Alf said to me.

'Tell me what?' said the O'sh.

I coughed. 'I'm putting most of my redundo dough on the horse. Five large on The Mumper, to win.'

'You're what?' said the O'sh. 'You had a bang on the head?'

'Look, I know what I'm doing. It feels right. I'm having it.'

The O'sh just shook his head, then nodded it in my direction. 'I know him too well, such a stubborn fucker, if he says he's doing it, he's doing it.'

There was a moment's silence as everyone got their nut round what was going on.

Fred broke the silence. 'Right then,' he said, clapping his hands. 'We ain't got time to stand here poncing about, they'll be off in ten minutes. Let's have your stake, O'sh, and then off you go, Gudge, mate.'

The O'sh took out the one hundred and fifty he had been holding back all day. He kissed it before handing it all to Gudge. I handed over my dough. My hands were trembling as I did so, but there was no turning back. Gudge looked me in the eyes as he took it from me.

I was waiting for him to say something. Instead, he put the money in his pocket, patted me on the arm and said quietly, 'All the Georgie, son.'

Gudge was now holding six thousand and six hundred pounds in crinkly notes. Six grand for the bet and six hundred for the tax. A lot of wedge in anyone's language. Alfie volunteered to go with Gudge to the bookie and put it all 'to win' on our horse.

'Keep an eye on him, Alf, nothing silly, eh?' Dave said. Alf nodded back in his direction. I had a lump in my throat as I watched them walk away.

'I give you one thing, Baxie boy, you don't do things by half, do ya, mate?' Fred said, laughing gently. 'In fact, there's a tiny part of me that fucking admires you. The rest of me thinks you're a complete plank. But then it always does, doesn't it!'

Gudge and Alfie made their way to the bookie we had been using all day, a fella who went under the title of Stan Vine of Nottingham. Just before they got to the bookie, I saw Alf stop and talk to his missus Lil. She was also putting on a bet. Then we watched Gudge and Alf talk to this Stan Vine. The bet was on.

'Right, looks like we're on, here they come,' said Dave, noting Gudge and Alf making their way back to us.

'All right, boys? Any dramas?' asked Fred as they joined up with us.

'Not really, boy. The bookie asked the bloke doing his ledger if he could handle the amount we were handing over. The bookkeeper didn't even look up, he just said "take it". We got thirty-threes in the end, so he's stayed solid in the betting. Want me to keep hold of the ticket?' asked Gudge.

'Yeah,' I said, 'you keep hold, and bring us some luck, eh?'

I stood there half wanting to run up to the bookie and say, 'Mate, there has been a terrible mistake, and I want my money back ... but I didn't, I just stood there rooted to the spot, with waves of hope and despair going through my body one after the other. The voices in my head just wouldn't shut up. Fuck, what have I done ... Nah, you'll be fine, he'll romp home ... No he won't, you'll be boracic for the rest of your life, son.'

Jesus, I was melting on the spot.

'Come on, Bax, they've found a spot in the stand, we can all be together and watch the race,' said O'sh.

After the experience of the Fontwell, when all the other owners and connections had sneered at us in their enclosure, we had decided to stand with the real punters and our mob for this one. As I walked towards where they were all standing, I spotted my mum, so went over and gave her a little kiss.

'Had a bet, Mark?' she asked.

'Yeah Mum, couple of quid, nothing big.'

'I've had a fiver each way myself,' she replied, 'you know I'm not a gambler.'

I had to stifle a laugh. My mum hated betting because my old man had the gambling bug bad. He often spunked all the housekeeping money, the holiday or the Christmas-club money. Eventually she gave him an ultimatum, it was either her or the horses. He went cold turkey there and then. That was one winner he got right. He often said that the local bookies, Gus Ashe, went broke because of that decision. Now here I was, following in the old man's footsteps.

I took my place among the south London contingent. Excitement crackled in the air.

'I've been racing loads of times,' said Persian Harry, 'but this is the first time I've backed a horse whose owner I know personally; blinding, mate, blinding.'

I smiled at Persian. From that one conversation six months ago or so in The Dutchman where Sefton's cousin tried to sell us that horse, to this moment, had been a long old journey, double-tough sometimes, but here I was, still standing.

'Which one is he, Gudge?' asked Doll.

'No good asking him, Doll,' Fred shouted over, 'he wouldn't be able to see the horse if he was bleeding riding it.'

'Oi, sarky,' said Gudge. 'I ain't that bad.'

Gudge then tried to look for The Mumper. 'That one, that's him in the blue and white,' he shouted as he pointed to a cluster of four horses trotting past at the same time. The truth was, he didn't have a clue.

'Right you are, Gudger,' said Fred, smiling at Doll. 'Give yourself a spotter's badge, son.'

The rest of the horses in the race cantered past to the start line. The Mumper looked fantastic as he went past us, head in the air, proud, coiled muscles, with Jimmy the jockey looking very smart in his 'Millwall' silks.

'Go on, my son,' shouted Shut Eyes, in his booming market-trader voice. 'Let's 'ave it, my son.'

I suddenly felt very calm. Removed from all around me at that split second, like I knew what was going to happen, like all this was somehow meant to be and I was just a bit player, powerless to control anything or anyone or any eventuality. I had the funny sensation that I was the lead role in a film, but the ending was still a bit of a mystery.

Suddenly, all the chat ended. The on-course announcer had started his commentary.

'Welcome to Newbury Racecourse for the two-thirty, The Arkwright Butchers' Steak Maiden Hurdle over two and a half miles. The going is officially good to firm. We have twelve runners for you, ladies and gentlemen, with number twelve, Maggio, favourite at 2/1, followed by number eight, Loopy Legs, at 3/1, number six, Harlow's Lad, at 4/1, and also Savvy Sailor, number five, at 4/1, 25/1 bar.

'He ain't mentioned your one, Alf,' said Lil. 'Don't tell

me we've come all this way and he ain't running now.'

'Shut up woman, will ya,' said Alf, the tension getting to him. 'He's there, but he's an outsider, ain't he, not in the betting.'

'All right, only asked,' said Lil, rolling her eyes at him.

She'll do you another of her famous casseroles for that comment, Alf, old son, I thought. You'll be crapping through the eye of a needle by the end of the week. The horses were all there at the tape, raring to go. I looked at Fred, Fred at Dave, Dave at O'sh, O'sh at Alf and finally all of us at Gudge. He nodded to us all.

The time had come.

The sound of the announcer kicked in again.

'And they're off, steady pace to start with, with The Snug the surprise early leader ... all safely over the first, still number four, the 40–1 outsider The Snug in front, followed by number five, Savvy Sailor and Harlow's Lad. Behind them Loopy Legs, Maggio, and making a move up the inside, the first showing of The Mumper.'

'Go on then ... kick on, son,' shouted Gudge, hearing The Mumper's name.

I watched silently as the field cleared the next three jumps and the horse carrying our dreams kept up a good pace.

'Mark, he's in there, son, he's in there,' Sefton said quietly, a reassuring confidence in his voice.

'A faller at the seventh there, the favourite, Maggio's gone. The Snug continues to lead, Harlow's Lad and Savvy Sailor contesting second place, The Mumper close behind.'

Suddenly, it was bedlam all around me, with shouts, screams and whistling filling my ears. I still hadn't uttered a sound.

I was deep in concentration, only seeing one horse in the entire field, my horse, our horse. It was as if the others weren't there. All I could see was Jimmy coaxing The Mumper along, nice and steady, slowly, ever so slowly going through the gears ...

'The Snug continues to set the pace on this second circuit, with Harlow's Lad slipping back, and now The Mumper's going third, Savvy Sailor in fourth.'

'He's doing rather well, isn't he?' said Vinny the Vicar, literally getting a little hot under his collar.

'Not 'alf, Padre,' said Dave, 'not 'alf. Come on, my son, come on, my son, kick on, Jimmy.'

For the first time I felt like shouting, but I was struggling to make a noise come out of my mouth. The tension was strangling my vocal cords.

'Coming to the second last, it looks like it'll be the two outsiders, The Snug and The Mumper, fighting it out, Savvy Sailor in third. All three safely over ... The Mumper goes into the lead for the first time. Just the last to jump and just The Snug to beat for this third-time runner.'

'The horse is gonna do it ... He's only gonna do it ...' Sefton was beginning to believe.

'Hands and heels, Jimmy lad, hands and heels ... save the whip for the run-in ...' Sefton said, coaxing Jimmy along.

All around me people were grabbing each other around the shoulders as they sensed The Mumper was going to win. I looked at my mum, and her and Doll were screaming at the top of their voices. Jimmy switched to outside of the rail, also switching the whip at the same time, he was now hitting our horse on his flanks, trying to get every inch of effort out of him.

'Tremendous run-in here, coming to the last, they jump together and land together. A pair of very brave horses giving their connections value-for-money rides. On the run-in there's nothing between them.'

The other horse, The Snug, wouldn't be shaken off. The Mumper and him were neck and neck. Fred and Dave were beginning to jump up and down in excitement in front of me. The O'sh was screaming the horse on, and Alf and Gudge had arms around each other's shoulders, willing the bloody horse home.

'In the final furlong now, too close to call ... The Snug, The Mumper ... The Snug, The Mumper ... coming to the line, it's ... Oh ... it's a photo ...'

'What the fuck happened, eh? What happened?' Alf was asking what everyone was thinking.

Confusion all round and on everyone's faces.

Sefton left us to make his way down to the finish, to check on the horse and talk to Jimmy. He was beaming from ear to ear. The run The Mumper had just produced was vindication of what he'd told us all those months ago: he had a good horse who would only get better with some decent training.

'Bax, did he get there, son?' Fred was asking.

'Freddie, boy, I just don't know. The geezer called it a photo.'

As I said that, the voice in the sky boomed out again and silence enveloped us.

'Here is the result of the photo finish for the two-thirty. First, number four, The Snug, second, number seven, The Mumper ...'

The rest of what he said was lost in the groans and shouts of 'fuck it', all around me. I stood there, numb from exhilaration to total despair in just two minutes. The horse was so close, so close to bringing me a small fortune. I was so proud of the bloody thing, but gutted at the same time. I felt empty.

'Never mind, son,' said Persian, 'he gave you boys a great

run, got a couple of quid coming my way, did him each way ... you?'

'To win, son, to win.'

'Tough titty, uncle.'

Tough titty indeed, Persian, old fruit. Six and a half thousand tough titties.

Fred and Dave were looking at me as if they didn't know what to say. As were Alf, Gudge and the O'sh.

'You okay, Bax son?' Gudge asked.

'I thought he had it. I thought it was ours ...' I said to no one in particular.

'No good for the jam tart, that's for sure. Mine was going thirty to the dozen watching that,' said Dave. 'I'm exhausted.'

'Weren't it great, though, eh? T'riffic really,' said Fred, smiling.

I knew what he meant. The Mumper had lost, but in a way we had won. We had each stuck a grand of our hard-earned bread into this, and had been caned for doing so, by many people we considered mates. Today, they all had to shut up.

The Mumper proved he was a racehorse, not a seaside donkey. He had silenced all those plums. All right, I had done serious dough, but, well, I had followed a dream. I had tried to do something. Got my digits burnt today, fair enough, I'd take that on the chin, but at least I'd put myself in the game.

I looked at Fred and Dave.

'I'm going to the khazi, boys, need to splash some water on my face, liven myself up a bit.'

'All right boy,' said Alf, 'we'll have a poodle down to the stables and try and find Seft and the horse. I want to give him my congratulations and give the horse a pat. See you in the bar, eh? Catch up with all the others and that.'

I nodded and started looking for a sign saying Toilets. As I did so, it suddenly hit me exactly what I had just done. I had blown all my dough on a bet. I didn't have a penny in my pocket. The realisation kicked in something awful, and it was such a horrible feeling, like an emptying of the soul. If only, if only . . .

I walked into the khazi and filled a basin full of cold water. I stood there looking at myself in the mirror. I had aged ten years in an hour. Gordon Bennett, what had I done?

I slowly shook my head and then splashed the water on my face. It felt good, refreshing. I wiped off the excess with a paper towel and then decided I needed to sit down, couldn't face the friends and family just yet, I needed to get my swede together first.

I went into an empty cubicle and closed the door. I left the seat and lid down and sat there with my head in my hands, mulling over what had happened. As I was still out of work, I wondered if I would ever see dough like six grand again. You plum, what have you done?

I decided to plot up here for a while. I couldn't face anyone just yet. After half an hour or so, I heard two guys enter the toilet, Northern voices, well, at least from the Midlands. They were discussing the day's racing and laughing, so I guessed they had had a good day. Turn it up, boys, I thought. All right for some, ain't it . . . mind my grief.

'Aye, had a good day today, Terry, took a nice few bob, sounds like you ain't done so bad yourself?'

'Too right, Stan, plenty of mugs out there as always, betting without a clue, most of them.'

'Mind you, I had a real strange one today, though.'

'Oh yeah? Go on, cock.'

'Yeah, for the two-thirty, a little fat fella walks up and tells me he wants to stick six grand on.'

'Jesus, that's decent dough, Stan.'

'Exactly, so I turned to Peter, my bookkeeper, like, and said, "We okay to handle that?" Peter said, "Take it."'

I suddenly pricked my ears up. This sounded very much like the story Gudger had told us after he had laid the bet.

'So the fella picks his horse, to win, and I take his money. Funny thing is, his horse came in at 40–1, but no sign of him. He didn't come back for his winnings. Weird or what, Terry?'

'Wonder what happened there, then? Maybe he got pissed and lost his ticket . . . Would you know him again if you saw him, like.'

'God knows what happened, but I would definitely know him again, if only from the shoes, he had a right pair of bastards on. He stood to pick up the best part of two hundred and forty grand. I've got the dough, but if he don't appear I'll keep it, damm right I will.'

'Oh yeah. His loss, ain't it? Fancy a quick one before you go, Stan?'

'Yeah, why not, Peter's driving today.'

I sat there, totally confused now. The Mumper was 33–1 and he came in second, so how had Gudger won? What have you done, Gudge, my son? What have you done? There was only one way to find out. I belted out of the cubicle and ran as fast as my unhealthy legs and body would let me, towards and into the bar where all my mob were congregated.

'Here he is . . .' said Dave, spotting me as I burst in, 'wondering what happened to ya, what you 'aving?'

'Where's Gudger?' I shouted.

'What, erm, he's over there with Shut Eyes and Henry, why, what's up?' Dave asked.

I spun round and saw Gudge in the corner.

'Gudge!' I shouted at the top of my voice. He didn't move. 'Gudger!'

The second shout did the trick and Gudge turned round, wondering what all the shouting was about.

'Who's that? What?' he sounded confused as he tried to focus his minces. I was on him in a second.

'Gudge, mate, where's the ticket for our race?' I demanded.

'Our ticket, erm, ain't got it boy, er ... gave it to Doll, she wanted it as a souvenir, why?'

Fuck me, I think, I don't need this.

''Ere, Bax, what's occuring, mate?' asks the O'sh.

'I need that ticket, I need that fucking TICKET!'

My mum appeared. She'd heard the shouting and was wondering what all the fuss was about.

'What's up, son?' she said to me. 'You in trouble?'

'Nah, Mum, really ... I just need that ticket.' I motion to Glen to come and get her.

'Look after her, Blue.'

'What's up, fella? You in the shit?' he asked.

'I'll explain all later. I just need the flaming ticket.'

'Doll!' Gudge shouted to his wife, 'Doll!' We spied her over by the fruit machines.

'What?' she said studying the lights.

'Give the boy the race ticket I gave you earlier,' Gudge told her. 'I stuck it in my handbag,' Doll said to no one in particular.

Doll started rooting around in her handbag, her hands shaking. 'It's in here somewhere ... Where is the flaming thing? ... Can never find anything in here ... Got it.'

She finally pulled it out and handed it over to Gudge, who gave it to me. I looked at it. It had the number four printed on it. By now I'd got the entire bar looking at me, wondering what the hell was going on.

'Gudger,' I said, in as controlled a voice as I could muster, 'The Mumper was number seven, right?'

'Yeah, I know, son, what's the problem, boy, tell me for Christ's sake!'

'Oh no, what's he done?' Fred had known Gudger long enough to suss something had gone badly tits up.

'Gudge!' said Doll, 'what you done?'

'I DON'T FUCKING KNOW, DO I?' shouted Gudger. By now everyone was looking at him.

'Right, okay ...' I said, trying to calm everyone down. 'Put it this way. Our horse was number seven, right?' Gudge nodded, 'Yeah, as I said, yeah ...'

'Well you, my old dumpling, put all our money on ... BLOODY ... NUMBER ... FOUR!'

'Gudge, you plum!' shouted Fred, exasperated. 'And you, Alfie, you were supposed to keep an eye on him!'

Alf looked lost in it all as well. 'I ... I bumped into Lil and ... and got distracted ...'

Gudger was speechless. He looked forlornly at our faces, desperate to make sense of it all.

'Jesus ...' I heard the vicar say.

'Fuck me, I've seen you pull some stunts in my time, but this takes home the first prize, son,' said Dave.

'Hold up, hold up,' said the O'sh, quietening down the rumpus that was now threatening to explode. 'You know what number four is, don'tcha? He stuck the lot on the winner, the BLEEDING WINNER!'

I stood there smiling, thankful that my ginger mate had worked it all out. The penny, along with the other thousands of pounds we were due, began to drop for everyone around us. The soppy old sod had somehow gambled on the wrong horse, the horse called The Snug, runner number four, and it had won, at odds of 40–1. Despite all our best efforts in shouting The Mumper home, The Snug had just done enough to win, meaning . . .

We had won. We had won two hundred and forty thousand pounds!

'Fucking hell! We're in the money!' laughed Fred, and then everyone joined him. Laughing and cheering filled the bar, as everyone began talking to each other, chatting it through and trying to work it all out. Gudge was stunned. He didn't have a scooby as to what he had done. I didn't have time to ask him, either; I needed to find that Stan Vine sharpish, before he pissed off back to Nottingham with our dough.

'O'sh, come here, son,' I said. 'We've got to find that bookie, mate. Get everyone who ain't too pissed out looking for him.'

'He'll be long gone, though, won't he?' said the O'sh.

'Doubt it, I heard him in the khazi five minutes back, saying he was going for one for the road first. Just got to find out where all the bookies have a drink.'

With that, we were off in pursuit. Me, O'sh, Fred, Dave, Jumbo, Persian, Harry Gossamer and Ricardo all spread out trying to track Mr Vine down. I ran up to the first steward I came across and asked him where the bookies hang out after the races. He looked at me suspiciously.

'It's all right, mate,' I reassured him, 'I ain't gonna hurt anybody, I ain't a punter looking for revenge. I'm a reporter doing a story on bookmaking, and I need a few quotes.'

After a few seconds, the steward pointed to a building right in front of me.

'They all go in there,' he said finally.

I ran up to the building, got to the front door and tried to get past the fella in the doorway.

'Hang on, hang on, where you going?' he said, barring my way in. 'Sorry, mate, members only. You got a badge?'

'No, mate, I just need to get in for five minutes,' I pleaded with the door bloke.

'No way, members only. Who you looking for, anyway?'

'I need a word with Stan Vine, the bookmaker ... he in there? Really important I speak to him, family illness, tell him.'

He looked me up and down, trying to work out what I was all about.

'Hold on . . Michael! ... Stan Vine in?' The door bloke shouted up some stairs to a colleague.

'Yeah? Tell him he's got a visitor.'

Found him! With that, I whistled to the others who were with me and they made their way over to where I was standing. A couple of minutes later, this fella Stan was standing in the doorway.

'Hello, chaps, can I help you?' He looked slightly worried, seeing so many faces looking at him.

'Yeah,' I said, 'been a balls-up our end, we lost a winning ticket for the two-thirty, but thankfully found it again. Come to collect, Squire.' I looked him straight in the eyes as I said that.

He looked at our ticket. 'Yeah, I remember that, six thousand pounds at 40–1, weren't it?'

'That's the one,' I replied.

'Wondered what was up when it wasn't collected, like,' he said. Then he stroked his chin. 'Got to be honest, chaps, I would rather see the punter who placed the bet before going any further, know what I mean, like. Make sure this is all kosher.'

I could see his point. I mean, for all he knew we might have kidnapped old Gudge and threatened him to get his ticket. Given how much dough was at stake, that was a possibility. Thankfully, Harry Gossamer had found Gudger wandering around the course looking like a lost sheep and was bringing him over to us.

'Here he is, Stan,' I said, indicating Gudge coming our way.

Stan looked down at Gudge's feet. 'Yeah, that's him,' the bookie confirmed, 'I'd recognise those shoes any-where.'

I had to laugh. Gudge looked down at his shoes with the red-and-grey fake snakeskin material and gold chains across the top, absolutely puzzled as to what the bookie meant. He was already in a state of shock, and now this geezer was taking the piss out of his shoes.

'Right, then, I'm happy to pay you, no problem,' the bookie said, pointing to Gudge.

'What I suggest is that this gentleman here, and you, follow me and I'll get your money for you.'

Me and Gudge walked away from everybody else towards Stan Vine's motor. On the way I had to ask Gudge what had happened with the bet. I just needed to know.

'I got all flustered up at the bookie's, boy, all over the shop I was,' Gudge said sadly. 'All the crowds, the noise, I lost my bearings. I kept thinking of your dad, how much I was missing him, and then holding all that folding, well, my hands were shaking something terrible. But how I ended up with the wrong horse, God knows. I just pointed at the number I wanted and handed over the wedge, I was so emotional, I couldn't even speak.'

I looked at him, and felt a lot of love for the fella. My family had lost a father and a husband. Gudge had lost a lifelong friend, and none of us have enough of those in the first place.

He was hurting badly, I could see that now. He was still an old plonker, though!

We arrived at the bookie's Range Rover, where Stan calmly wrote a cheque for the full amount. Cash, of course, would have been preferred, but, to be fair, it was such a whack of dough there was little chance of him having that about his person.

As I stood there waiting a while as he wrote out all those numbers, I spotted his bookmaker's chalkboard on the back seat of the car. I noticed that all the number sevens written on it had a line through them, like they do in France, and in Europe in general.

I smiled to myself as the thought occurred to me ... those sevens would look like a number four to a bloke with terrible eyesight and bad shoes.

Merci beaucoup or, as we would say, murky bunkup! I suddenly loved being a European, God bless the Common Market and the Channel Tunnel!

12

The Blind Man of Camberwell

I was woken by a shaft of bright sunlight coming through some pulled-back curtains, and by the simultaneous rattle of glasses, which seemed to be threatening the onset of World War Three.

I could feel a George Raft on the back of my neck, which made me open my eyes, and it's then I realised I was lying under a table.

Suddenly, a dam opened and pain rushed into my head, filling it up from top to bottom.

Still, at least I couldn't hear bagpipes ...

Slowly, very slowly, I began to piece together the how and the why.

After me and Gudge collected the cheque from Stan the betting man, we'd made our way back to the bar and the syndicate. I kept looking at the cheque, hardly believing my eyes. TWO HUNDRED AND FORTY THOUSAND POUNDS!

That was a lot of readies, ackers, spons, wedge, bread, shekels, poppy, folding, crinklies, de niro ... whatever your personal word of choice is for money, that was a bundle. I personally had two hundred thousand pounds coming, which took some taking in, believe me. It was decided there and then to stick it in the bar's safe. I didn't fancy that falling out of my pocket at some stage of the evening. I asked the manager to have a look at the cheque.

The fella stared at it for a second or two in silence. Finally he gasped, 'Stuff me gently . . .'

'Mate,' I said, 'we've had a right result today, as I am sure you can see. Trouble is, all our capital is locked up in that, and I haven't any cash on me. Obviously, I want to give them out there a drink on me tonight and want to lump over five hundred pounds behind your bar. I also want to give you and your staff a couple of hundred quid between ya, in the hope that you'll stay open and work late for us tonight whilst we have a little Russell Harty. What d'ya say, fella?'

It was a lot to ask – I mean, he didn't know me from Adam. The manager thought it over for a further second or two, and then looked back at the cheque.

'What you drinking, pal?' he asked.

The scene in the bar was joyous, chaotic, exhilarating, miraculous. Everybody heard the news of what had happened, how we had cleaned up, and before too long a full-scale party had erupted. Mr Patel discovered an old upright piano under a sheet and was tinkling the yellowing ivories to a few old favourite songs that all and sundry around him were now loudly murdering. The free bar was going down a storm, and the drinks were well and truly flowing. In the middle of all the madness, I wandered past my mum. She just laughed when she saw me.

'I hear you had a bit of a bet, son!' I smiled back at her. 'I should slaughter ya, really . . . but come here,' and with that she grabbed me in a hug, laughing all the while. 'You'll be the death of me, boy,' she said with a big smile.

I was beginning to get right royally pissed as the vodka and diet coke coursed through my body, and it was a lovely feeling. There was no way that coach was going to go back to London tonight; everybody was beginning to settle in for a lock-in. I told Vinny the Vicar we would pay to put him up in a local B&B if he wanted, but he said he would rather stay at The Russell. The Lord does indeed move in mysterious ways.

'Here, Bax,' said Dave at one point, 'I've just seen Gudge talking to old Shut Eyes, and he's still trying to work out what he did. You've got to laugh, mate, ain'tcha?'

Poor old Gudge, by getting his fours and sevens all arse about face, had pulled a right stroke ... it could only have been him. Sefton had arrived with Jimmy, the jockey who had ridden The Mumper in the race. They were welcomed like conquering heroes.

'What you drinking, Seft ... Jimmy?' asked Fred.

'We'll have a quick half of lager each please, Fred, 'cos we need to get the horse back and settled,' said Sefton.

'Where is the horse?' asked the O'sh.

'Outside in the horsebox. Amy the stable girl's looking after him,' Jimmy replied.

'Would really like to say goodbye, if that's all right,' the O'sh continued.

'Sure,' said Sefton, 'just don't make too much noise, don't want him spooked.'

With that, O'sh left, and half the bar followed him downstairs to give their best to the horse. Sefton, half a lager still in his hand, opened up the box and led The Mumper out on the threadbare grass at the front of the bar. A polite round of applause broke out, and The Mumper responded by throwing his head back and making a neighing noise.

'Hear that, Gudge?' said Dave. 'Even the horse is saying you're a plum!'

Laughter swept around the assembled. What a moment this was. I knew I had to savour it right then because, well, told you before, days like this don't come around very often, and when they do . . .

Gudge walked up and patted the horse, and one by one the syndicate all did the same. He had done us proud.

'Good horse,' said the O'sh. 'You're a diamond, mate . . .'

I just stood there looking at this great big animal, smiling 'til my face hurt.

'Right, we better be getting back,' said Sefton, 'want to get him all tucked up safe.'

I walked up and first hugged Sefton and then Jimmy, and thanked them for a great day. Sefton just smiled at me, as if to say *my pleasure*. We stood and waved as they drove off, and then we made our way back up to the bar.

The next couple of hours are a blurred memory, to be honest, but at some point I had obviously thought that the spot of carpet under this table was an inviting resting-place, 'cos there I was with a burning light in my eyes and a head that was thumping to its own tune. I pulled myself up and looked around me. There were bodies all over the place. Some were laid out on the chairs and the sofas, the majority on the carpet.

An old girl, who I guessed was the cleaner, was walking in and out between the various legs, collecting up the empty and part-filled glasses with a bemused, half smiling look on her face.

'All right, love?' she said, noticing me looking at her. 'Had a party last night, did ya, wedding was it?' she asked.

'Wedding?' I asked her.

'Yeah, you know, man marries a woman, a wedding. Going by the clothes you've got on, I've got you down as best man.'

I smiled at the sarky old sort.

'Wedding, no. Day at the races, yes. Anyway, had a good

day and decided to have a night cap, so to speak.'

'Well, by the state of some of these,' she said, nodding to the prone, out cold, snoring mass around her, 'I don't think they were drinking Ovaltine.'

I had to chuckle. I stood up, with my back aching and as stiff as a board, and made my way to the khazi, where I splashed cold water on my face and then went into the back room of the bar. The manager had already arrived and was settling the books from the night before.

No wonder he had a smile on his face. He gave me the bill, as we had run over the five-hundred-pound limit, by three hundred or so. My mob knows how to spend when they go out. Must have been his best night for years.

'All right, mate, enjoy yourself last night?' I said.

'Your lot certainly seemed to,' he replied.

'Can I get the kite we left in your safe last night, please, mate,' I said. I needed to make sure it was still there, felt I needed it about my person, know what I mean?

He opened the safe and handed it over. It went straight into my back sky. I strolled downstairs and out of the bar, onto the spot of rough grass where we had saluted The Mumper the previous evening. I found Vinny down there and a few waifs and strays who had woken up before me, also milling about.

'Morning, young Mark,' Vinny said.

'Morning, Vinny,' I replied, 'you okay?'

'Splendid, splendid. Had a great time last night, lovely to see so many people enjoying themselves.'

'That's nice to hear ... Give me an hour or two, and I'll round everyone up and we'll get cracking.'

'Yes, that'll be fine. I have already rung Brian back at the office and explained the situation. I'm afraid there will be a surcharge for the coach, but under the circumstances, I presume that isn't a problem.'

I just smiled at him. You presume right, padre, you presume right. I found my mum, Glen and Tracey amongst the early birds, and made sure they were all okay.

'Look a bit weak round the gills there, Blue,' Glen said, and I wasn't going to give him much of an argument.

'I'll be all right when I wake up,' I said.

After an hour or so, the majority had woken and made their way out of the bar. A fella running a burger van was in the process of setting up for the market that was held at Newbury racecourse on Sundays. Before he knew what had hit him, he had a swarm of hungry south Londoners all around his van, getting in the teas and sausage sandwiches. With the last customer, he had made enough to pack up and enjoy the rest of the day. Money can do such lovely things sometimes.

'We're gonna be on our way soon, just got to make sure everyone is all on board,' I announced to the throng who were busy stuffing meat and bread into their faces.

Slowly but surely, we made our way to the coach and within half an hour were on our way back to the smoke. In contrast to last night's rumpus, it was pretty quiet on board. Most were asleep within ten to twenty minutes, catching up on some badly needed kip. All apart from Alf, who I could hear reminiscing about the old days when he used to go to the tracks.

'Oh yeah, there was a protection racket in force,' he said to no one in particular. 'The bookie wasn't even allowed to sponge his own chalkboard down, he had to pay a local 'erbert to do it for him or they'd turn his pitch over.'

'Was that in the good old days then, Alf?' O'sh said on a wind-up.

'Bloody right,' Alf retorted. 'You got a better class of villain in them days, son, not like these drugged-up ponces that are about now. Happy days, boy, happy days.'

A few of the hardcore brigade at the back had cans open and were discussing getting a beer back at The Dutchman. I just wanted to get home and put the cheque under the floorboards, along with all my 'valuables'.

'So, Baxter,' Persian asked me, leaning forward in his seat, 'how much then?'

Nosey fucker you, ain'tcha? I thought, although I guessed a few would be curious.

'Not sure, Persian, not counted it yet.'

'Put it this way, Persian,' Fred said with a little hint of anger in his voice, 'there's enough there to get a packet of fags out of it, got me?'

Persian Harry got the hint, smiled and went back to his tin of warm lager. He never asked again how much we had won.

Vinny made good time, and we were back outside The Dutchman within an hour and half, arriving at around half-one. O'sh tried his best to get me in for a quick one, but I had a special girl I had to attend to, plus I was determined to sort out the dough.

'Nah, son,' I told him, 'I'm done in, buckling badly. I'll catch up with you in the week.'

He nodded, and I took my old girl's arm and walked her home.

On the way there, she said, 'Thanks for a great time, Mark. Your dad would have loved that, you did him proud.'

It was lovely to hear that, coming from her, and I couldn't help hoping he had watched the whole adventure from up above. I should have had a word with Vinny the Vicar, see if he could have put a word in with the Big Fella upstairs and sorted that one out. At home, my old girl offered to cook something up but I was too tired to eat. I went upstairs, put the cheque in an envelope, placed it under the floorboards and breathed a sigh of relief. As I did, a wave of tiredness engulfed my whole body. I went down and slumped in front of the television.

The big match was on. 'See Millwall lost again yesterday,' said my mum, entering the room.

'Polish, that mob, Mum,' I said, 'polish.' Soon enough, my eyes were flickering, I was struggling to keep them open, and before I knew it, I had nodded out cold.

I'm climbing the longest staircase I have ever seen, going up and up in a never-ending line in front of me. Grey wispy clouds are all around me as I continue to climb. Occasionally I see a sign saying 'This Way' with arrows pointing up. Even though I'm climbing for what seems like hours and hours, I don't get out of breath. I just march on. Finally, I can see the end of the line in front of me. As I reach the last step, I see a doorbell with the name 'Thimble' on it. I press the bell and it makes the sound of a horse neighing. The door opens and I walk in to be confronted by a fella dressed all in white, waving his hands about, tic-tacking the latest odds over to a woman, again all dressed in white, who is standing by a cooker with a frying pan in one hand and an umbrella in the other. I walk past them both and arrive at another door. The name 'Thimble' is once again under the doorbell. I press the bell and hear a loud ringing sound, the sound gets louder and louder and then I hear Mark, Mark! ... Mark it's me ...

'Mark, it's me, Mum, the phone for you, wake up, son.' I jumped up in a start. 'You been dreaming, boy?' she asked.

For a fleeting second, I wasn't sure where I was, and then I started to recognise the things in the front room. Christ, that was a weird one. A bookmaker and my nan Connie ...

What had I been drinking last night?

It was the O'sh on the dog, just wanting to talk, making sure yesterday really happened, and that it wasn't just a dream. He was beginning to doubt it all, as the lager rushed through his veins and confused an already tired mind. I pulled myself up and out of the chair and jumped in the shower. I needed to freshen up, get my own swede together.

I dressed and then set about sorting out who would get what, once I had the cash. By my reckoning, Gudger and Fred would get eight grand. Alf and O'sh would pick up six, while Dave picked up a very handy twelve. Me? Me, I'm looking at the best part of two hundred grand. Fucking hell ... what a result. What will I do with the dough? My mind conjured up the answer. I saw wardrobes stuffed full of beautiful handmade suits, rails and rails of them, with gleaming loafers and brogues placed neatly underneath them on the lush, carpeted floor. I saw myself on a beach, cocktail in one hand, bronzed beauty in the other. I saw myself taking hold of the keys to a massive house and opening ... Nah, the dough wouldn't stretch that far. If only I'd put ten grand on, or twenty. Fuck me, what would that have been ...? *Shut up, Bax, you've got two hundred grand coming your way and now you're moaning to yourself because you didn't put enough on. Tart.*

Thankfully, the doorbell went, bringing me back to my senses. 'Markie, it's O'sh,' shouted my mum up the stairs.

I looked over the stair rail and down the stairs, and saw a ginger head coming up towards me.

'Hello, O'sh, you all right, son?'

'Yeah, mate, just thought I'd nut in, make sure you're still in the country ... besides, I needed to get out of The Dutchy, I seem to have more friends than I had a couple of days ago,' he laughed.

Word was beginning to creep out we'd had a touch.

'Yeah, still here, can't get a flight to Rio 'til tomorrow ... Nah, I'll be straight down to the bank in the morning.'

'Sweet, looking forward to that six large, mate.'

'Worked it out, then?' I said, smiling at him.

'Just a lucky guess,' he laughed.

The following week went by so slowly. It seemed like the cheque took for ever to clear, especially as I had a lot of time on my hands, with not working. Christ, I was sure something was going to go wrong. Every time the phone rang I thought, That's it, the game is up. Stan Vine has declared himself bankrupt, or has been involved in an accident and all his accounts are frozen ... or the bank is about to be robbed. Terrible, how my mob and all of us who span off from it thought we were not worthy enough for luck to shine upon us. Finally I had notification that it had gone through. I arranged to collect forty grand from the bank on the Friday lunchtime, leaving my two hundred in there. Then I rang everybody up and arranged to meet them round Gudger's on the following Sunday night.

O'sh had taken the day off work sick and came with me to the bank. He was already starting to panic.

'A lot of the slags round here were in The Dutchman on Sunday, they know we've had a touch, but thankfully don't know how much,' he told me.

'Hopefully keep it that way, son, eh?' I replied.

'Best come with you, though, safety in numbers and all that.'

I appreciated what he was saying, and we did the collection in record speed. Back at my mum's, we divvied up the dough into brown envelopes, wrote names on them and dropped them under the floor.

On the Sunday, I gave The Dutchman a swerve and

instead took my mum out for a spot of Sunday lunch at The Greyhound pub, which is near to Oval tube station. I would be seeing the boys later that evening, I reasoned, so I could afford to miss this session.

It was good to get out for an hour or two with her, and it was even better to see that she was finally beginning to think of the future. Ever since the old man had gone, she had been too scared to put a foot forward.

'What you going to do with all the money, son?' she asked, as we tucked into our roast chicken dinner.

'Not sure yet, Mum, but I'll look after Glen. Give him and Tracey a few bob, so they can sort out a nice gaff.'

My mum smiled at me. 'That's good of you, boy, that will make me and your dad . . . very happy.'

I smiled back, and thought I'd spend every tanner of it if it would bring the old man back.

Back at the house, I loaded up the envelopes into my green Adidas bag and then waited for the O'sh. Once again, the O'sh was my shotgun man. He arrived and we left my gaff, getting a jog on, didn't want to dwell with that amount of dough in the bag.

Walking towards Gudger's, we both looked around every now and again, in case some cheeky slag decided to have a pop at us. Thankfully, Gudge and Doll lived in a council block not too far away. We got into the lift that smelt of bleach, and it climbed to the fourth floor.

When we arrived, the others were already there. We sat down in the front room, which was decorated with a loud patterned wallpaper, set off by a busy carpet. Picture frames were everywhere, mostly containing photos of their grandchildren. We both gave Doll a kiss on the cheek as she ushered us in.

'Cup of tea, boys, nice bit of cake?' asked Doll as we greeted the chaps.

227

'Yes, please, Doll, we're Lee and Hank Marvin.'

'So, here we are then, girls. All safe and well,' Dave said. 'Bloody hell, I just keep smiling.'

Like the rest of us, the man was in a great mood.

'Know what you mean Dave,' said Alf, 'been a long week, though, waiting for that phone call, son.'

'And all because of the Blind man of Camberwell,' Fred said, nodding towards Gudge.

'You leave my Gudge alone,' said Doll as she came back into the room with cups of tea and slices of Dundee cake on a tray.

'Yeah, without me you wouldn't have a pot to piss in today, would ya?'

'Oh, do leave it out, Gudge. You'll be telling us next you meant to do it,' said the O'sh.

'Well, as it happens ...' Gudge sounded like he was going to take the credit for the bet then, but he was drowned out by the rest of us.

'All right, all right, it was the minces, it was the minces,' he admitted, laughing.

'Well,' I said, getting the envelopes of money out of my bag. 'You can go and get yourself a new pair with this.' With that, I threw Gudger his packet.

'Ta, boy,' Gudge said as he caught it. He didn't open the envelope straight away, he just looked at it, like an expectant kid on Christmas morning. Only his smile was bigger than any kid's I had witnessed. I handed out the rest of the packets. We were all very jolly boys now.

'Fucking 'andsome,' said Alf. 'I know exactly what I'm going to do with this.'

'Wassat, Alf, mate?' Gudge asked.

'Me and Lil have had our eye on a caravan down in Rye for a couple of years. I'll buy it next week with this.'

'Good luck, Alfie, you've earned it,' said Dave.

'Be lovely to relax down there,' Alf said. 'Been at work since I was fourteen, reckon I've done my bit, eh?' said Alf.

''Course you have,' said Dave. 'I'm off to the States myself. Memphis, Detroit, New York, Las Vegas, Florida, gonna do the full bifta, can't fucking wait. Stax, Motown, here I come. Always wanted to see where all that wonderful music came from. Also gonna catch a show or two at Madison Square Gardens, Tony Bennett or even the guv'nor, Francis Albert, and I've always wanted to buy a couple of shirts from Brooks Brothers on Fifth Avenue. Now, I'm having it.'

Dave's smile stretched from ear to ear.

'O'sh, what you got planned, mate?' Fred asked.

'Gonna tell the Royal Mail to poke their job up their arse and going to crack on with the Knowledge. Pack up work for six to nine months and do it full time. I swear to you, on my last day at Mount Pleasant I'm going to walk around bollock-naked, excuse the language Doll, with that top hat of mine on, smoking a big cigar.'

We all laughed at the thought of that, even though it was a horrible one to contemplate.

'I'm going to do the shop up ... yeah. Give it a right once-over, all glass shelves and chrome. It'll look the bollocks. I might even dust.'

At long last Fred could have the West End shop he'd always fancied, even if it was still going to be technically in Camberwell.

'I'm also gonna get the best ranges of shoes I can. I'm belling that Johnny Moke up next week, get some of his tasty stuff in, there'll be queues down the road, mate.'

Doll looked at Gudge. 'Go on, tell 'em'. She looked at Gudger again, and he looked at the floor.

'Tell us what, mate?' asked Fred.

'Well … it's like this, see … I ain't been too well lately, nothing too bad, but I do need treatment.'

'What's up with ya?' I asked, feeling very concerned.

'It's me breathing and all that. Got to have a heart bypass. Been on a waiting list for a while, as it happens. I can go and get it done private now.'

'Told him he'll have to knock the fags on the head,' said Doll.

'I told ya I will,' said Gudger laughing. 'It'll be a piece of piss, won't it?' We all smiled at him, but inside I was gutted to hear this. Gudger had been a permanent fixture in my life, never ill, not as far as I ever knew. And now this.

Us without him meant there was no us. Simple as. Gudger bound us all together. He was the presence, the one we gravitated towards. Gudger was the leader. We'd fall apart without him. We'd already lost one of our table recently … couldn't let another get away from us … The whip couldn't take it!

'You'll be fine, Gudge, they can do wonders now,' said Alfie.

Fucking hope so, Alf, mate, I thought, really hope so. I couldn't take Gudge bowing out, not right after my old man's terrible departure.

'What about you, Bax, son, what you got planned?' Fred the Shoe asked.

'To be honest, Frederico, nothing planned, really. Would like to sort out my own gaff, but I'm needed at home for a while, want to make sure the old girl is all right. Didn't really believe I'd ever see this much dough in my life. I'll give my brother a few bob to get him out of his council gaff, give him a chance of getting a decent place. As for the rest, don't know. One thing is for certain, I ain't working for no

J. Arthurs again. I'll go self-employed, maybe get a unit or a little shop, buy and sell a bit of antiques and collectables.'

'Fucking Steptoe, ain't he?' said O'sh laughing.

'If I know you, you'll be getting most of your stuff out of skips, son.' As always, Fred stopped me getting too carried away.

After the laughter subsided, it went quiet in the flat for the first time since me and O'sh had arrived. We all seemed to be contemplating the future, and it was strange that when we did so, none of us could see anything but goodness. Normally, when you peeped over the barricades you got a horrible feeling in your stomach. Not this time.

I couldn't ever remember feeling so contented in all my life. Nor could the others.

Slowly, smiles broke out on all our faces and it was a wondrous thing to behold. On the following Sunday, we all agreed to meet up at the usual table in The Dutchman. During the previous week, I had the local *South London Press* newspaper bell me looking to do an interview, to get the story on The Mumper and the money we had won. I told them, 'I'll get back to you,' but I didn't. Yeah, we had some dough, but we had no intention of shouting all about it in the local rag. People knew we had won a few bob, but not how much, and I personally wanted it kept like that.

As I walked into The Flying Dutchman, all was as it should be. The card school were all present and correct and Wavy Davy was wobbling about more than ever.

'Here he comes, old slippery bollocks!' Brenda the barmaid shouted I as walked in. Never could resist a thought-provoking, analytical comment, that girl.

'Thank you, Brenda, for that very welcoming salute.'

'Usual is it, Lord Baxter?' she replied.

'Grazie, Brenda, grazie.'

'We don't seem to have any grazie I'm afraid, will vodka and diet Coke do ya?' And with that she burst out laughing, as did the rest of the punters that had heard her.

I paid her and picked up my drink, shaking my head as I made my way to our usual table. Gonna be a long lunch-time, I reckoned, with her in that form ...

Next in were Alfie and Gudge. As per, tenners were put in the whip, joining mine. I got up and collected their usuals, which Brenda had already started pouring. Fred and Dave came in now, not too far behind, their brown drinking vouchers quickly thrown onto the table. Then the O'sh followed them, stopping briefly at the nearest fruit machine to stick in a couple of nuggets. Old habits ...

'How we doing, boys? All well, I trust,' I asked the assembled table.

'Yeah, you?' asked Fred.

'Sweet,' I replied. 'How you doing, Gudge?'

'All right, boy, me and Doll went up to Harley Street and booked up to get my tubes seen to, go in on Monday week. Got to get through ten packets of B&H before then ...'

We laughed.

'Good luck with that, Gudge. Mind you, fuck that sur-geon's luck when he cuts you open, he'll need a blow torch, mate,' I said laughing. 'The old man always used to say that when Gudge dies if they cremate him he'd burn for a fortnight!'

Laughter to cover the fear and pain, us boys were the world experts. 'I see that Eddie Shah got his *Today* paper out then,' said Alfie.

'Yeah, all that grief and strife down at Wapping ain't achieved much, has it, not for the worker anyway. Murdoch and the others were always gonna win that war. It was a carve-up between the money men, the government and the rozzers, I'll tell ya.' The anger I felt about all that still burned in me.

The table fell silent as we all thought of people, like me, who had lost their way of life over that. But as ever, gloom doesn't settle for too long at this table.

'I was in The Corrib one lunchtime, in the week, having a lively one, when old Smurf Murphy comes up to me,' said Dave. 'He asked me in that broad London Irish accent of his, "Dave, that right you won a couple of grand at Newbury with that gee-gee of yours last week?" "Yeah, that's right, it did okay, Smurf, won a nice few bob." "What you gonna do with all the begging letters then?" he asked me, laughing. "Still going to send them, son, still gonna send 'em . . ." You should have seen his face,' Dave said. 'It was a picture.'

'I was thinking about The Mumper last night,' I said.

'What about him?' asked Alf.

'Well, the jump season's over, and we've had a nice few bob out of him, thought he might fetch a few bob if we sell him. To a decent owner, of course.'

'Thinking along those lines myself,' said Fred. 'Had our fun, ain't we? Besides, the thought of seeing O'sh in top hat and tails again fills me with the horrors.'

'Fuck off, at least I didn't look like an overdressed garden gnome!' said the O'sh.

'Another saucer of milk for Miss O'Shea, please, Brenda,' said Dave. 'Seriously, though, we selling?'

Everyone looked around at each other and nodded. I think the overriding feeling was that we had got away with something. We had pulled a stroke. We had gambled good money and struck it lucky, got more back than we ever imagined possible. And as lightning rarely strikes twice, it was time to jog the horse on, get out with our noses in front.

'He gave us a great ride for our money, but think it's time

to cash in the chips.' Fred had spoken for us all.

'Right, then,' I said. 'Only one way to do it, ain't there ...'

I stood up, had a swig of vodka and diet and cleared my throat. 'Everybody,' I shouted, 'listen up.'

Everyone in the pub slowly turned to look at me, and the pub fell silent.

'Ladies,' I said, 'and gentlemen, any of you ever thought of owning a racehorse?'

The Mumper Glossary

Dave Sainsbury and Ricardo Spaghetti

All the Georgie: 'All the best', as in George Best
Ammo: ammunition
Apple tart: (slang) fart / to break wind. *See also* Trouser cough
Arrers: darts – derived from bow and arrows

Bark: shortened, polite way of saying bastard
Barnet: (slang) barnet fair – hair
Beano: an 'any excuse will do' day out / trip
Bedlam: long been used to describe lunatic asylums in general and later used to describe chaos and confusion
Bell: as in 'bell me' – to phone someone
Big 'un: 'give it the big 'un' – to be boastful
Bins: spectacles, derived from binoculars
Bird: the female of the human species
Blinding: excellent / fantastic / amazing
Blouse: a weak man. Derived from 'you big girl's blouse'
Blowout: a big event / a party
Blue: a nickname
Boat: (slang) boat race – face
Bods: bodies
Bombing: speeding along / to go as fast as you can
Bookie: bookmaker / turf accountant
Boozer: pub / drinking establishment

Boracic lint: (slang) skint (broke). Boracic lint was a type of medical dressing

Bottle: (slang) derived from Aristotle – bottle – bottle and glass – arse

Brahms: (slang) Brahms and Liszt – pissed

Brass monkeys: freezing – 'Cold enough to freeze the balls off a brass monkey'

Bread: (slang) bread and honey – money. *See also* Poppy

Brown: a ten-pound note

Bruv: abbreviation for brother; also used for friend

Bugle: nose – as in blowing your nose like a bugle

Bunce: a nineteenth-century word for money or profit. An informal windfall

Bunking off: playing truant from school or work

Butcher's: (slang) butcher's hook – look

Butter: bald – derived from 'He's as bald as a butterball turkey'

Cake'ole: someone's mouth. 'Shut yer cake'ole, you'

Caned: do something to excess. 'I caned it, fella'

Chant: to sing

Cheese-cutter: (slang) flat cap

Claret: blood. Same colour as a good claret

Clobber: clothing

Cocker: mate / friend

Cough all: nothing / nil

Cow son: early twentieth-century English saying, meaning similar to son of a bitch

Darby: (slang) Darby Kelly – belly. 'Darby Kelly' was the title of an old folk song

Deep-sea diver: (slang), a fiver – five-pound note

Dickie bird: (slang) word

Dicky: feeling unwell. *See also* Tom Dick

Divvie up: to divide and share

Divvy: waster or sponger. Possibly derived from 1950s Unemployment Dividend, i.e. dole

Dodgy one: something suspect. 'You put me on a dodgy one there'

Dog: (slang) dog and bone – phone

Done in: finished / all over

Donkey's years: a long time. Supported by the belief that donkeys have long lives

Dosh: money. Almost certainly derived from the word 'dosshouse', meaning a very cheap hostel or room, in Elizabethan England, when a 'doss' was a straw bed

Dough: money. From the cockney rhyming slang and metaphoric use of 'bread'. *See also* Bread *and* Poppy

Dozy mare: stupid woman

Drinking vouchers: bank notes

Duffer: an English word meaning 'an incompetent or clumsy person'

Dummy: a stupid person

'Erbert: a young tearaway

Farmer Giles: a person with a countryside accent

Flapping track: an unregistered racetrack / course

Fleet Street belly: beer belly

Folding: cash / bank notes. 'He's holding folding'

Full bifta: everything / all

Gaff: Irish word for residence / house

Game as a pebble: very determined / will keep going

Garrity: mad / lose temper. Thought to be derived from

Freddie Garrity, lead singer of the pop group Freddie and the Dreamers

Gavvers: Traveller word for the police

Gee up: to encourage / to incite

Geezer: a man. A working-class *Everyman*

George Raft: (slang) draft. George Raft was an actor / film star

Glorias: (slang) Gloria Gaynors – trainers

Go spare: to lose control / be furious. 'She was going spare'

Gob: Scottish word for mouth

God-botherer: someone who spreads the word of the Almighty, and inflicts it on others

Going off alarming: to go crazy / make a lot of noise

Gordon Bennett: an exclamation of surprise. Probably named after James Gordon Bennett, founder of the *New York Herald*. He was known for his outrageous lifestyle and newsworthy stunts

Grand: a thousand pounds. *See also* Large *and* Long 'un

Gravy boat: Something that requires minimum effort but which yields a profit

Grub: food

Hank Marvin: (slang) starving. *See also* Lee Marvin

Hook, line and sinker: as in, 'Fall for it hook, line and sinker'. To believe or be duped into believing something completely

Hopping: harvesting the hops. To go hopping in Kent was the only 'holiday' the majority of the working class would have

J. Arthur: (slang) J. Arthur Rank – wank(er)

Jam tart: (slang) heart

Jekylls: (slang) Jekyll and Hydes – strides – trousers. Also used for snide (fake) goods

Joe Loss: Gudger-speak for a waste of time. 'He was a right Joe Loss'

Jog on: to move something on / give it a push or a nudge

Juggling: when things are going well. 'I'm juggling, mate'

Jump: a pub bar or shop counter

Khazi: lavatory / toilet

Kip: sleep. 'I could do with a good night's kip'

Kite: a cheque (that will probably bounce)

Knocking his pipe out: working hard

Kosher: (Yiddish) clean / good / perfect

La-di-dah: (slang) cigar

Lagging: being truly wasted on drink

Large: a thousand pounds. *See also* Grand *and* Long 'un

Laugh like a drain: laugh loudly

Lavender: a gay man

Lee Marvin: (slang) starving. *See also* Hank Marvin

Leg over: the act of sexual intercourse. 'To get one's leg over'

Lemon: fool / idiot

Lively: get stirred / wake up

Lob: an erection

Lock-in: after-hours drinking session

Long 'un: a thousand pounds. *See also* Grand *and* Large

Long johns: long-legged undergarments

Lord-mayoring: (slang) swearing

Lugs: ears

Malarkey: nonsense

Mare bag: a term of offence

Methers: severe alcoholics who drink methylated spirits

Minces: (slang) mince pies – eyes

Monkey's, A: as in, 'I don't give a monkey's toss'; not to care / of no interest

Monkey nuts: peanuts still in their shells

Moriarty: (slang) party. Moriarty was the arch enemy of Sherlock Holmes

Mouth on a stick: someone who talks loudly but with nothing to say; likes the sound of their own voice

Mugged off: to be disrespected / made to look a mug. 'You've been mugged off, mate'

Muller: to beat or break someone. 'She mullered me'

Mumper: scrounger / ponce / beggar

Mush: a male person / Romany word for a good friend

Nada: nothing / zero

Narked: annoyed

Nause: abbreviation for nauseating / annoying

Nebbish: (Yiddish) a nobody / a weakling

Needled: irritated / upset

Nish: nothing / zero. 'Leave it out, I got nish, mate'

Nugget: a pound coin

Nurse: (in a pub) the barmaid

Nut: head. 'You're doing me nut in'

Off their boxes: out of their minds / insane / crazy

Off your trolley: out of your mind / insane / crazy

Old bill: the police. Named after King William IV, whose constables were an early form of police

On one / it: intending to enjoy yourself. 'He's on one tonight'

Parky: cold / freezing

Pearlers: teeth

Peckham: (slang) Peckham Rye – tie. Peckham is an area of south London

Pie and liquor: (slang) vicar. Pie, mash and liquor is traditional London working-class food and has been since the eighteenth century.

Pisser: the male appendage

Pit: bed. 'Come on, get out of yer pit!'

Plank: idiot. Someone who is as thick as a piece of wood

Plum: idiot / stupid person

Plot up: sit down

Polish: useless / hopeless

Ponce: English word for pimp. Someone who gets something for doing nothing

Pony: (slang) pony and trap – crap. Of poor quality

Poodle: slow walk / to meander

Pop: to scold someone. 'You having a pop, son?'

Poppy: (slang) poppy red – bread – bread and honey – money. *See also* Bread

Poxy: horrible / inferior. Derived from the word pox (syphilis)

Puff: breath / life. 'Never in all my puff have I seen that'

Puke: vomit

Pull the ladder up: stop / have a rest

Pulling my chain: when someone is trying to take advantage of you for a laugh. 'You pulling my chain, fella?'

Punter: a customer

Pup: a young person

Rabbit: (slang) rabbit and pork – talk. 'She can't half rabbit, the bird'

Raspberry: (slang) raspberry ripple – cripple

Redundo: redundancy payment

Reeled in: been caught / duped / suckered. 'Got ya, reeled you right in'

Rolling: drunk / heavily intoxicated

Rozzers: policemen. Thought to be Polari (homosexual slang)

Russell Harty: (slang) party

SP: abbreviation for starting prices in racing terminology. Also means to know the situation from the start. 'You know the SP, yeah?'

Salmon: (slang) salmon and trout – snout (cigarette)

Sarky: short for sarcastic

Sauce: alcohol / booze

Savvy: well informed / shrewd

Scab (worker): strike-breaker / someone hired to replace a person on strike

Schmutter: clothing. From the Yiddish word *Schmatte*, meaning rag

Scooby: (slang) scooby doo – clue. 'He ain't got a scooby'

Score: twenty (pounds)

Scuppered: overwhelmed / ruined

Septic: (slang) septic tank – Yank (an American)

Sherbet: alcoholic drink / Australian slang word for beer, first recorded in 1890

Shithouse: big and solid. 'Built like a brick shithouse' / also a term of abuse

Shlep: (Yiddish) drag / haul

Shtum: (Yiddish / German) quiet

Sickie: be off work as a result of being unwell

Sid Nicholas: (slang) ridiculous

Skirt: a young attractive woman. Often preceeded by 'A nice bit of …'

Sky: (slang) sky rocket – pocket

Sky pilot: a member of the clergy, especially a military chaplain

Slag: can mean a petty criminal or a woman with loose morals

Slash: to urinate. 'I'm busting for a slash!'

Smother: overcoat

Snide: fake / false

Snots: money / cash. 'Cost me thirty snots, that'

Sod: a mild insult. From the word sodomite

Spar: Jamaican slang for friend / pal

Spiel: talk / say something. From Yiddish word *Shpil*

Spliff: a joint. A cigarette rolled together with cannabis and tobacco

Spruce up: to make neat / tidy yourself up

Spunker: (in this context) a waster / to waste

Starter's orders: get ready to go. 'Come on girl, we're under starter's orders'

Stone me: an exclamation of surprise or annoyance. 'Stone me, son! You sure?'

Strides: trousers. Originated in rural England. *See also* Jekylls

Stronza: Ricardo tells me it's Italian for prick

Sweats: old men, who have seen and done it all before

Swede: head

T-las (back slang) salt

Tackle: junkie speak for drugs. 'He's on the tackle, mate'

Tater: potato

The World Upside Down: Old Kent Road pub

Three parts: very close to being very drunk. 'He's three parts, mate, look at the state of him'

Tickle up: to adjust / make good

Timber: to fall down like a tree / carrying a bit of extra weight

Tin-tack: (slang) sack. To lose your job

Titfer/titfer-tat: hat

Tit-headed: the shape of a policeman's helmet

Tits up: broken / wrong. Also means to fall over (on your back), 'All gone tits up, ain't it'

Togs: clothing. *See also* Schmutter

Tom Dick: (slang) sick. *See also* Dicky

Top: commit suicide. 'Topped himself'

Totty: a good-looking woman, or man. Possibly from the Romany word *taati* meaning a woman who is warm

Tough titty: tough luck / unlucky. From the phrase, 'Tough titty, said the kitty as the milk ran dry'

Twenty-up: twenty minutes to the hour. 'Not time yet, it's only twenty-up'

Twonk: idiot. Thought to derive from the Edwardian era, meaning lower-class foreigner

Under-fives: young people. Someone who has left school to learn a trade

Up the stick: pregnant

Wagons roll: to get a move on / start something

Webs: shoes – derived from webbed feet

Wedge: money. The expression is from when coins were cut into wedge-shaped pieces to create smaller money units